THE MORTEM CYCLE

DEATH HOUSE

DEATH SHIP

DEATH BEYOND

DEATH CUISINE

First Edition
Published by
Nordic Press
Kindlyckevägen 13
Rimforsa, Sweden.
2022

This is a work of fiction. Similarities to real people, places, or events are entirely coincidental.

Death Magic
978-91-987509-0-4
Cover Design by
C. Marry Hultman
Compiled and Edited by
S.O. Green

DEATH MAGIC

S.O. Green, Jessica Chanese, Joel Hunt,

K.B. Elija, Marcus Bines, Clint Foster, Aaron Hansen,

Carrie Gessner, Holley Cornetto,

Alanna Robertson- Webb, Nerisha Kemraj, Kim Rei

Foreword

S.O. Green

"I pray that which was buried remains buried, insensate, in perpetual rest with closed eye and stilled brain. I pray it lives, I pray it sleeps…"

~ Tamsyn Muir, Gideon the Ninth

Necromancers are bad guys.

Maybe it was growing up during the Nineties that taught me that. Whether it was Shang Tsung using his magic to steal people's souls, or the Umbrella Corporation resurrecting the dead with experimental viruses, the ones trying to disrupt the natural cycle of life and death were always the villains.

They say only two things in life are certain: death and taxes. Well, the truth is, we didn't always pay taxes, but we have always died. The idea that someone might cheat the system, escape that fate, is a source of horror as much as of fascination. Collectively, we seem to agree that it would be a bad thing. We also agree that it would exact a toll. A blackening of the soul, maybe, but then if we believe we'll be judged in death, only the guiltiest would try to avoid that judgement entirely.

And the villain of this book is no exception.

Alvard Lestrange started out life as a villain in an unpublished short story of mine, but he stood out from the other characters, despite having such a small role. This book has gone through several changes, including a change of publisher, but Lestrange has always been the bad guy of this piece, ever since the original pitch.

I had the privilege of putting together an amazing crew of writers, all of whom I admire and respect greatly, when working on this project. Each of them brought something different, something uniquely theirs, to the finished book. Horror stories, heroic stories, stories of madness and love and betrayal and loss. You'll find them all in here.

But this isn't a book about a necromancer. It's a book about the victims of a necromancer. The real measure of a villain is in the people they hurt and the lives they destroy. Eleven authors put their talents towards telling the tales of the souls who suffered at his hands and I have been privileged to work with this talented group to bring you Death Magic, part five of Breaking Rules Europe's Mortem Cycle.

They sent him to death, but death was an old friend…

Prologue

Death of a Necromancer

At noon, beneath a grey sky and shrouded sun, they dragged Lestrange to the gallows.

He still wore the robes of a Grand Mage, even now. They hadn't stripped him and they hadn't beaten him like other prisoners. Afterwards, the guards would say he was a dead man already. Why dirty their hands? They never spoke of the way his dark eyes crushed the anger from their hearts and left only cold fear behind.

He walked with head held high, hands folded behind his back like he was strolling in the gardens. Only the faint rattle of chains betrayed that he was shackled.

The noose was tied. The executioner stood ready at the lever. The press of bodies in the square, wealthy and poor alike, from all the districts of Kingsgate, stood silent for the absurd spectacle of eight guards in full armour, swords drawn, escorting a single, slender man in fine but crumpled robes.

Not a single one of them doubted the necessity. Here was the most dangerous man in Guardiana. And they had come to watch him die so that they might sleep better at night, knowing it was over.

"Alvard Lestrange, formerly Grand Mage to the Crown of Guardiana," the magistrate announced. Even if he'd whispered, he'd have been heard in that sepulchral silence. "King Vertice has heard account of your deeds and judged you accordingly. For the crime of murder, you have been judged guilty. For the crime of conspiracy to commit the act of murder, guilty. For the crime of graverobbing, guilty. For the crime of wrongful imprisonment, guilty. For the crime of torture and dismemberment, guilty. For the crime of damage and destruction by proxy to the city of Kingsgate, guilty. For the crime of violating the sanctity of our treaty with dragonkind, guilty. For the crime of practicing forbidden magic, guilty. For the crime of treason..." The magistrate took a breath and lowered his parchment. "Guilty. There can be only one punishment."

Sentence had been passed that morning. It would be known as King Vertice's finest moment. The only remarkable act of a weak and inept king. A man who had let his court jig to the song of a necromancer, content to let his coffers fill and his belly grow while undead monsters rampaged across his country with impunity.

Until someone traced those monsters to Lestrange. Then it was time to act. Time to sever ties. Time for justice to wake in the royal palace and clear away the mess that men had made.

"How long do you suppose this farce can continue?"

The crowd craned necks, searching for the speaker, with his strong, calm voice. It was only when Lestrange lifted his jaw through the straight, black hair curtaining his face that they saw the smile on his lips and realised he was the one who had spoken.

"Lords and ladies, fear is what motivates these people. It is what keeps them in line. How will you contend with their discontent if it is allowed to fester? Fathers and mothers of the Faith, how will you shepherd them without wolves? Soldiers of the Crown, would you rather face a real enemy? At least a rotten foe crumbles easily under a mace."

All those questions, but only silence answered. Even so, they listened. They heard. They considered.

"Guardiana is mine. It has always been mine. It will always *be* mine. You send me to death, but death is an old friend of mine. I will not reside there long before I return. What you do today will throw a shadow over your children and your children's children. I give you this warning in gratitude for the service of your fathers and mothers, your sons and daughters, your sisters and brothers, for their bodies and their souls have aided me in my endeavours all these years while your king sat idly on his throne and your masters came to me with their petty complaints and your faith reaped the benefits of your terror. Without you, I could have achieved none of this."

He bowed his head in silent thanks. Disgust wriggled in every stomach.

They fitted the noose around his neck. He was still smiling when they opened the trapdoor. His neck didn't break when the rope jerked him to a stop and there was some justice in that, the people decided. Even the great necromancer, Lestrange, would dance to that old tune.

No one stepped forward to pull his feet. But he had darkened every heart in the kingdom so perhaps it was fitting that there was no mercy left for him. They listened to his silken voice grunting and choking for thirteen long minutes. There were no curses or apologies in that insensible gurgling. He had already said his piece.

When the only noise in the square was the gentle creaking of the rope, they cut him down and loaded him into a cart. A procession formed behind the guards. Every man, woman and child in the crowd followed them to the yard where they tossed his corpse onto a pyre and set it alight.

When he was nothing but blackened bones, they decided they could finally be sure. Lestrange was dead.

They brought the black steel gauntlet he had worn as Grand Mage from the jail and, by order of the King, sealed it in his quarters. His study, his laboratory, his bedroom. Nothing within had been touched. They already had evidence enough to hang him. Why disturb the tools and trinkets he had gathered through the years? They were cursed. Lingering in their presence would only bring misfortune.

They sealed the doors. The new Grand Mage, a faithful man never touched by the corruption of the capital, took the key himself and decreed that no one would ever again set foot in the chambers of Alvard Lestrange.

And that was why no one heard the objects in those rooms whispering and crying and laughing and screaming in the darkness.

A Storm Approaches

S.O. Green

"Are you sure we're safe in here?"

The storm had come on suddenly. Nothing but blue skies and then the eerie green light, the gathering dark, the sound of a thousand voices shrieking in misery and pain. They'd scrambled into an old, wooden shack that trembled like it was being whipped. Howling faces whirled past the window, made of ghastly smoke.

Feran hadn't made it. They'd watched it descend on him while he was still a dozen feet from the door. Lyssa already knew, from the reports, what would happen to him.

I wanted to study a soulstorm up close. Couldn't get much closer than this.

"We should be fine," Captain Merrick muttered.

There was a little too much prayer in his tone. "So long as we're not open to the sky."

"Let's hope the roof holds up then, shall we?"

Lyssa flashed him a reassuring smile. She got the feeling it didn't touch him the way the circle pendant around his neck did. Faith was funny that way. You could believe more in a piece of jewellery and an idea than in the flesh and blood across from you.

Understandable. Flesh and blood wasn't feeling too potent right about now.

"I'm sorry about Feran."

"That makes two of us."

"Take me to his family when we return to Kingsgate. I'll break the news myself. They can blame me if they want."

"That's not something your predecessor would have done."

"My predecessor was a dick."

Maybe not the biggest dick who'd ever been a Grand Mage though. Lyssa had read the accounts. Three centuries hadn't done much to diminish the notoriety of the necromancer, Lestrange. In fact, she was reasonably sure she had that same bag of dicks to thank for this current predicament.

I don't know how you made this happen, but I am going to stop it.

Caught in a soulstorm, you only had one option. Wait for it to blow itself out. Lyssa was about to suggest breaking out her tarot deck for a game of cards, as a more entertaining alternative to prayer, when someone knocked on the door.

"Wha-?"

"Don't open it."

"Give me some credit. I wasn't going to."

That wasn't strictly true. It took considerable effort to keep from doing just that because, if someone was knocking, it meant someone was still alive out there. Maybe Feran.

Except that life wasn't binary anymore, was it? They had Lestrange to thank for that too.

The knocking ceased. Then something slammed against the door, rattling the hinges, straining the bolt Merrick must have drawn, shaking the walls of their crappy, little shelter.

"Looks like he's done being polite."

Merrick gripped his blade, knuckles white. "By the Circle, I prayed against this."

"Get behind me."

"I'm supposed to be protecting you, Your Magisty."

"Who says I need to be protected?"

Another crash against the door. The screws tore from the wood, splintering. It burst open, just as the last wisps of the soulstorm swept over the barren earth and the last of the screams died into silence.

Feran, skin grey, features slack, eyes white, mouth frothing, lunged for Lyssa with only dim-witted murder in his stalled heart. He let out a gurgling rasp and she remembered how sweet his voice had been when they'd ridden out from Kingsgate and she'd coaxed a travelling song from him.

"I'm really, really sorry about this," she grunted, and focused on a single, potent word.

Fire.

It erupted from her palms like dragon breath. Feran walked into it like he was trying to battle a high wind. He staggered back under the weight of it as his livery, then his skin, then his sinew, scorched through, turned to ash and blew away. When there was nothing left but bones, he folded to the cabin floor and finally lay still.

"Ouch! Shit!"

Lyssa patted her hands out against her cloak, still swearing. She really needed to find an arcane focus. She'd always thought staffs and wands were just phallic compensation but there was something to be said for using something other than your hands to handle naked flames.

"Are you alright?" Merrick asked, moving around to study the pile of charred bones that had been his lieutenant.

"You worry too much."

"I think his family will be happy to hear that the Grand Mage oversaw his cremation personally," he said.

Lyssa wondered if he was joking but the grim line of his mouth disagreed. He was being serious.

She still wasn't used to this 'Your Magisty' stuff. She'd become Grand Mage to watch over Queen Camelia. It was only after taking office that she'd realised how screwed up things were in Guardiana.

Someone needed to fix this shit.

There was just one problem. Even face-to-face with a soulstorm, she was still no closer to figuring out what caused it. Or how to stop it.

◉◉◉

"I hate this."

"Your Magisty?"

Merrick looked around, confused. They'd made camp under a rocky outcropping jutting from the sun-baked ground. The horses had been safe there during the storm but they'd be riding home with an empty saddle.

They hadn't actually reached the site of the storm Lyssa had come to investigate. The storm had come to them.

Merrick was cooking supper because the only thing Lyssa could do with food was eat it. She'd lit the fire though.

"*This*," she clarified, gesturing at everything. "I hate the mess those other dicks left me with. I hate that they never tried to fix these things themselves. I hate how many people have died—no, scratch that, I hate how many people are *still* dying—because of these fucking storms. I hate that everyone keeps telling me I'm the most powerful mage Guardiana has ever seen and that all that power is, basically, *useless*. And I fucking hate Alvard Lestrange."

She kicked a stone away across the cracked earth with a growl. Merrick turned back to the mess tin he was holding over the fire.

"Good talk, Captain."

The silence that followed didn't last long. Lyssa heard hooves in the dust and turned to see a rider approaching. Merrick reached for his sword. She held out a hand to calm him.

It might have been a bandit. It might even have been a bandit in stolen Kingsgate livery. And, if he was, she'd make sure he didn't live long enough for Merrick to need his blade. She didn't want him to draw attention to himself. She'd lost one bodyguard today already.

"Grand Mage Lyssa," the rider said. It wasn't a question.

"That's me."

"A message for you. From the capital."

"From the Queen?"

The man shrugged and handed her a roll of parchment. She took it with a grateful nod and slit the wax with her thumbnail. She could already tell it wasn't from Camelia. It didn't smell like her perfume the way her letters normally did.

It was written in flowing, graceful handwriting she didn't recognise. And it wasn't signed.

Return to Kingsgate immediately. Alvard Lestrange's chambers have been unsealed. Your queen has sold his possessions.

"What the actual fuck?"

"Your Magisty?" Merrick asked, jumping to his feet and still playing with his bloody sword, like he thought he'd need to set about the letter.

"If this letter is right then our queen has just done something very, very silly."

She showed him the parchment, watched his eyes roving. Then he turned pale as Feran had and circled himself.

"No time for supper," Lyssa grumbled, and stuffed the letter into her pouch. "We're riding home tonight."

She rode out of the Red Lands, through the north wall of Kingsgate, through the Miners' Quarter, where the crimson dust gathered in the cobbles and the lungs and the guildhalls were large and powerful, and up into the noble district. Captain Merrick peeled off for the guardhouse. Lyssa rode straight for the palace.

She jumped off her horse at the gate and waited just long enough to shake red earth off her robes before marching to the throne room.

She'd been rehearsing what she was going to say the entire ride home and then she saw Camelia in her seat of power, magnificent, golden hair luxurious around her bare shoulders, long legs crossed at the knee and neckline plunging, and the lecture she'd prepared evaporated from her tongue.

"You're home!" the queen said, sitting up. A smile bloomed on her full, scarlet lips and Lyssa remembered why she served. "I wasn't expecting you for another week."

"We never reached the place," Lyssa said, forcing steel into her voice. "Another soulstorm dropped on us. I lost Lieutenant Feran."

"Oh, Lyssa, I'm so sorry. But... You know how to stop it, don't you? Now that you've seen it?"

A knife of cold slipped between Lyssa's ribs. She stared into the other woman's hopeful eyes and knew that she had to disappoint her. She had a duty to tell her queen the truth.

"No, Your Majesty."

Camelia's expression crumpled. The knife twisted.

"But I *can* find a way stop it. I just need some more

time. Leave it with me."

Her queen nodded. "You have my complete faith."

Lyssa sighed. *Now you're a failure* and *a liar. Good job.*

"I received a message, Your Majesty. It said you'd unsealed the chambers of Alvard Lestrange. And sold his possessions."

Camelia put a hand to her chest and Lyssa couldn't tell if she was surprised by her knowledge or the barb of anger in her voice.

"Please tell me you didn't."

"I can't tell you that."

"Because you did?"

"I wanted to build an infirmary. A place where the people could come to have their ills treated instead of dying in the streets or putting their family's lives in the hands of the apothecaries. Half of them don't even know what they're doing. I wanted them to have a place where they could shelter from the storms. But we didn't have any money in the treasury, Lyssa. I needed money."

"Your Majesty, Kingsgate is the richest city in the realm."

"Oh, don't patronise me. Besides, you're wrong. Kingsgate is a poor city full of rich people. And when I asked those rich people if they would fund my vision, they told me that they owed nothing to the Crown. That my father's edict abolished taxes and absolved them of their responsibility to me. I mean, they employ my subjects in their hellish mines and their disease-ridden plantations. Why would they possibly owe *me* anything? Why should it matter to them that poor people are dying?"

Lyssa sighed. They were both suffering from the legacies of the men that had preceded them. The former Grand Mage had been a feckless pervert who'd used his magic only to court the merchants' wives and noblewomen. Lyssa had ordered the bed in his quarters burned when she'd taken office. She'd spent the first year at her post just trying to claw back the respect he had lost for her. What a guy.

Camelia's father had traded his power for wealth. He'd turned the crown of Guardiana into a figurehead so that the merchants could do as they pleased without interference. Only now the money was running out and Camelia, who actually wanted to change the world, was as influential as the peasants she wanted to help. Just better dressed.

"How much money did you make from the sale?"

"Enough."

Lyssa arched an eyebrow, surprised. The people of Guardiana were sicker than she'd thought. She wouldn't have given her last coppersheet for a piece of necromancer treasure. Fuck that.

"Well, that's something, I guess. Did you keep receipts? Bills of sale? I need to track those items down before they hurt people."

"I can't give the money back, Lyssa. It's already spent."

"Your Majesty, if I don't find those artefacts, there might not *be* anyone to give the money back to."

Camelia sighed. Lyssa hated to see her pout. She hated being the bad guy. But someone had to be. "Ozma has the records from the auction. She can help you."

"Thank you, Your Majesty." She bowed. "One last thing. I know you had someone take the key to Lestrange's chambers from my quarters. I need it back."

"I value your privacy more than that," Camelia insisted. "I took it from your quarters myself."

She reached into the neckline of her extravagant gown and fished a plain, iron key from under her bosom. Lyssa was of two minds about teaching her that trick. It wasn't very dignified for a queen, certainly, but on the other hand, the key was *very* warm in her palm.

"If I'm sure that they pose no threat to the people of Guardiana, I won't cause a panic. I hope you trust in my discretion."

"Of course I trust you, Lyssa. You're the *only* one I trust."

She could summon fire from her palms, so it wasn't too much of a stretch to keep the glow off her cheeks at the queen's praise. Even so, as she bowed again and withdrew from the throne room, she felt like she'd failed to impress upon the queen exactly how dangerous this situation was.

Lestrange's rooms had been locked for a reason. Just because they didn't know what those objects did, didn't mean they were safe.

If the queen had thought a soulstorm was bad, it was nothing compared to the unholy shitstorm that might have been about to unleash itself on her realm.

\#

Lyssa unlocked the door with the key that had nestled beside her queen's heart and put her forehead against the wood, summoning the strength to keep moving.

"Alright. Let's do this."

She let herself into the room and shut the door behind her. In the dark, she conjured a spark to a sconce on the wall. She could tell what was missing before she even unfurled Ozma's scroll. There were empty spaces on the desk and table and dresser, where things had been lifted from the thick dust. There were empty patches on the walls and scuffs on the floor where the servants had carried away the most impressive objects.

On the desk, Lestrange's black steel gauntlet lay where it had been for the past three hundred years. The servants hadn't touched it. Neither had the dust or the rust. Even the light seemed to be having trouble with it.

Could have been worse. At least you're still here.

She took a breath and flicked open the parchment the royal scribe had given her.

"Okay. Number one. Painting of the Saint. Purchased by the Kingsgate Priory. Well, this is going to be fun."

A BRUSH WITH ETERNITY

CLINT FOSTER

Movement? For the first time since… I cannot remember.

There was movement, once. Ripples passed up the canvas, within which I have so long been captive, shivering what might, at one time, have been my bones. The wanton touches of wanderers who resonated with my predicament, perhaps. The hot breaths of the gossipers and sycophants who passed beneath my frame in the parlor of that mad wizard.

But he never moved me. Not an inch. By the disarray of the place, his death, if that be what it truly was, did more harm than good for the fortunes of the royal family.

Yet their disgrace might prove my benefactor. I long to grin as the calloused hands of servants grip the sunset-wrought frame that holds me imprisoned. I see the world tilt and spin, flipping and sliding in a blur I cannot track.

I see only what he wanted me to see. Only what my gilt window permits. I see Lestrange in every shadow, every nook of darkness, for it was darkness that bore him, and to which he returned in death. A darkness all too good for him.

The darkness that takes me is uneasy. Liquid. Agitated. Filtered brilliance dazzles my eyes through what must be an untrustworthy burlap sack. I am being taken. Taken away from the castle? Perhaps, but certainly away from Lestrange's study.

For so long, I stood sentry over the shoulder of the Grand Mage of Guardiana. Even longer, in my trance of unending days, sunrise and sunset, since the last time he set foot in those unhallowed halls. Where now am I whisked? I care not to ponder.

The past comes back in that flood of glistening shadows. Of the artist who painted my likeness and the deal he made, whetting his lust with handfuls of money, black with blood. I knew not of it, nor would I, obviously, have consented. However, I am cowed by my time in the confines of this canvas.

As a mortal, as a man, I was frail, and perhaps worse than all things, normal. I was ordinary, albeit born of demiroyalty and raised like it. Hand-me-downs of great quality and high thread counts. Dinners of sumptuous, day-old roasts and what cakes were left behind by the palace. The crumbs of greats were surely better than the plenty of poverty.

Yet, how I longed to be more than an afterthought of the royal line. I was, at the best of times, seventeenth in line for the throne, hoping for the happiest of tragedies. Silian, son of Soran, son of…someone else.

My reverie is shattered by the brusque hands of the movers once more, by the rasp of the course sack on the delicate frame in which I have been housed so long. I can nearly feel scrapes against the oil and resin and canvas that is my skin. To feel again, even the heat of a rash, would be euphoria.

By the Circle! I wish they might drop me so my painted flesh would bend and twist in ways unnatural to the living, if only to scream in silent agony at the sumptuous feeling of my own bones breaking, my own skin tearing like so much leather before the tanner's hot gloves.

Alas, I remain still, and my eyes see only a glimpse of cobbled path. A threshold, though not one wrought of even so precious a metal as iron. A few pairs of shuffling feet upon which cling desperate shoes long in need of repair, or better, replacing.

The words of those around me are as they always have been. They are muted, distant. Whispers into a thick fog, garbled to me like the regurgitations of some eldritch monster. Horrible things that wash against my mind and dim it the further for having heard them.

Yet I am wont to listen intently, for what else might I do, save hope to drown in madness? It would be a blessing.

I can tell they disagree about something. A brief argument, perhaps? Let them argue. Let one of them rage beyond reason and pull a knife from his belt, gashing me with a flick of the wrist. Let them dash me to the flagstones and trample the greasy paint into the dust.

More movement. I am given.

After so many years, their number beyond my tally, for I have naught but my mind upon which to etch those many sleepless hours, I am free of Lestrange. I am bequeathed unto a new hell of monotony. Immortality came at a higher cost than this new home paid for it. I could laugh.

I need not wait long for my new perch to be revealed, for I am hoisted via pulley near to the ceiling. A dull, wretched face blocks my view until the very end, and I am forced to watch the brutish, beady eyes of the creature judge distance from one beam to the next. Suddenly, his eyes give way to a forehead that lasts long enough to worry me, a wistful cloud of used-to-be-thinning hair, then a gleaming bald patch, and I behold my view.

After so long trapped in the dreadful lair of that creature—the Magus—I find myself where I had always dreamed my portrait might rest. I am at rest above the mantle of the ever-burning hearth of my own monastery.

The Monastery of the Perpetual Journey. Home. Paradise. I could sigh, content and pleased with my station after so long.

Was it worth the horrors glimpsed over Lestrange's shoulder?

My mind is drawn back to a memory of his study. Of my sentence. My time as the witness to unadulterated sin. Lestrange saw no merit in the Circle. Indeed, he openly mocked our religion, and the occasions on which his besmirked, wicked lips twisted at the discovery of wrongdoing by my beloved children were myriad.

He called us, by the writings in his diary, "A cluster of filth. A disease that needs more than leeched, but indeed a purging of the direst sort. They linger at the King's hand and tug at his conscience in a way that impedes my progress and potency. Let them be judged not by the best of them, but by their worst, by the filth in their ranks. Let them be purged from His confidence, and thus, their station."

I could laugh, thinking of such blasphemy. It is, in the end, not to come to fruition, and I am grateful to know the Faith still sits in good standing with the royal line. From his frustrated writings and vehemence toward all those people of the Faith, I could tell, even without grasping the meaning of his words, that his plans of usurpation had been thwarted time and again. The Circle lives on, even when Lestrange does not. The cycle continues, and the guilty are purged. Lestrange will not be reborn; he will be cast into the Void like the abomination he was.

Of the two of us, I will be the immortal one.

Brought back to the present, I am, as always, surprised to find my body unresponsive to action. Even after so long, I am shocked to have no agency over myself upon waking from a daydream. It does not last, for I remember my plight, my hell, my salvation.

What could be better for one who longed to dwell within the Circle after death than to live out eternity in observance of that which he loved most?

My paradise is long overdue, and I have suffered

much at Lestrange's hands. Yet, I endured, and I have been granted salvation.

Settling into my new home takes little time, for I have no need of sleep and grow easily accustomed to the routine of the monks of the Circle. Each morning, when I can scarcely see the first honey of a rising sun filter through the oft-shuttered windows to the east, a series of newer brothers to the Faith sidle into the cloister on their way to begin cooking breakfast.

My own admission had been much the same. It is with the fondness of one who has undertaken this rigorous task, and reveled in it, that I recall the snapping of bacon on skillets the size of a door. The sizzling of eggs frying in moments upon the hot flames of the grill stove. The smell of grease burning to pans whose crusted scrapings I knew would become my responsibility come noontime. It was a joy to cook for the Faithbrothers, the Faithfathers. To serve as a tiny part of the Circle that binds us all was a greater fulfillment than I had ever known.

I long to feel the bubbles of boiling grease burn my wrists again. To choke on the steam of the ovens. To sweat over meals of which I would taste but morsels.

I wore the crisp, itchy, mustard-yellow sacking cloth robe without complaint. I tied my belt tighter with every prayer to close the Circle about my waist. So much incense smoldered beneath my nose that I could grow no beard, and in skipping my morning shave, gained a few precious moments to devote back unto the Circle.

My Faith. My legacy.

It is with no small satisfaction that I watch the Primarch of today—Leonardo, they call him—enter the cloister, flanked as usual by the ranking acolytes of his cloth. In my youth, Primarch Magnus was always quick to shame me, to tear me down, to tighten the Circle around me and remind me how small I truly was. I never forgot.

Magnus would descend from his dais, when the Faithfathers had gone, and he would appraise me as though I were a possession to be owned or sold. He would bow his head in the slightest manner, so little it was perhaps meant as an insult, and slink away, back to the dim halls of his personal chambers.

I knew little enough about him then. I long to return to such times of blissful ignorance.

Years later, I learned that Magnus had been one of Lestrange's puppets.

Leonardo is different. A true paragon of the Faith. I watch him lead prayer in the hall. I hear him singing in the kitchens, working side-by-side with his children, wringing impurities from his soul with honest labour.

Ten years? A moment to me, and my observance has allowed me the pleasure of watching the Monastery led by a wise and benevolent man. The corruption Lestrange tried to sow amongst us failed to take root and I wonder if my own time as Primarch helped to turn back Magnus's darkness. I see nearly two dozen Faithbrothers become Faithfathers, and as many Faithfathers rejoin the Circle.

As far as I can tell, judging by the other paintings within my view, no new Saints have been ordained since my own ceremony. Perhaps the Faithfathers simply died too soon.

Death is but a part of all things, and the Circle honors the dead by casting their ashes among the meals of the living in sparse quantities. Ash is delivered also to the castle gardens and to Kingsgate, for royal ceremony. I could laugh, imagining someone daring to ask Lestrange why he needed a vial of monk ashes, but I know the answer and it is no laughing matter.

None dared question that man. He was above us. Yet that laughter of mine that no longer has a throat through which to leave is caught and choked by the knowledge that my ashes were never given to my children here at the Monastery, nor scattered among the gardens to nurture new life. It is a bitter thought.

One young monk in particular has caught my eye, and I have observed his growth fondly. An orphan left before the doors of the cloister—the child of an outcast, hiding among these snowswept crags, perhaps—he did not take to the Circle for some time. They named him Lawrence. The Faithfathers are patient, and his brothers are obedient, and he did not suffer or want during his stay. So great was their hospitality that he eventually donned the sacking cloth of an acolyte, and I have had the pleasure of seeing him grow in his faith through his adolescence into adulthood. I watch him elevated to Faithfather, and from there to Prior, serving directly under Primarch Leonardo. It is a privilege.

Paradoxically, any time I revel in the joy of my present, I remember the pain of my past.

Just imagining Lestrange makes my body, such as it is, writhe and itch. A monster more than anything. As I brood upon him, I see, for the first time, a fleck of my paint drift away. It is the merest satisfaction. The tiniest scrape against the itch of three centuries. A balm of the mildest sort, but a balm nonetheless.

The flame in the hearth roars below me, and the heat, it seems, has finally cracked the oils that have for so long imprisoned me. It is now I realize there is an end. A blessed end, not just to my cruelly bound soul, but to this existence. To be reborn in the center of the Circle. True paradise at last.

Lawrence does not notice the fleck of paint fall, nor should he, for bigger things are on his mind. Though I cannot hear them, I know what the texts the Faithfathers carry signify, and I recognize the eager hush of anticipation. Today is a day of great sadness and great joy. Primarch Leonardo has rejoined the Circle. Now, the boy I have watched grow into a fine man, a fine Faithfather, will become Primarch in his stead. I could not have been prouder had he been my own son.

In all my time upon the mantle of the cloister, I have not recalled my own ordainment. It has been a conscious thing, my avoidance of such a memory, for it is simultaneously my greatest and my worst. The pinnacle of my brief moment among the flesh, and my demise.

Lestrange, in his generosity, was having a painting commissioned for each of the previous, and current, Primarchs of the Faith. Even Magnus was included among them, despite his profligacy. It was on the day those paintings were revealed that I found my own likeness not among them.

The Fathers had voted in enclave. I was to be a Saint!

In my mind, I occasionally find myself mimicking the staccato, piercing laugh of my life. It was a horrid thing, one I always wished was otherwise. Yet, for all my worry, I never could change how my humor found expression. I imagine such a thing, and for a moment, it is pure and wonderful. Until the laughter becomes uncertain, becomes nervous, becomes screams.

I see, just as clearly as I would now from the mantle, myself standing proudly before the artist. He squints and dashes his brush against the canvas—against what is now my flesh—with such care, such grace. There is not a move he has not choreographed, not a droplet, not a hair out of place.

The idiot's grin on my fool mouth never wavered. Not even when Lestrange stalked out of a closet behind the man. It had been hours, and though my cheeks ached and my brow was starting to sweat, I had scarcely blinked. The Grand Mage's grin, wicked and wide, proved the more impressive.

With a wanton gesture of his gauntleted right hand, I felt my body freeze. No longer was my smile my own by effort and strain. It was frozen upon my face. Chiseled from stone as much as it was to be painted in oils. Then he touched the painter gently on the nape of his neck, and I watched a thousand years pass in an instant. His flesh wrinkled and grayed, mottling and molding, before becoming pocked with holes and maggots, consumed, and finally drifting to dust. Lestrange's grin never faltered.

Neither did mine.

I could find my voice, and I screamed through gritted teeth until blood gurgled in my throat and my vocal chords thrashed themselves to pulp. I screamed louder than any bell could ever ring, than any thunder has yet tolled, but none came to my aid. I remained frozen while Lestrange took over the stool from the artist, not even bothering to wipe the ashes away, and raised up a brush of his own.

It was a wicked thing, one suitable to his intentions, and he did not dip it in the paint but lashed the rough horse hairs against the canvas with a singular concentration. Those appraiser's eyes of his, the ones that so often found my children wanting, never blinked nor strayed from the painting.

It was but a moment before I felt the first touch of the brush upon my face.

The present hits me in a cavalcade of unintelligible noise and blinding torches. The flame behind me sends monks scurrying away. The inferno roars on the day of Encirclement, just as it did on mine. I am glad to see Lawrence, the orphan I have watched so dutifully throughout my time there, amid his fellows. They smile and hold their candles higher for their comrade, soon to be elevated, and it would have warmed me to the quick to see such a ritual performed for such a deserving candidate.

Instead it is the flames at my back that warm me, and several more flecks of paint fall amid the celebration. I am joyous. I am happy.

The cold memory of my own ordination lingers, but I am soothed.

Not even a month has passed since the Encirclement, and I am still aglow with the ritual. I feel at peace with my predicament, for each passing day sees more of the old oils that make me up dry, crack, and flake away. Away from the material world, away from this curse. Away from Lestrange.

The new Primarch is here at an odd hour, for it is dark, and the fire in the hearth beneath me is scarcely embers. I recognize the subtle hunch of Lawrence's shoulders, the hitch in his gait. He throws open the door to the cloister and there, silhouetted against what few stars are out tonight, are two clandestine creatures clad in noxiously noble raiment, whom he admits with a gesture.

It is thus for many nights, and weeks pass wherein I see these hushed discussions, their content unknown to my mind that can no longer grasp the words that are spoken.

Mute, deaf, and dumb, I watch Lawrence fall to his debts, to his failures, to his sins. Men come to threaten him; they come to beat him, to strip away the Faith from his belt by the fistful. He is shamed and confused, and I long now more than ever to be free of my prison, to descend to the aid of this man—a man like I once was—

struggling as so many of us have, and offer the wisdom of centuries.

I see men enter; I see men leave. Still, I can no more move than I can threaten them with divine justice. I am helpless. I weep in tears of falling oils.

Oh, the months of fear and pain I saw. To have those returned, when I thought the new Primarch to be one of the good folk whom misfortune had viciously waylaid!

Lawrence is a demon! No Lestrange, but a foul beast in his own right. Nightly come his henchmen, and they report with bloody knuckles and wicked grins. Scalps and sliced ears. Trophies of his reign of terror, brought forth to quell the doubters among the common folk. They had been stirred by promised gold from local criminals, hoping to make a coin for their words against the new Primarch, to discredit him. He proved his mettle by succumbing to corruption and wielding the deep pockets of the Circle through his own personal army. They threatened and beat the thoughts of insurrection from the common folk, no better than the criminals themselves.

And yet the mockery of the Circle within which they claimed to dwell continued to shroud their evil. They met in the mornings and prayed, tightening their jute belts with solemnity, with reverence! They prayed to join the Circle, to tighten it around the people of Guardiana and lead them into the Centre. They communed, and fasted, and meditated, wrote canticles and burned incense, just as I had when I was so honored to be among their number.

Tonight, when I think his blasphemy cannot grow, I see the flash of silver on his belt. The streaks of red as he slides his cool knife over the pale throats of kneeling, praying Faithbrothers. Oh, the tears of color I wept then, such that they need sweep them away in the morning!

Brothers—true Faithbrothers of the Circle—murdered by the Primach they were duty, honor, and faithbound to serve! They deserved better, and I pray that the Circle closes around them. The flagstones I once felt it a blessing to scrub upon my knees grow sticky with their blood as the Primarch grins with pride. As I once grinned.

As Lestrange had grinned.

This man—this abomination—is Lestrange's monstrous corruption made flesh. I sense his hand in it, but how? Lestrange died three centuries ago. I could shiver for the chill that crawls up my canvas spine.

In the morning, I see other brothers come upon the scene. In the afternoon, I see the Primarch condemn one of them to a sentence befitting the crime. In the evening, an innocent young man, not yet with hair upon his cheeks, is put in a noose and strangled. He suffers the same fate as the truly guilty. The same fate as Lestrange.

Again, I weep.

Something new happens when Primarch Lawrence, grown older now, as though in the blink of an eye, kneels before me as though to ask my absolution. In mock prayer to a faith he has betrayed. His shoulders are draped in the robes of a Saint. My robes. I would have spat upon his bowed head.

To any observing, it was an innocent moment between new Saint and old. None but I can see his snarling grin as he rises to deal in wickedness once more.

It is too familiar, and I am once more thrust into the moment when I lay beneath Lestrange's wicked brush. Each fiber of the thing feels as though it has been dipped in acid, and with each progressive stroke, I can see, from the extreme periphery, gashes of my cheeks torn away, set to the canvas. I feel each momentary lash of the brush as it steals my form and shreds my soul. Lestrange has a cruel, crude hand, even in art, and the horse hair brush may just as well be a cat-o-nine. It rends my body from reality and crudely cements it to the canvas, and I feel every moment, every stroke of his wicked brush, just as I did then.

When he is done, the sweat runs heavy over his brow, and the gauntleted right hand quivers from fatigue. He is pale, weak, and in that moment even a peaceful man could have overcome him. Alas, none came until much later, when Lestrange directed his servants to carry me to his study where I would remain for so long. So long.

Watching my child, Lawrence, turn to such wickedness cannot but remind me of my imprisonment. In the screams of the innocent begging for his mercy, I hear the wailing of the victims given to Lestrange for his cruel experiments and tortures. I remember seeing wheels of spikes that grew in length set against gears that turned them slowly, cruelly outward, ratcheting into place to cause small punctures across the entire body. There were rags dipped in foggy potions that, when applied to flesh, caused an instant rot that left behind white, wrinkled pits of meat that wriggled with disease and parasites. Chairs, upon which one might be shackled or lashed, that vibrated with such violence as to turn the innards to slime.

I watched more people than I care to remember fold in on themselves as their bones dissolved and leaked out of every orifice.

When it was Lestrange, it was somehow easier to take, for seeing this creature—I shan't call him Saint—turn so quickly to evil is a tragedy of the highest order. A child that may have offered the realm a future of good and light turned to torture, to wicked magic, and to fear.

All the while, I watch, and I will the oils in my painting to fall the faster that my sentence might be commuted, and my time served. Let my soul fall away to bits and join the Circle, as I rightfully should have so many centuries ago. Let me die! Oh, to die and be free at last of this cursed eternity!

I lament without a voice.

I weep without tears.

I ache.

I wake from my despair to have lost what must have been decades. The wicked Primarch is old now, and though I have no memory of the intervening years, I recognize his walk, the way his feet shuffle heavily on the stones, and his furtive, hunched shoulders. His bearded face is fat, and his belt far looser than it had been when last I remembered. I would have laughed at the caricature of himself he has become. A glutton, a criminal, a false prophet.

Lawrence's crimes may have served him well in life, but the Circle will not be so kind. He will find his next life a hard, short, and painful one.

A life he deserves.

At his guidance, the Circle has turned from good and service toward vice and sin. They leave in their wake naught but suffering and hollow, weeping creatures unfit even to claim humanity.

Torture? Torture, I thought I knew, watching over Lestrange's shoulder as he used his foul magic to rip souls asunder, to cook living flesh and force it upon the starving host from which it was harvested, to inflict nameless putrefactions and diseases upon the living and observe, always with that grin. The one that haunts me still, though I am naught but colors on canvas.

I see, in the Primarch's life, a rebirth of the ideals of Lestrange, if not his methods. It brings me to despair to know this is the reward for those who once dwelt within the Circle in life.

My only solace comes from the fading of my paint. I somehow know the painting to which I have been bound is nothing but splotches within an antique frame. The heat of the hearth has plied at me, tearing away flecks, creating microscopic tears, such that now I must be less a picture and more an eyesore.

The Primarch has moved most of his operations to Kingsgate. The Monastery is too secluded. How will he exert his control? How will he revel in his debauchery and excess in so far-flung a place?

The building falls to disrepair. I pray daily that they might throw me into the flames and end it. I pray to fall at last away, and be joined in the Circle where I belong, for my faith has never wavered even in these centuries of blasphemy.

I know my reward, and I have long since earned it.

A funeral for a Faithfather is a nominal affair. Even a Primarch is only another revolution of the Eternal Wheel. But the death of a Saint is momentous. Unprecedented.

For one who rules with terror, who proclaims dictatorial rule over a people who scarcely know the true mission of the Circle, it is a glorification. A deification. This Primarch, this Saint, this beast, becomes a symbol of the Circle incarnate in the eyes of the common folk of Guardiana.

I weep in tears that fall unseen in the abandoned cloister where once I served. None come to tend the flames behind my aged frame. None come to sweep away the fallen pieces of my soul, though still they peel and drift upon windless airs to rest on the smooth flagstones.

None check on the withering stones that tear away, bit by bit, with each passing storm.

Time, I must assume, passes.

The ravages of the Violet Range—blizzards, avalanches, the predations of wyrms—see the Monastery fall to ruin. The once-stout ceiling falls away, giving beneath a heavy storm one hellish winter, which I can only assume Guardiana deserves. Benches, tables, pulpits and candelabras all about me are smashed to splinters, yet the wind, somehow, never reaches me, so high upon the hearth I rest.

I know that there are but the merest specks of paint left upon the canvas. I am nearly gone from this realm. My sentence in hell, though undeserved, is nearly done. I elate at the falling of each new particle. I would weep at how many seem to remain.

The cloister is hardly a ruin, I must imagine, overlooking the might of Kingsgate below, consumed by its iniquity. I am forgotten, blessedly forgotten, and through the lack of tending I have fallen apart the faster.

Let me die! Oh, my voice would have shaken these mountains from their moorings had I been able to scream!

I count each falling raindrop; I measure the depth of the snow by the weathering of the skeleton of a door frame that remains. I can no longer keep the rising of the sun and moon. I must, by now, be but eyes, only eyes left to stare in pain upon a world I once held in such esteem.

The Faith which I followed with rigor and zeal is no more, and I have been witness to this bastardization of the Circle within which I still pray to dwell, in eternity.

And yet, I cannot help but wonder at the depth of eternity. Another century must have passed since Lestrange's study was unsealed and I was brought here, and still I am forced to suffer so. The crimes of my past lives must have been truly immense to deserve such a punishment. I bear it stoically. I am strong in my faith, and the Circle has made me strong.

Bits of me cast away with a hearty breeze.

One eye is, at last, blind, and I feel a quivering behind the other. I see but half a world. Half a future. I am soon to be Encircled. I rejoice!

Even as only a fragment of me still rests upon the canvas, I survive one last storm. It rages, shattering stones about me and screaming death to me in a language I can finally understand, and though it threatens, and flicks its lacerating winds against my frame, it leaves me. I cannot remain thus for long. The storm, as all things, comes to an end.

I hope soon to do the same.

A man shuffles through the foot-deep snow that has accumulated in the rubble of the cloister. He kicks at some of the tables, shaking loose a shower of powder, just as I hope to shake loose from the canvas. He prods at the petrified ashes in the chimney behind me. He frowns at a rotting robe in one corner.

He looks up the chimney toward my rotting frame, toward what is left of me upon the canvas. With a gesture and a glance back toward the door, he summons others. They bring a ladder, and still I think of how I am to die at last.

They pry me from the stones and wrap me, lovingly, in a soft cloth.

Movement? For the first time since… I cannot remember.

I am hardly a painting, hardly a soul. A mere fragment of what once had been a devoted Father, a Primarch, a Saint of the Circle remains, and that soon to fall.

At last, I may die!

Yet the jostlings of my carriage bode ill to me. I am removed from my cloth bag, set so gently that the loose flecks that remain do not peel away. Oh, that I had finally been stripped away then by rougher handling.

Before me looms a stool. Beside it rests a table and a painter's palette.

By the Circle, the screams I willed what used to be my lungs to issue forth! The fearful, hot tears that would have drenched my living cheeks! I roar to the stool, *Let me die! LET ME DIE! I have served my sentence and the Circle awaits me!*

A door behind the stool opens, and shuts, and in the half-light of a low torch I see the wicked grin of my waking nightmare. He sits upon the stool with a flourish and draws forth his evil brush with a gauntleted right hand.

All too soon, after hours of pain as my flesh is ripped from unreality and viciously pasted upon the old canvas, I am whole once more. New oils anoint my body, and a frame of fresh mahogany imprisons me. I am hoisted presently above a new cloister of a new Circle. A horrid, inbred creature that has consumed the Circle of my life. By day, I am prayed to, and worshiped, and praised as a hero to them. By night, I am forced to watch as his influence lingers in their hypocrisy and debauchery and sin.

Eternity has passed me by, and I remain. The Circle continues.

I thought, after all this time, that I knew hell.

Lestrange clearly knows it better.

Perpetual Journey

Kimberly Rei

Aiferd stood outside the Prior's office, summoning the courage to knock and get through the door. He had been requested, after all. He wasn't there on a whim, and he wasn't interrupting. He was expected.

Why was he expected? What had he done wrong? His mind raced for any indiscretion or misstep. Yes, he had stared at the swell of Marie's breast, but who wouldn't? Marie was curvy and beautiful. She was made to be peered at. And yes, yes, he had taken more than his share at dinner the evening before, but he had worked hard all day and he'd been famished.

With one hand on the door knob and the other raised to knock, he stood like a statue, locked in his own spiralling worry.

The door pulled out of his grip. Prior Daniel stood on the other side, looking amused. "Precisely how long were you intending to stand at my door, wheezing? Come in, lad. Come in. Take a seat. And a breath."

Aiferd tried. His rasping stilled to more of a church mouse's squeak and he tucked his shaking hands into his robes. When he attempted a formal greeting, the Prior waved him off.

"Never mind all that. You'll pass out in my office before you finish. I have a task for you."

Aiferd blinked. Not at all what he'd been expecting. Instead of inquiring, he gratefully sipped at the weak ale Daniel placed before him.

The Prior settled in his chair and leaned back. It was a plush office, as things went. Daniel believed in a great many pious things, but the Vow of Poverty was not on his list. Leather boots, tied carefully with sturdy cord, landed on the desk, crossed. Daniel's arms followed suit over his chest. He looked casual. Calm.

"You've always been a smart lad. Which is why I'm sending you to the Violet Range. The Brothers of the Perpetual Journey are deliberating on a new saint, and it would mean a lot to our chapter if they would name one of ours. The Kingsgate lot got in first with some portrait or another, but we have a treasure of our own that's sure to beat some old painting. Why they make the most vital decisions of the Faith in that forsaken, icy hellscape, I'll never know."

"B-but… But they… They have… They…"

He'd overcome his stutter years ago, but it still surfaced when he was anxious.

"Dragons? Yes." Prior Daniel sounded equal parts amused and concerned, "Not to worry though. Chances are good you won't run into them. But if you do, just try to look unappetizing."

Aiferd's lips flapped soundlessly like a Blue Haven bass on a riverbank. Daniel dropped his feet to the floor with a thud, conversation ended. He rose and gently guided the young monk to the door.

"You'll be fine, Brother Aiferd. See Brother Nikolai tomorrow morning. He'll have all your supplies and a good, strong horse, along with the gift. The brothers at the Range will restock you for your return trip. No questions? There's a good lad. Off you go, then! Get a good night's rest!"

The Prior was extra jovial as he closed his office door and turned the key. Two irritations taken care of at one fell swoop.

Aiferd spent a restless night, tossing and turning, caught in visions of dragons—black, white, red, but all huge, all terrifying, all brimming over with flame. And then there were the violet wyrms, named because they could blend into the mountains and effectively disappear. Many a bard sang tales of the violet dragons, the last sight of so many victims. Assuming you saw them at all.

"No one has returned from such an encounter.," they said.

Aiferd had once asked how such things were known if none remained to bear witness.

It was the last time he visited an alehouse. The smell of rotten fruit still brought on his stutter.

Perhaps the mockery added to his fear.

The next morning, he wondered at the bruises on his arms and legs. Remnants of his thrashing. But he could not recall the dreams. He trembled with excitement and raw terror. Prior Daniel was not there to see him off, but Brother Nikolai left a fine steed tied to the post outside his cell. Aiferd thought the beast black until the sun peeked out from behind a cloud and the deep blue of a Haven Rain glimmered.

It had been bred for one purpose, but the war-horse was retired. His languishing in the pasture had not dimmed his glory in any way. Wide at the shoulder, standing tall enough to invite vertigo, he would have no trouble navigating the Range. A travel saddle, more comfortable than the standard fare and more valuable than Aiferd's entire hide, was strapped in place. The horse's rump was hidden under a bedroll and a plethora of bags.

Aiferd gave the horse an awkward pat and carefully stepped past. He made his way to the stables.

Brother Nikolai was standing on a stepladder. He was brushing down a graceful, silver mare. Brother Nikolai stood an impressive four foot, four inches, but his way with their equine brothers and sisters was unmatched. He smiled over the mare's back.

"Ah! Brother Aiferd! All ready for your trip? The kitchen has packed good, solid food and rations. The stuff only keeps so long, but the rations will get you home, no doubt. Fire dust, water and, well… Everything you'll need is strapped onto Beryl." Nikolai laughed.

"He is shaped like a barrel, isn't he? Fine lad, though, fine lad. He'll keep you safe. Wicked kick to him."

He began to wave Aiferd off, then paused and snapped his fingers.

"The gift! Hurl me into the Void, I almost sent you off without your mission."

He patted the mare, tossed down a fresh bale of hay for her to munch, and stepped into his office. It was no more than a converted stall, but he'd made it into a place of magnificent productivity. Nikolai knew what every bit of parchment contained and exactly where it rested. He knew the lineage of each horse the Priory owned, including the ones rented to farmers and travellers. Aiferd always imagined Brother Nikolai had a map of the realm in his head and could tell you at any time where each horse was, even as they moved.

What a fascinating tool that would be to possess!

The diminutive monk returned with a long, slender box. The box itself was nondescript and bore no grand seal or engraving. It was simple wood, well-made but unremarkable.

Until Nikolai opened the lid.

Aiferd recoiled at the wave of nauseating wrongness. He couldn't put voice or word to his instant fear. He hadn't yet seen what the box contained. But he was afraid, to his very core.

And then, just as swiftly as it came, the feeling was gone and he was left with only curiosity, fear already forgotten.

Nestled on a bed of King's Silk, a shimmering scrap that was illegal to possess without written and sealed permission from the Crown, lay a quill of Glory. Not glory. No. Nothing so mundane. This was kissed by the divine.

The feathers, for there were enough to clad a small bird, layered over each other in a rolling burst of fiery colour. The palest of peach at the tips. The colour of the sun setting on nights the Faith offered grace. A shade that would wash out to white if neglected and leave one all the poorer for the loss. From there, a richer but still gentle glide through the spectrum, reaching a red so deep, so tainted by spilled blood, so terribly dark it caused souls to shiver. True, black thread, a near impossible shade, wrapped tight to hold what could have been the end of a feather or a very long talon.

Aiferd wouldn't bet his place in the Circle on the origins of this gift, balanced between Glory and Malevolence. He swallowed hard, some primal instinct trying to remind him of the dread from just moments ago, then squared his shoulders to match Beryl's. He could do this. It was his duty.

And so, he and the warhorse strode from the monastery without audience or ceremony. He focused his eyes on the path ahead, getting accustomed to the sway of such a large creature, praying to the Circle to keep him centred.

Aiferd expected his first night on the road to be a sleepless one, full of strange sounds and banditry. He was delightfully wrong. He found that, aside from the occasional insect annoyance, he quite enjoyed sleeping rough. He was able to stare at the stars, get lost in the wonder, until he drifted off under a cool breeze to the songs of distant, gentle creatures.

That wonder began to fade after a week. He'd been fortunate to find humble inns twice, but otherwise he was on his own. Setting up camp and tending Beryl had become routine. Everything was routine. Focusing on the Circle was routine, and that was disrespectful.

One night, out of desperate boredom, he pulled the plain wooden box from its saddle bag. While the squirlen he'd caught for his meal spit and hissed over the fire, he withdrew the quill. That same dread flashed and faded so fast he barely registered it. By firelight, the feathers came to life. They sparkled and he could almost swear they were aware of him.

He knew he was getting closer to the border. The air was starting to take on a bite and he had to add a second layer to his cloak. It was nearing dark and he had yet to find a good place to stop when he saw the young woman on the road.

She was sitting in the dirt, half in a wagon wheel rut. She looked angry, glaring at a bared ankle. Normally, such things would cause the monk to avert his gaze, but the bruised swelling did nothing for his loins, so he brought Beryl to a halt and slipped out of the saddle.

"M-madam?" He hoped she was a madam. Married women were far easier for him to cope with. "M-might I offer a hand?"

She looked up and he was struck by the greenest eyes he'd ever seen. It was in his heart to make the sign of the Circle as a ward, but he didn't want to insult her.

She might be armed.

"That would be most kind, good monk."

Her voice startled him. He was expecting a rougher accent. She was, after all, dressed in what might have once been a fine gown, but was now tattered and dirty. Blue, he would have said. It was both surprising and not. They lived in Blue Haven, but it was a colour most desired across Guardiana and certain hues were only granted to the royal family, never sold. That would be gauche. To avoid censure, the weavers happily gave away the cloth, in exchange for donations.

And if they weren't happy, they were at least smart enough to appear to be thus.

And so, Aiferd found himself helping a lovely, somewhat filthy, but utterly entrancing young stranger to her feet. He braced himself as she tucked her arm into his and leaned into him. He hadn't been so close to a woman since his mother last hugged him. He'd been five and she was leaving him to the monks. For his future, she said. Later, he learned it was because she couldn't feed him.

She certainly hadn't felt like this stranger.

He patted her hand and realized, foolishly, that she had no choice but to lean on him. That ankle wouldn't hold her.

He moved slowly, using his free hand to reach across his front and grip her elbow, giving her a little more support. He gave a sharp whistle and Beryl strode forward to stop in front of them. He marvelled again at the obedience of the warhorse. No, obedience was wrong. No one could tell Beryl what to do. He'd shown amazing intelligence on the journey, once Aiferd learned to ask instead of command. The horse seemed to know the difference.

"If I m-might, my lady? I f-fear you'll struggle to c-climb into the saddle yourself."

She looked him over with those disturbing eyes, then burst into delighted, but slightly cruel, laughter, "Lady? Monk, you are a treasure. Yes, indeed. I would be most grateful for your touch upon my flesh."

He cringed. There was no need for vulgarity. What manner of creature was she that such words flowed so easily? He controlled his scowl and carefully but firmly gripped her waist. He set her side-saddle, swallowing hard as she twisted to swing a leg over and settle like a man. He cast his gaze aside and swung into the saddle behind her.

She wiggled back and tsked soft. "It's a pleasure to meet you too, monk."

His cheeks flushed bright red, but there was no way for him to move away from her. He nudged Beryl forward, praying silently to protect him against the push and sway of her backside. Thoughts he had not endured since he was a teenager rose. They were not helping.

They did, however, inspire him to find a suitable camping spot. By then, she had ceased teasing him and was breathing ragged.

"My la- What is your name, please?"

Her laughter was soft and not at all cruel, "You learn fast, monk. You may call me Nyasha. And you?"

"I am Brother Aiferd. B-but you don't need to use the Brother part. That might be a bit odd, actually. No, don't use that. Aiferd. Aiferd is my name and that is what you should call me."

He was babbling, and he knew it. Belatedly, he realized she had said, "You may call me…" which didn't exactly offer her true name. He had heard of woodland creatures that could ensnare you with such trickery and he had flat out given her his name. He winced, feeling every bit an idiot.

He helped her off the horse. She was slight enough that making the attempt herself would likely damage the other ankle. Carrying her to a fallen tree where she could rest brought back the blushing, but she was weary enough not to torment him further.

Aiferd did his best to gently ignore her while he set their camp for the night. It was obvious he would need to find somewhere civilised to leave her before he crossed into the Range. He certainly couldn't leave her out in the forest or back on the road. His mind worked as he went about his business. He had but one bedroll, but his cloaks would be enough. She would take the roll; he would take the earth. He was proud of himself for sorting the snarl so quickly. And then she spoke.

"Aiferd? I… Erm… Well, there are no facilities here and I'm afraid I cannot balance on one foot and tend nature at the same time."

The crimson roared back to his cheeks. Faith would repay pride, just not often with such brutal swiftness.

He helped as best he could, then distracted himself with preparing the evening repast. He started a fire, found a nearby stream to fill a small pot with water, hunted down roots and wild vegetables, and pulled a pouch of precious meat from a saddlebag. While he was preparing the stew, Nyasha asked him about his journey. Where had he come from? How long had he been traveling? Where was he going?

"The Violet Range. The Brothers of the Perpetual Journey are expecting me." He started to puff up at the thought of the mission he'd been entrusted with. "I am taking a gift to Primarch Leonardo."

Her head tilted slightly at the name, eyes narrowing. She began quietly muttering to herself.

Aiferd returned to the stew that was starting to hiss and pop. When he handed her a bowl, she looked thoughtful, but there were no signs of her reaction.

After their humble meal, and before bedding down, he wrapped Nyasha's ankle as tightly as he dared. He dug into his precious supply of numbark and offered her a pinch. "Between the lip and the gums. It tastes like grave dirt, but works like a charm."

She met his gaze steadily and with a touch of malice. The first he'd seen from her.

"You've no notion what grave dirt tastes like, monk. Do not dare to presume I do not."

But she took the bark, wincing as she tucked it into her lip. She rolled over on his bedroll, offering him her back. Aiferd's brow wrinkled. He shrugged and dampened the fire so it would keep them warm but offer no danger. Eventually, he drifted into a deep sleep.

Fresh air and exercise were good for the body and soul, it seemed.

Nyasha waited until the monk was snoring. She

took great care sliding out of the bedding and paused to savour the chill in the night air. How long since she'd felt the kiss of cold? So invigorating! She wanted to dance and stir the air. She wanted to sing and watch the clouds of frost drift from her lips.

She sighed silently, knowing she'd have to accept that puff of cold and nothing more. She couldn't disturb Aiferd.

What did the good monk say? A gift. A gift a gift a gift. Could it be?

She grew very still and listened. There was too much noise, but under it all—maybe, perhaps, perchance—it was there, behind all the racket.

With more grace than she should possess with a twisted ankle, she moved to Beryl. He stamped slightly, eyeing her with suspicion. A sweet cube from Aiferd's pack and a brush over his shoulder calmed him. She moved carefully to his haunches, staying on his side and away from those powerful back legs.

She glanced at her companion and carefully dug through the saddle bags. She threw out bits of cloth and neatly tied packages of rations. Books flew through the air to land in the dirt. If Aiferd woke, he'd likely keel over in apoplexy.

"Aha!" The barest of whispers, but still, she snapped her head around to peer at him. No need. Still snoring away. She pulled the wooden box out and stroked it lovingly. "Hello, my love."

She opened the box as the clouds parted and moonlight struck the feathers. They lit up, inner fire sparkling. She made a soothing, loving sound and reached out with a single finger to stroke the length of the quill. It responded. It shivered, shade sliding from oranges and reds into greens and blues. The glow flared, then exploded and left glittering shards behind.

"Mmm… There you are. Who changed your nature, hmm? Was it that monk? I've been gone too long. I'm sorry. No, I don't know what happened. He did something. Lestrange. He hurt me. And then he did something. Some—"

"Nyasha?"

The voice was sleepy and came from the fire. For a moment, she thought it was the fire. Was it angry that she'd returned the quill to its original state? That she'd stolen the fire from it?

But no. It was the monk. Her cooing had woken It. Him. *Him*. Remember, boys are him, not It.

Lestrange was Him. Always and ever. She'd forgotten once and slipped into It language. He didn't let her dance for a month. The bastard.

Aiferd's voice snapped her back to the present.

"Nyasha, what are you doing?"

She hissed under her breath and tucked the quill carefully between her teeth. She dropped into a crouch, knees splayed wide, hands on the ground in front of her. Aiferd glanced at her ankle, but she was ignoring it. Not feeling pain anymore. She scrabbled forward and he squeaked, trying to untangle from his cloaks. He'd managed to get one leg free before she was on him. She straddled, like a malicious demon or a lover, leaning down to sniff at him. Aiferd froze, praying to the Circle for protection and control of his bladder.

"Did you change it? Did you harm it? Tell me true or I'll chew your throat out. My teeth, your neck. Guess who wins?"

She grinned then and her teeth looked sharper than before. Much much sharper.

Aiferd couldn't find his voice. His throat had closed up under the threat. He shook his head violently. He needed her to believe him. He didn't want his throat ripped out.

"No? No. You aren't clever enough."

The tip of her tongue swiped out and tapped the end of his nose. He squeaked.

"It's the gift, isn't it? For Lestrange. Do you know him? Have you met him? Did you help him? Did you enjoy it?"

She was babbling. Aiferd struggled to keep up with what she was saying. Lestrange? Who? Help him with what?

He wanted to ask but his words had fled again. He was beginning to doubt her sanity and most of his mind was occupied with getting out of this alive.

"No. You're not clever enough for Him, either. Which means you aren't useful enough. So sad. Tragic. Oh, dear me."

It happened too fast for him to react. One moment she was hovering over him, the next his life's blood was spilling into the dirt. The wound at his throat didn't hurt, but he knew something was terribly wrong. He pressed his hand to the ragged gash. Shock kept panic at bay, leaving him confused and sad. He was going to die on a forest floor and he couldn't see the stars or the moon. The clouds had become heavy and menacing.

There was so much more he wanted to do. So much more he had to offer. His last thought, watching Nyasha dance around the fire, was that her wings, running green to blue, were beautiful.

Nyasha sang as she leapt and spun, Brother Aiferd's blood flying from the quill in bursts of claret rain:

Nyasha, you gifted me,
Nyasha, am I,
I spin with the moons,
And leap with the winds,
Dancer am I,
With the grace of the soul,
Free am I,
You son of a bitch...
The Range. So that's where he's hiding...

Not bothering to wait for morning, she began packing up. As she was strapping the last bit to Beryl's rump, she glanced up. Aiferd was standing on the far side of the fire, looking miserable.

"Go away! You're dead!"

She turned away and sat on the log near the dying flames. They were taking longer than Aiferd had. She rested her damaged ankle across the opposite knee and began to take the bandage off. Beneath the cloth, her skin was pale and smooth as the rest of her. No swelling, no bruising, no indication of the sprain that looked so ugly just hours ago. She smiled, stroking the curve of her leg. The fire extinguished and as the smoke surrounded her, she slipped away to another time. So very, very long ago.

"My dear, you cannot fly. You do not have wings."

Fenella batted him away impatiently, "That is simply not true. Or at least, not true for long. I just got them, you see. I need to practice. Learn how to use them."

She straightened her shoulders and flexed those magnificent wings, partly in defiance of Lestrange's dismissive tone and partly because it felt so good.

"See?"

He shook his head, "No, sweetest. You have a stunning and unique power to let others see what you want them to see. That is all. They are not real."

She turned on a heel and stormed out. She'd had enough of his arrogant disbelief. She put up with odd behaviours from him and frightening losses of memory. She'd lost entire days, but she never doubted him and his love for her. And she never asked for anything. Nothing! She danced for his friends, to that never-ending harp music, she held entire audiences in thrall in standing room only shows. All at Lestrange's behest. She was his puppet and she enjoyed her strings. But she needed him to believe in her.

She stared up at the sky, one hand lifting to shield against the blazing sun. She should have brought a hat.

Birds coasted by, lazy on-air currents. Her heart wrenched. She longed to join them.

Tossing a scowl at the door she had exited; she

stormed around the side of the building and began to climb the tower stairs. It was high enough. She should be able to catch one of those currents and prove him wrong, once and for all. She had to tuck her wings closed on the climb, but that was alright. She would stretch them soon enough.

Lestrange had been puzzling over a twisty alchemical formula when he heard the scream. He knocked over quill and ink as he ran to the door and outside. Fenella sat on the ground, sobbing and clutching her ankle. It was wrenched in a most unnatural fashion. His own joints throbbed in sympathy.

He raced to her side, "Oh, Fenna. What did you do? I told you. You cannot fly! Come. Let's get you inside. I'll send for a doctor. That does look nasty."

She saw. He thought he'd turned his head enough to hide the smile, but he didn't. He wasn't as clever as he thought. She wasn't as dumb. She saw.

And she loved him even more for it.

Nyasha's fingers twirled on her ankle and then she bounced up, spinning on her 'wounded' leg. It was so easy, making them see.

"Well, that's enough of that!"

She glanced up, across the fire. The monk was gone. Good. He was dead. He should have better manners than to still be poking around.

As she climbed into the saddle and patted Beryl, she tipped her head back and inhaled. The night air was crisp with a deepening cold and rich with the scent of doused fire. It would be good to stay there, in that moment, forever. It wasn't flying, but it was almost as heady.

She couldn't though. She had work to do. Places to see, people to kill. She may have loved Lestrange for his smile, but that had twisted to hatred when he stole her joy.

The border wasn't far. She didn't have a cloak. Aiferd had gotten blood all over his. That was fine. Weather rarely disturbed her. She was wrapped in feathers, after all. Blue and teal, green and cerulean. Most couldn't see them and that was also fine. Nosy-nosy questions were tedious.

Every hour that passed grew colder. Beryl's breath created an interesting fog to ride through and Nyasha was enchanted. She had piled her hair into a messy nest on her head and stuck the quill through to hold it all in place. It meant she could listen to it whispering.

Come back, dancer! You are treasured and missed. Come home…

She ignored it for the most part. When it spoke of the old days, reminding her of both better times and why she was making this journey, she eased into the murmurings. The rhythm of the warhorse lulled her into a hypnotic state. Her mind wandered through the past and the present.

She yanked the horse to an unceremonious halt.

How did she get here? Where had she been? Everything was a bit of a blur, but there was a great deal that seemed odd. Different. She felt out of time and out of place.

"Lestrange… Le… Strange…"

The whispering wasn't coming from the quill. It was coming from inside her and it swept away all doubts in a tsunami of rage. She had to find him. She had to avenge something.

Something...

She looked up to nudge Beryl forward again and hissed, "You are dead! Go away! Get! Rude monk, go away!"

Aiferd stood on the road, arms crossed and hands tucked into his sleeves. The blood was still bright red and wet on his cloak. Nyasha didn't care. She was in a hurry, damn it. Memories and destiny were pushing at her.

She closed her eyes and waved her hands wildly. She tapped the horse's backside and he began moving. A chill shivered over her as they passed through Aiferd.

More hours. She ate in the saddle and stopped only to tend bodily needs. Beryl stopped when he felt like it. On the crest of needing to find a place to spend the night, preferably out of the elements, she saw a small camp with four men. In any other circumstance, she would have searched for a way around them, but these men were dressed in monk robes and cloaks.

Aiferd, who once more stood in front of her, looking sad to see his breathing brothers, hadn't mentioned a welcoming party.

They hadn't seen her yet, so she led Beryl into the woods to watch for a moment. She tugged the quill from her hair and tucked it back into the wooden box, not bothering to clean the blood off. She couldn't see it anymore anyway. Some part of her knew it was there, but it was invisible to her.

There, not there. Didn't matter. No one would see the quill until its great debut.

She was smiling as she approached the monks, noting the swords and daggers all carried. They were bristling with danger and Nyasha pushed away a surge of ecstatic joy. She envisioned a battle, just her and the quill against trained men with blades. She shivered and drew close enough to call out.

Every man had a hand instantly on a hilt.

"Brothers of the Perpetual Journey? Greetings! I come bearing news and a gift."

Hands fell away, save one. He kept a steady gaze on her. "Hail, Lady. You are not who we were expecting."

"And who were you expecting?"

"Never mind. Pray, tell us your news."

Too calm, this one. Nyasha recognized the predatory stance. Admired it. And was properly wary of it.

"It is not happy news, I am sorry to say. Your Brother Aiferd fell ill on his travel to you." She paused. This was the tricky part and she needed to be as convincing as possible. "I met him at an inn. He was suffering from a terrible fever. The local cleric declared the cause unknown."

It took everything in her to not hiss as Aiferd stepped forward to stand between Nyasha and the monks, arms crossed and disappointment on his stupid face.

Stupid monk! You'll give the game away! You'll spoil everything!

The brother looked unconvinced.

"He knew he was dying. He asked me—begged really—to bring you this gift for your Prior. It seemed so important to him, I could not say no. It's poor form to deny a dying man's wish, is it not? I would be cast into the Void if I refused such a noble cause."

Still he stared, silent. She sighed inwardly.

"Well? You were waiting for him, were you not? Is that not why you are here? To escort him? Will you escort me then?"

"We don't host women at the monastery."

Her smile held steady, "Poor Brother Aiferd asked that I deliver the gift to Primarch Lestrange and none other."

His brow wrinkled, "You mean Primarch Leonardo?"

"Yes, of course. Leonardo."

I see through your ruse, Lestrange. I see!

The monk kept staring. A wind picked up, dusted with frost, swirling around her, adding to the cold. She held steady and still, waiting. Looking as innocent as possible.

Finally, he nodded and she swallowed a whoop of triumph, "Right. Pack up camp, boys."

Nyasha looked up to the darkening sky, "Should we not wait for the morn?"

He snorted, "If you've a mind to meet dragons face to face. There are no nocturnal wyrms this close to the border. We'll get to the monastery by mid-morning if we ride straight through. Sleep in the saddle as you like, but strap yourself in. We're not stopping if you fall off."

That was a lot of 'if'. Nyasha hesitated. Whispering rose from the hidden box.

Once more, she painted her voice with a smile, "I shall follow your expertise, Brother…?"

He turned away to tend his men, not deigning to offer his name. No matter. Name, no name. There, not there. Nyasha, Fenella. Only one truth mattered.

Halfway through the night, Nyasha caved to the irritating monk's suggestion and strapped herself to the saddle. She wasn't sleeping, exactly, but she was swaying. Darkness here was quiet. There were no creatures skittering around, no birds in the trees. Just snow. The wind had died. The stars and moon spoke nary a word. She was soon lulled into a trance, mind drifting.

"Fenna. We must, my heart. You've turned an ankle, broken two ribs, and dislocated your shoulder, all in attempts to fly."

She hissed at him. It was a sound she had come to embrace. He didn't approve, but one fight at a time. He needed her.

"No. Hear me. Clipping your wings is the only answer. This will hurt, but do hold still. Thrashing will only make it worse."

He had strapped her to a table, wings spread out. Slowly, with precision, he began to saw away at precious feathers. She sobbed. She screamed. She howled. For hours.

He stopped often to give her water and wipe her forehead. But her pleas fell on deaf ears. Eventually, she passed out.

Lestrange leaned back, grinning with something

akin to, and yet far removed from, glee. He glanced down at the floor. His hands. Fenna's body.

There were no feathers. No blood. No wings. It was all in her head.

He rose and went to a workbench. With a tenderness he never showed his subjects, he opened an ornate box and peered at the quill inside. It was all in her head. And soon, it would all be in the quill's feathers.

They arrived at the monastery just before terce. Lunch would not have been served yet. Many of the brothers would be preparing for mid-morning prayer. Nyasha tried to smile as the only monk to speak helped her down from the horse. She stumbled, stiff from the ride and the cold.

She straightened and tried to run a hand through her hair, wild tangles halting her fingers. She laughed brightly and dipped a curtsy, "Thank you, good sir! Will you take me to the Primarch now?"

He kept his composure, held his expression in check as he looked her over. Clothes torn and filthy, hair not fit for a bird's nest, eyes wild and frenetic. She'd been talking in her sleep. Crazy mutterings about experiments and pain and revenge on someone named Lestrange. He'd thought about leaving her to die, but that would beckon the Void to claim him.

He couldn't abandon her. He most certainly couldn't allow her near the Primarch. He suspected she had killed Brother Aiferd. He needed to make a report. But first, he needed to get her settled. Safely.

He tucked her hand under his arm and patted her fingers, "I'll see you to your room first. The Primarch will be in prayers soon and we don't want to disturb that. It is no way to offer a gift. We'll have a meal and water for a bath brought to you."

Nyasha swallowed a hiss. She played along, but the whispering was getting louder and the urge to find Lestrange was overwhelming.

"Will you bring my saddlebags?"

"I'll have them brought along, Lady. Your belongings are safe here. No monk would dare disturb what is not theirs."

He chatted with her as he led her into the monastery and through a maze of corridors. Her impatience grew.

He stopped at an open door, "I must apologize. We live simply. But you'll find a bed and desk here. A brother will be along in a moment to bring everything you'll need."

He motioned with one hand and as she stepped into the bare room, he gently shoved her forward, then yanked the door closed. It slammed with a reverberating thud. She heard a key turn in the lock.

She pulled on the door handle. It didn't move. She pressed an ear to the solid door and heard him say, "Ignore anything you hear. She's to stay here until we sort out what to do with her. She's clearly touched and likely a murderess as well."

Betrayed!

She felt a scream rise. She turned to examine the room for another door or a window. Anything. Any possible way out. What she found was Aiferd, looking both sad and relieved.

She hissed at him.

And then, smiled. Her eyes fluttered and rolled back. She held out one hand. Giggles bubbled up until they spilled from her lips. She looked at her palm, at the small but growing ball of blue light flickering. Slowly, it began to take on the ghostly form of the quill.

No pious, arrogant monk was going to stop her. She would have his blood to quench her rage. Fenella would reclaim her name. She would have her revenge.

"We'll make them see, my love. We'll make them *all* see."

Interlude One

The Mountain

S.O. Green

The painting emitted a faint glow, like a dying ember. Honestly, Lyssa couldn't tell if the imprisoned soul was even aware. At the very least, she didn't think it would be able to cause any mischief up there.

Three hundred years in Lestrange's study hadn't been kind to the canvas, but the eyes were still strangely vivid, awake and yet distant. She was tempted to wave a hand in front of it and ask if anyone was home.

She'd rather have played it safe, exorcised it and then burned it in the hearth, but the Perpetual Journey folks seemed quite eager to keep their Saint where he was. Besides, there was kindness in those eyes. She tried to keep in mind that he was a victim too.

"He belongs here," the envoy who'd met her on the road had said. "Not in the chambers of some Void-damned necromancer."

"I suppose it's fine," Lyssa decided, closing off her third eye.

"Good. No doubt the Saint has seen enough despair over the last three centuries. He will be at peace here."

"Sure, why not? But I'd appreciate a message if anything weird happens. Unexplained fires and whatnot."

"As you wish," the envoy said, all flinty eyes and granite tones.

He'd met her on the road with a small welcoming party—actually, the word warband had sprung to mind—but she supposed it was to be expected. She was the first Grand Mage to set foot within those walls since Lestrange himself. There was bound to be some bad blood there.

And she'd tried to be polite, but she'd risen because of her mastery over the elemental forces of existence, not her skill at diplomacy. She'd be happy if she managed to get home without deeply offending them all.

"One other thing," her host said. "A woman arrived at the monastery just before you. She seemed quite mad. I believe she intended to harm Primarch Leonardo, so I had her detained in a cell in the east wing."

"You know, I really don't feel like this 'no girls at the monastery' thing has been good for you."

He ignored her. "She had in her possession a gift intended for the Primarch from the Priory in Blue Haven. A feather quill of rich colours procured at an auction in Kingsgate."

Lyssa's skin prickled at that. She'd learned the list of Lestrange's missing artefacts by rote, and the quill was on that list. Was it really the same one? What did it mean if the objects were starting to cross paths?

The envoy took an ornamental box from one of the other Faithbrothers and presented it to Lyssa. He opened the lid to reveal a dull, grey feather lying on the crimson velvet inside.

"Sorry, you did say 'rich colours', right?"

"After we locked her away, we checked the artefact she had brought. We found it like this. Changed."

Her next question was, obviously, 'Can I see the mad woman?' Before she could ask, she was interrupted by another of the Faithbrothers running up, features dripping sweat and anxiety.

"She's gone," he said.

"Well, that's not good," Lyssa muttered.

"What do you mean 'gone'?" the envoy demanded.

"We checked her cell on the hour, as you instructed, but she wasn't there. We couldn't see any sign of escape, but…"

"Send men to watch over the Primarch. Rouse the brothers. Scour the monastery. Find that woman and re-capture her." As the others scurried off, he rounded on Lyssa. "You had best leave."

"If she's got magic, you might need a mage."

"I don't need mages and I don't need women. Your kind were not supposed to set foot in this monastery. We have ignored our own rules and nothing but trouble has come from it."

"You know Lestrange was a man, right?"

"Go about your business, mage, and we will go about ours. Primarch Leonardo has pledged to send his most skilled investigator to assist you in your search, but until then you are on your own."

Lyssa scoffed. They'd have been better off letting her stay, especially with magic afoot, but they clearly thought they knew best. And she had work to do.

Two items ticked off. Neither of them had enough soul power left in them to make any trouble. But the Circle only knew how many others were still out there.

She went to retrieve her horse from the stable. She should have known really. If there was one place you were guaranteed not to get a warm welcome, it was somewhere with this much snow.

She left the monastery behind and rode back towards Kingsgate. Her horse was sure-footed and knew the route better than she did, so she sat in the saddle in her fur-trimmed cloak, feeling about as useful as tits on a Faithsister.

The monastery fell away among the peaks and snow. She longed for the palace and home, the smile of her queen. Ascetic monks must have been lining up for a place in those drafty rooms, to purge themselves of the sin of this life, but it wasn't for her, that existence.

All the suffering in the world, all the pain her queen's people felt, she couldn't just lock herself away in a frigid, stone fortress making bread and chanting the day away.

She rode until she hit the Adventurers' Quarter

and there stopped to take care of her perishing thirst at the nearest tavern. Sitting at the bar, she considered Lestrange's objects, how they could be anywhere, anything. The tankard she was drinking from, the tarot deck those drunks were playing with, the staff in that woman's pack.

Wait a second...

She ordered a second tankard and walked to the stranger's table. She sat alone—her broad shoulders and general demeanour precluded company—and didn't look up until Lyssa placed the ale in front of her.

"It's not free," she said, with a grin. "I'm just curious to know where you got a staff of power from."

"Is that what it is?" The woman gave a shrug. She reached for the tankard and Lyssa glimpsed the blood under her fingernails. "I don't really care, so long as it's valuable."

"Oh, it's valuable. I might even be interested in buying it myself. Lyssa, by the way."

"Pip."

"I'm still interested in hearing where it came from."

"It's a long story."

Lyssa pulled out a chair and waved to the bartender. "Well, the drinks are on me until you finish. Deal?"

The Lengths We Go

Carrie Gessner

Pippa reared back as she let her opponent land a punch to her jaw. Pit fights weren't her preferred way to earn coin, but when jobs were hard to come by— jobs that didn't require her to completely abandon her morals, at least—pit fights were what she had to fall back on. The blow knocked her head back, but she kept her footing. It was good for the fight to drag on a bit, for the audience to see some excitement. Meant they bet more; meant her cut was higher when she won.

And she would win. She hadn't earned the surname 'Painbringer' for nothing.

The noise of the crowd assaulted her ears as she danced around her opponent, throwing a few light punches to lure him into complacency. He was a big guy, but she was big too. Built to be a fighter, for better or worse. She'd never really had a choice in the matter.

She let him land a blow against her abdomen, reacting more than was warranted and letting out a pained grunt. When he grinned, thinking he had her, his guard loosened. She took advantage of that overconfidence, as she always did, slipped in beneath his guard, and landed two quick blows on his chest. That distracted him enough that he left his face unprotected, and she pummeled him, each punch harder than the last, until he staggered backward and fell on his ass in the dirt, face bloodied. He groaned and writhed. His body would heal in a few days, maybe a week at the most. His pride might take a bit longer.

The cheers grew louder. The referee came into the ring to lift Pip's arm in victory. Pip didn't smile. Not liking pit fights didn't mean she didn't know how to work the crowd. They ate it up, noise growing.

She exited the ring in favor of the small enclosure where the fighters readied themselves. She splashed water over her face, wiped away the blood, stretched out her muscles, and threw on a fresh tunic. Fresher than the one she'd fought in anyway. It was still dirtier than most people's clothing.

A runner, just a kid, came in to hand off the purse she'd won and then darted out again. Pip dumped the coins into her hand and frowned. Not as much as she'd expected. Not as much as she'd planned. Still, nothing she could do about it.

She pushed her way through the fabric door of the enclosure and nearly ran straight into a man. What a stupid place to be standing.

"'Scuse me," she muttered, trying to navigate around him. She was accustomed to men not having the sense or decency to move when they were in someone's way.

"Oh, no, I actually came to talk to you," he said.

She turned to look at him. He was middle-aged, brown hair receding, and dressed in the kind of fancy clothes you didn't see often in the so-called 'Adventurers' Quarter'. The staff he was carrying had to be worth more than every purse she'd ever won.

"Why?"

It was rude, more of a grunt than a word, but Pippa couldn't bring herself to care. She wanted supper and a decent night's sleep, not to talk to some man.

He stuck out a hand. "My name is Kallus Pridehall. Perhaps you've heard of me."

She lifted an eyebrow at the hand and said nothing. Whatever he wanted couldn't be more important than food.

"Ah, well. I saw you fight."

"I figured."

Why else would he have stopped her just outside the ring right after her bout had ended?

"Yes. Right. I have a job for you. A job *offer*, actually. I've seen lots of fighters, spoken to a great many… adventurers, here in the Quarters, and you're the one I want to have at my back."

Pip straightened up. That got her attention. "What sort of job?"

"I'm a treasure hunter, you see."

She looked at his outfit skeptically. "*You're* a treasure hunter?"

"A financier of treasure hunting expeditions then, but this one is different. I have information that something I've been after for a long time now—a very priceless something—is hidden in the Violet Range and I need people I trust to find it. That means me and, possibly, you."

Pip snorted. "The Violet Range? Nothing there but death and dragons."

"You might be right. I have reason to believe otherwise."

"Whatever you're paying, it's not enough," she said, striding past him.

"Oh really? Try me."

She stopped again and turned around, uncertain whether he was joking. But his expression was benign, and she named an outrageous number, more gold than she would need for the rest of her life.

"Done," he said, without a second thought. Off her look of confusion, he added, "The treasure I'm after will fetch so much more than that. I can give you five hundred today, the rest once we've completed the hunt."

Pip considered. Even five hundred gold would set her up for a long while. And if he could go that high with the payment, what else could he provide?

"I need new equipment."

Hers was in acceptable condition, but she'd need better than 'acceptable' if they were going to the Violet Range. Besides, if he could pay her that, he could buy her better armor and weapons.

"Done," he said. "I've already procured a sword at

an auction the palace was hosting. It's quite a thing. But we can go to the market right now for armor. I want to leave as soon as possible, so I'd rather get you set tonight. No time to waste."

Not a lot of notice. Pip hesitated.

Journeying to the Violet Range was insanity, most likely a death sentence, and Pridehall was soft. She'd probably have to carry him up the mountain. With any luck, he'd loosen his bowels at the mere sight of a blizzard and give up on the whole venture, leaving her five hundred gold richer.

There was just one more thing to settle.

"And I don't kill," she said.

That was her line; the one she wouldn't cross. Mercenary or not, at the mercy of the rich or not, she wouldn't take another's life. She'd rather take her own.

"We're after treasure, my dear, in a place that's nearly uninhabited. Not another human soul for miles. I don't expect it will be a problem."

"Oh," she said, "and don't call me 'dear'."

"Of course not."

He tried for a smile, but it didn't hide his fear.

She let him stew in his discomfort for another second before saying, "Let's go to the market then."

"Excellent!"

The Adventurers' Quarter was populated mostly by sellswords and freebooters. The lucky ones hired on to Blue Haven cargo ships or Red Land militias. The rest occupied the limbo of the Violet Range, hired on to find treasure or mineral seams or unusual creatures in a never-ending cycle of life-threatening contractual obligation.

The market sold weapons and armor and only those things. It smelled of molten metal and leather tanning, sounded like hammers on steel, and the desperation in the air tugged at Pip's guts. Anyone with real money went north, into Kingsgate proper, to buy drink or cheap company.

As they entered the market, Kallus assured her that money was no object. Pip traded in her tattered and cut leather armor for newer, freshly oiled armor. It was light and fit her better, and the buckles weren't rusted like on her old outfit. Next was a new pack, not patched and worn and falling apart like the one she currently carried. Larger too. She was able to fit all of her belongings in it and have space leftover.

"You said you had a sword," she said, with a frown.

She favored a zweihander, and it was unlikely he had picked out a decent weapon with the right weight balance and good craftsmanship, especially at a palace auction. She cringed at the thought of the ornamental blade he'd show her, nothing but gold and gems, so brittle it'd snap the moment she tried to land a decent hit She wandered toward the smith's stall, which had a variety of well-made blades, hoping she could convince him to let her take a 'back-up'.

"Ah, yes," he said, turning her hastily away. "It's back with my things at the inn. I'll take you there now."

He was staying in the best inn the Quarter had to offer—all the patrons stayed there. To her astonishment, the weapon he'd bought at the palace was a broadsword. It was old but in excellent shape. She assumed it had been freshly polished and sharpened, but he swore it had laid untouched for three centuries.

Her palm wrapped easily around the wide handle, and the weight of the thing was a comfort rather than a burden. Simply by holding it, she could feel the power residing within. It seemed to call to her. She could do a lot of damage with such a blade, and if it turned out to be less useful than she hoped, she could always sell it down the line. It was ornate enough to fetch a pretty price, either here or in Kingsgate itself.

Upon closer inspection, she found an inscription on the quillons. The etching was small and weathered, but readable. On one side, 'Only to a warrior pure of heart,' and on the other, 'Will I reveal my wealth of secrets.'

"Huh."

She flicked a glance up at Kallus, who seemed unbothered. Perhaps he hadn't even noticed the inscription. No matter. It was a silly riddle meant for silly people.

She swirled the sword through the air a few times and Kallus cringed when she nearly cleaved the bed in half.

Yes, this would do very nicely.

Kallus put her up in a room in the inn where he was staying for the night, probably to try to make sure she didn't run off and take his investment with her. She'd given her word and that should have been enough for him, but she wouldn't complain at a night in a real bed with actual sheets.

Something woke her halfway through her rest, when the moon was high in the sky. It was a whisper, hoarse and far away.

What is this place? What happened to me? How long... have I been...asleep?

But it was only a dream. She inhaled deeply, rolled over, and went back to sleep.

Kallus had procured them fine horses, and they made good time on the first day. He turned out to be quite talkative. Pippa didn't care much for what he said, but she didn't hate it enough to stem his words either. After all, she would put up with a lot for five hundred gold, and more down the road.

And since she was doing the job, why not find out what it was all about?

"The object I'm after," he said, "they don't come around very often. This might be the first the world has seen in centuries."

He paused then, and she knew he was waiting for her to ask. So she did, because it was a long journey and conversing might help it pass quicker.

"I'm glad you asked," he said. "It's a dragon egg. Black as midnight and the size of a large pumpkin. Perhaps bigger."

Ours. It does not belong to him.

The words tickled her mind. She shrugged them off.

"Wait. A dragon egg? As in, with a baby dragon inside?"

"Oh, no. Perish the thought. It's just a name for a very rare, very valuable treasure. Something a collector would pay an obscene sum for, I assure you."

Pip nodded. True dragon artifacts were priceless. Was that all Kallus was after? Money?

"I thought you said we were digging something up, not stealing it."

"And it probably is buried. Under a hoard or something."

"The hoard of a living, fire-breathing dragon? Do you have any idea how territorial they are?"

"There's really nothing to worry about. I've been studying this for years now, and I can say with absolute certainty that the dragon to whom this particular hoard belonged is now dead. And there are enough stories around the cave being haunted and out of bounds that I'm also sure no other dragon has taken up residence there."

"If there's no danger, they why do you need me?"

"No danger from dragons, my dear. There have been people following me every step of my journey, and they will try to stop me. You're here to deter them."

"Why's it so valuable? It's just a gem, right?"

"Oh, ho, ho," he chortled. "'Only a gem!' Imagine! No, no. Far from it!"

Pip clenched her jaw. She bore no ill will toward people in general, but the way most assumed she was stupid grated her nerves. "You can just tell me," she said icily.

"Right." He sobered. "Forgive me. I get so excited when I talk about it. It's a gem, yes, but it has magical properties. Dragon magic. With the help of this gem, we'll be able to cure ills, grow crops that don't fail, experience endless summer for the rest of our days. With time and study, we might even be able to eradicate soulstorms and rid this world of the dragons themselves. I will be the creator of a better world."

"It sounds powerful," she said.

"It is. Just wait. We're going to change the world."

She tried not to scoff. Someone like Kallus wasn't going to change the world; if he did, it probably wouldn't be for the better. Honestly, she'd settle for getting paid.

That night, with so few travelers on the road, she didn't bother keeping watch. They pitched their camp in the lea of some large rock spires and fell asleep to the sound of howling wind. Nothing could creep up on them without tripping over Pip, who kept her sword to hand as she slumbered. Kallus proved not to be as soft as she'd thought and snored like he'd probably done back in the Adventurers' Quarter.

He was still asleep when a voice woke Pippa up.

Nothing is right anymore. So much...has been stolen.

She looked to Kallus, who was still snoring but not talking in his sleep. She kept still for a moment, straining her ears to hear the voice again.

Tell me... Tell me how I have come to be trapped in this vessel. Tell me why this bastard schemes to steal our secrets.

Pip sat straight up. What the hell was going on?

Either she had gone mountain crazy or something she didn't understand was happening.

The voice came from the blade sheathed beside her bedroll. The ancient sword Kallus had bought at the palace. A talking sword wasn't out of the realm of possibility, she supposed, but she hadn't expected one to fall into her hands.

"H-hello?" she said softly. Whatever this was, she didn't want Kallus waking up for it.

Who…speaks to me? Who are you?

"Uh, my name is Pippa Painbringer. But I go by Pip."

Pip. I am Miraghan. Where am I?

Pip furrowed her brow. "In the Violet Range."

Ah. I thought I felt the call of home.

The call of home? "You…you used to live here?"

Nothing lived in the Violet Range. Like she'd said to Kallus, nothing but death and…

"You're a dragon?"

Miraghan let out a low, bitter chuckle. *That is what I once was, yes. Now, I'm merely a trapped soul.*

Pip scratched her eyebrow. She didn't know much about magic, but this didn't seem like a typical use for it. In fact, it reeked of something foul. Something evil.

"How did you come to be trapped?"

A mage. He hunted me, killed me, stole my soul.

How awful it was to be stuck like that. Pip sometimes felt that way, entombed alive, because of the scarcity of choices open to her. It was why the five hundred gold had been so enticing.

"I'm sorry," she said. For whatever it was worth.

You are not like him, Miraghan said. *Thankfully, you are not like him.*

"How do you know?"

This mage who'd entrapped Miraghan sounded like a bad man. If Pip wasn't like him, then it followed that she was good. Goodness, though, was a hard thing to believe in.

You feel remorse. You have a line you will not cross. Purity in your heart. He did not.

So simple. She had no time to dwell on that.

Is your destination in the Violet Range or beyond?

"No, it's here. He's looking for treasure. Some artifact called a dragon egg."

I know. He has been using you to find the way.

"Me? But I don't know the way."

But I do. Through our connection, I have been leading you. Did you not notice that he gave you no directions? That he never once took the lead?

Pip shook her head. She hadn't noticed. She'd assumed he was just letting her scare away bandits or secure the trail ahead of him.

"How do you know the way?"

Because it is my home he seeks. My hoard. My kin.

"There it is," Kallus said, pointing ahead of them. "The cave we're looking for."

"How can you tell?" Pip asked, though she already knew the answer.

Now that she knew to look for it, she could feel Miraghan's pull in her mind, leading her onward. This was why Kallus had hired her. Not as a bodyguard, but as a guide.

He'd found what he was looking for. Did he still need her?

She felt a sort of warm hum from the sword that she guessed meant Miraghan recognized the location.

Before either of them could move, a shadow swooped out of the mouth of the cave. She ducked down behind some rocks and pulled Kallus with her.

"That," she said, "is definitely a dragon."

"No, no, no," he whispered. "This cave was supposed to be empty. The dragon's dead. Three hundred years. It's soul…"

Pip looked at him. He pursed his lips and fell silent. How much did he know about Miraghan? More than he was letting on.

The dragon soared out around a peak, dropped low on the turn back, picked something up in its claws, and flew back into the cave.

"Damn," Kallus muttered.

"What are we going to do now?" Pip asked.

"We've come too far to fail now. I want that egg."

She arched an eyebrow. "That's not an answer."

"I'd like to see you come up with an idea," he spat.

"Didn't pay me for ideas," she pointed out. "Only for protection."

"Yes, and you've got your work cut out for you, so you better be worth the money."

Pip stayed quiet, as she always did when employers got close to insulting her. In these moments, she reminded herself that she was simply a means to an end for them, just as they were to her, the end for her being a slightly heavier coin purse, a hot meal in her belly, and a roof over her head for the night.

Except that this time was different. Kallus had deceived her from the start, and there was more to this than he pretended.

"We obviously can't go in while he's in there," Kallus mused aloud, "so we could…wait out here until it leaves again."

Brilliant. "In that case, I suggest we split up, one of us on either side of the opening. When he leaves, you go in for the egg. I'll stand watch."

"Yes, yes, that could work. All right then. You take the eastern side, and I'll take the western."

Taking the west meant he didn't have to go very far at all, whereas she had to either loop around or sneak across the opening, far enough away from the threshold so as not to attract attention. Still, she'd risk it for the separation, which would give her time to converse with Miraghan again. There was so much going on that she didn't yet understand.

"Fine," Pip said.

Staying low to the ground, she walked as far away from the cave as she could get in the mountainous area and sneaked across to the eastern side. Once there, she settled against the rocky wall and unsheathed her sword.

"Miraghan? Miraghan, are you there?"

She didn't know how this worked. Maybe Mirghan was napping. Could a soul trapped in a sword nap? Did souls without bodies even need to sleep?

"Miraghan?"

Yes?

"We're here, at your cave. But there's another dragon here. How do we get the egg?

You cannot take it, Pippa. The child does not deserve to be a slave.

"He said it was just a name. For a gem. A piece of treasure."

He lied. If you help him take it, you will imprison that child as surely as Lestrange imprisoned me.

"But…is it true what he says? That it could cure ills? Eradicate the soulstorms?"

I don't know. It is possible. Dragon power was once beyond the imaginings of mortals, but you may have progressed far in these intervening centuries. He may be able to find a way. Even if he could, I do not believe that is what he will do.

"What do you mean?"

Dragon scales, dragon fangs, dragon bile. These things fetch high prices in your human realm. Why settle for studying a dragon egg, or making an ally of a hatchling, when he could chain it, cut it apart and sell its pieces? There are many ways one can exploit a dragonling. Great power can be wielded for good or for evil, and humans are not to be trusted with it.

"I can't let him do that," Pip said. "I won't."

Hours later, the dragon swooped out of the cave and flew south. This time, he didn't make a quick loop and return. Pip held her breath as she watched. When her lungs burned, she let the breath out and signaled to

Kallus to head into the cave. Standing, she scanned the rocky surroundings for any sign of activity.

"Painbringer!" Kallus shouted. "I need your help!"

Pip scoured the sky once more, quickly, before darting into the cave. Kallus had lit a torch, and sunlight filtered in from a few crevices in the cave's ceiling, so she was able to see well enough. The dragon's hoard was enormous, separate piles of varying heights comprised of coins, gems, jewelry, weapons, and other valuables.

Kallus was at the far end of the cave. The egg, gleaming black, lay at his feet, ringed by piles of coins and jewels. It was far bigger than he'd told her. By the look of it, it was far bigger than even he'd realized.

"I need your help lifting it."

"How are we going to get it down the mountain?" she asked.

"We'll carry it. I'm paying you for your muscle, woman. What's so hard to understand about that?"

"If it's heavy enough that it needs both of us to lift it, then we're never going to make it down. We'll need a harness or something. Or a way to drag it."

"I am not dragging something this important!"

Pip bit her tongue once more as Kallus yammered on. He should have planned for this. If he was such a treasure hunter, such a researcher, he would have known the plan never goes to plan and he'd have prepared for something to go awry.

"We should just leave it," she said.

"Leave it? After we came all this way? After all the sacrifices I've made? Don't you understand how important this is?"

"I just…" She didn't have a choice. She was going to have to tell him that she knew. "I can't go through with this. You're talking about stealing a child, Kallus. Using it for your own gain. I can't let you do it."

Kallus looked surprise for a moment. Then his face turned hard. Suddenly, he wasn't the affable financier who'd hired her for a treasure-hunting expedition anymore.

A shadow darkened the cave. When it didn't immediately pass, Pip turned around, unsheathing the sword as she did.

Only to face a giant fucking dragon. It was a lot larger on the ground than it had seemed in the sky.

Well, she had known it was a possibility as soon as Kallus told her they were going to the Violet Range, and their plan hadn't exactly been well thought through. It had relied on a dragon who'd been dead for three hundred years and a woman who made her living by punching things very hard

"Humans" the dragon said, sounding affronted. "Here? How dare you set foot in my home after all that you have taken from my kind?"

"Stay back, beast!" Kallus exclaimed, brandishing his staff.

Pip, however, remained quiet. A dragon stood before her, massive and monstrous, and the soul of a dragon resided within the sword in her hand. That had to mean something. Miraghan had led her here for a reason.

"Miraghan," she said, holding the blade out and upright, where the dragon could see that she meant it no harm. "Miraghan, we've found your kin."

Yes, I recognize him. Ghalthrugan.

The dragon peered at the sword curiously but seemed to understand. "Miraghan? No. It isn't possible. You were lost to us, three hundred years ago. How have you taken this form?"

The work of a mage and necromancer. I was wronged, and I have only just woken up. I have much to relate.

"And I will listen. But first, I will eat."

Or you could let them leave, Miraghan said.

The dragon laughed. "Leave? They have come to my home and intend to take a child. If I let them leave, will they not simply return in greater numbers, with more powerful magic? I don't think so. What would you do, Elder? What would you do if they had come for the children under your care?"

"We'll leave in peace and never tell a soul what's transpired," Kallus said, even as he glanced at Pip and mouthed, *Do something.*

Ghalthrugan glared at him. "Why should I believe you? All humans do is lie."

He spat a burst of flame in Kallus's direction, but Kallus only planted his staff on the floor and a bubble of protection sprang up around him, protecting him from the heat.

So, that was his plan. He would protect himself while Pip was burned alive. She'd thought he was just an investor, but it turned out he had some magic of his own. Would he have enough to get away with the egg?

She thought through her choices. What if she could prove herself to the dragon? Prove she wouldn't share her knowledge of this place with other treasure hunters, that she would keep her mouth shut and let him continue on with his life in whatever counted as peace for a dragon.

She could show him that not all humans were the same. That some could see the wrong that had been done to him and his mother, despite their differences.

Not all humans lie, Miraghan said. *I believe one here is trustworthy.*

"Then show me," said the Ghalthrugan.

"How?" Pip asked.

You know what you must do, Miraghan said.

Kallus gestured wildly. "I've had enough of this. I didn't come all this way, spend all that gold liberating that sword from the palace, just to be cheated out of my due. The egg is mine."

From within his cloak, he drew some kind of phial. Something to use against Ghalthrugan, Pip guessed. She gnawed at her bottom lip. That made her decision a mite easier. Just a mite. But it came down to what was right, and there wasn't much choice here.

Still… There would be no going back.

"What do you intend to do with the egg?" she asked Kallus.

His expression was incredulous. "I think we have bigger things to worry about right now."

But Pip knew the dragons would wait.

"No. Tell me what you're going to do with the egg. If you're going to do what you said you would, will you destroy it in the process? And if you don't do what you said you would, will you sell it to the highest bidder?

I've seen the price a single scale can fetch. I can only imagine what an entire egg will. Or will you incubate it, wait for it to hatch, make a pet of it? Treat it cruelly so that it'll wish you had killed it instead?" She hardened her voice so that he understood. His life depended on his answer. "Tell me."

"This is ridiculous," he spat.

Scoffing, he faced the dragon towering in front of them once more. His fingers clenched on the phial

It was too late though. She had seen it clearly in his eyes. Kallus was every bit a monster as the mage that had imprisoned Miraghan.

"Kallus," she said, and when he turned toward her, she shoved the sword through his middle.

His eyes widened in surprise, but as soon as she pulled the sword away, it was over. He slumped to the cave floor.

What a sorry waste of a life.

She stared up at Ghalthrugan, a challenge in her gaze.

"Very well," said Ghalthrugan. He tossed his head toward the entrance. "You may go. The Elder has vouched for you, and you have proven that you are not like the rest of your species. Perhaps not all humans are liars and schemers."

"Human or dragon, some things are always wrong."

He nodded, then turned his attention to the egg, still sitting at the heart of its nest of treasure. "You're on your own to make it down the mountain."

"I think I'll be all right," Pip said.

She was used to taking care of herself. She was the

only one who could.

She glanced down at her sword, still wet with Kallus's blood. "Miraghan?"

She waited but heard only silence.

The dragon's eyes seemed to soften. "Can you not hear her?"

Tears burned in Pip's eyes. She looked down at the cave floor, gathered herself, and shook her head. "Not anymore."

The sword's inscription glimmered. *Only to a warrior pure of heart will I reveal my wealth of secrets.*

Pure of heart. Someone who hadn't killed. Someone Pip no longer was.

She wiped the sword on her trousers and set it down on the closest pile of treasure, murmuring a goodbye in her head to Miraghan the dragon. Then, with a twinge of regret, she took Kallus's staff and the phial from his unresisting hands. On his belt, she found his coin purse. No sense in wasting them. She took the rations and supplies in his pack, dropped them into hers, and walked to the cave entrance.

She paused without looking back. She wanted to ask Ghalthrugan to take care of the dragonling when it finally hatched, but what could she tell him that he didn't already know?

She walked out. It was still light outside, which seemed wrong. The sun shone brightly up here, and she had to squint against it. Her legs trembled, and her chest felt heavy. The wind wiped the tears from her eyes.

Even if it took her the whole return trip to forgive herself for this transgression, she would do it. Doing the right thing had never been particularly rewarding, but maybe she'd gone some way to fixing some of the damage the mage Lestrange had done. Besides, with only herself to rely on, she couldn't be at war with herself.

When she got back to civilization, she would need a new sword.

Pip began the descent.

JUST A GAME

ALANNA ROBERTSON-WEBB

Day grinned as she set the game box in Niv's outstretched hands. When he opened his eyes, the joy dancing across her friend's cheeks told her the impulse purchase had been well worth the extravagant number of silversheets she'd spent.

"Is this a Tenes set?" he asked, amazed.

"That's right! More than three hundred years old, believe it or not. And still in excellent condition. Apparently, it was just sitting around in some dusty old academic's study."

"You will indulge me with a round, yes?"

"Of course! I was hoping you would ask. It's been too long since we allowed ourselves some time to relax together."

Niv plopped down onto the blanket Day's servants had spread upon the riverbank, unlacing his sandals so that he could slide his aching feet into the soothing water. Day opened the board and set up the pieces. Tenes was the game of lords and kings, and someone with Niv's means could never have afforded to own a set. Now he owned the very finest set in Guardiana. What were friends for?

Day had heard the game had come from a distant, sand-shrouded country past the Red Land. In those far reaches, Tenes was more than just a game. It was used for divination. Each of the 30 tiles represented good or bad fortune, depending on where your pawn landed for the final turn. Throwing sticks determined which direction the wooden board was traversed in, and those with an ear toward rumors of dark magic often claimed that the board doubled as a conduit for departed spirits.

She just thought it looked fun.

It was not often that they got to spend much time together lately—not since Day had to take over her ailing father's business—so the little moments they could salvage were precious to them both. She knew Niv would never have admitted it, but he missed her when she was gone.

It was a warm, sunny afternoon, and with the hustle and bustle of Crow's Cove in the distance, the duo could enjoy some time away from the grind of daily life. It would have been a nice day to propose, if a man were in the mood.

Once she was done with the board, she waved a small, delicate hand in front of his face. "Helloooo?

Niv, is anyone at home up in that head of yours?"

He reached out, fingers lacing with hers as their eyes met, sapphire and emerald gleaming in the daylight. He leaned in towards her ear, breath gently ghosting upon her neck.

"I am always home, as long as you are by my side."

Day felt a soft flush spread across her skin, fingers lingering between his for longer than was proper before she finally pulled away. She turned back to the board, head tilting to the side as a wave of ginger curls partially obscured her face.

"I, um, I… Ah, yes, you are. Always. Oh, umm… Well, let us play…"

Her gaze dropped back to the board, the pieces enduring a much closer, more prolonged scrutiny than they really needed. His intimations were so strong sometimes, but he was a poet and had a poet's soul. Probably to be expected he'd speak that way. Any woman across Blue Haven, across the whole of Guardiana, would be lucky to have him. She just hoped she could remain his friend, no matter what.

She gestured to the game. "Sh-shall we play?"

Today was the day. Niv knew he would need to be direct. Day was shy, and too proper a lady to think he would be romantically forward. If he waited too long— if her father passed before he admitted his feelings—the people of Blue Haven would think him a cad and her a fool, that he was proposing because of her inheritance. So it would be today.

He would tell her that he wanted her to be his wife, that he wanted to show her the beauty of Guardiana beyond the bounds of Blue Haven, and that he wanted to be by her side through all the ups and downs that life would cast their way.

"Niv! Hellloooo? Goodness, whose forehead do I have to tap to get some attention today?"

While he'd been daydreaming of whisking Day away, she had finished dressing the board, squinting at the small, square sheet of papyrus with its scrawled instructions barely legible. She had picked their pawn sets—hers with a water lily carved on top and his with a curved sword etched along the side—and the pieces balanced precariously on the edges of their tiles.

They almost seemed to vibrate, eager to be used again after decades of neglect.

"Alright, how do we play?"

What followed was a vigorous half-hour battle of pawn swapping, blockade forming and stick tossing, both players hoping to see the colored side of their sticks land face-up on their turn. It started out fun and reminded him of all the things he loved about her, but as the game progressed, a creeping sense of dread began to thump along Niv's spine. There were only five 'bad' tiles out of thirty—tiles that denoted misfortune or negativity—but Day managed to land on all of them. They were supposed to tell her future, to portend what would soon happen, and Niv was not pleased.

Fear

Sorrow

Lost

Trapped
Alone
His own tiles weren't much more encouraging.
Run
Swiftness
Grasp
Run? From what?

He tried to ignore the feeling of dread pressing against his ribs, the sense that something was wrong as their turns unfolded. Niv chose instead to focus on Day, her glittering eyes alight as she carefully maneuvered a pawn over a three-pawn blockade, ending with her piece on a tile engraved with a vortex-like swirl.

That move lost her the game.

Her folly allowed Niv to jump his last piece over hers, and with his dozen pawns off the board he had triumphed.

"Looks like I win!"

Niv grinned rakishly, shooting Day a wink and trying to push back his disquiet. She rolled her eyes playfully.

"Fine, fine, my big, strong man wins! Now, what does my ending tile mean? This is supposed to be the part that can prophesize our future."

He picked up the instructions papyrus, heart thudding. She had called him 'her man', however subconsciously, and a small bloom of hope unfurled in his chest. He focused on referencing the tiles Day's remaining pieces rested on. Their unique configuration would give a message specific to her fate, supposedly.

But with how wrinkled and torn the paper was, the

only part he could make out were the words 'the afterlife rides a storm'. It looked like some parts of the prophecy were missing. He read it aloud to Day, who wrinkled her nose in response.

"Well, that was disappointing. What about you? Does the winner get to see their future?"

"Not quite, but it says here the winner may cast the sticks one last time. If four or more land color-side up then it denotes good luck."

Niv gathered the nine, thin sticks, their brittle bark crackling like lightning beneath his fingertips. He gently tossed them, and every single one landed color-side down.

For a moment, he was glad that superstition did not run in his veins. He might have felt even more unsettled. Caught up again in his musings, he didn't realize he'd scooped up Day's final pawn. He turned it over in his hands, fingertips tracing lightly over the surface, the lily carved into the top, then jerked his hand away as if the pawn had burnt him.

He'd heard a voice coming from it.

The playing piece dropped, nearly rolling into the stream until a small rock blocked its descent.

"Niv, what is it? Are you alright?"

Day's brows scrunched together; alarm clear in her features as Niv sprang up off the blanket.

"By the Circle, did you hear the woman? She said… She said we'd played the game with her bones… That her skin revealed our fates!"

Day shook her head and took his hand, trying to pull him back down. "No. I heard no one, save for us. What did you hear?"

"Madness. Three hundred years of madness. Seeing the future without eyes. No mouth to speak the prophecy. She's been waiting for someone to listen, Day."

"Niv, is this a new piece you're working on? You're starting to scare me."

"Where… Where did you find this board?"

"A friend of father's had it at his estate in Kingsgate. He bought it at auction, but he couldn't get the box open. I bought it from him rather than leave it to gather dust. I just wanted to give you a gift."

Niv refused to meet her eyes, trying to smooth his expression into a calm, unreadable mask.

"That was very kind of you. I just, ah, remembered that I accepted a shift with Baker Thomas. I must get to his shop immediately, alright? Maybe we can play again some other time?"

He fell to his knees, started stuffing the pawns and papyrus and sticks back into the box.

Whatever was wrong with this game, he had to get it away from Day.

He was lying.

Day realized this was the first time Niv had ever told her a falsehood. Less than an hour ago, she had passed Baker Thomas and his family as they left to visit kin just outside of Blue Haven, and whenever this happened his shop would close for the day. She visited Crow's Cove, visited Niv, often enough to know that. There was no way he would be about to start a shift there, especially not in the middle of the day.

"By all means," she whispered. "Mayhap I will see you later today, after you finish working?"

Niv gave an absent nod. Normally, a promise to see him that evening would have had him brimming with enthusiasm. Instead, he barely seemed to notice. He ran to the edge of the gently churning water and snatched the runaway piece. He was fixated on the carved, yellowed pawn as though it were hypnotizing him; he barely even grunted an acknowledgement at Day, wide-eyed gaze glued to the thimble-sized object. As he turned to face her, skin flushed like he had just run a great distance, he seized the board from the picnic blanket and tucked it under a trembling arm.

"Niv? Please, tell me what's wrong. It's just a game, and this isn't like y—"

"Shut up! Shut up, shut up, SHUT UP!"

No one had ever dared scream at Lady Daylinia Vassanar de Minthey, daughter of Baron Reginald Vassanar de Minthey III, heir to the de Minthey Trading Company. Day cringed, raising a hand between herself and the one person she had always seen as unshakable.

"Niv, stop! This isn't you! Please, just explain this to me. Please…?"

Niv's head shook violently, whipping from side-to-side. His eyes glazed over. A white sheen covered those beautiful sapphire orbs, his body twitching like a crushed ant and his jaw hanging loose.

"He returns! Bewa…Lestran…agic…deat…stor…"

The young man began choking, a trickle of spittle leaking from the corner of his mouth, chest heaving. His head jerked to the side, the unnatural angle making his spine press visibly against his flesh. There was a pause, a moment where the world seemed to hold a breath, and then Niv blinked. His eyes were once again blue, pupils dilated as they took in the sun's harsh glare. He straightened, looking around groggily as though waking from a deep sleep.

"D-Day? Wh-What happenned?"

Day, hands clutched over her mouth, could only shake her head, sobs escaping from between clenched teeth. Niv's eyes widened. He stared at the board in his hands and she couldn't figure out what was going on in his mind. What had happened to him? What had taken control of his body for that short time?

"Day, this game… It's…wrong. I have to get rid of it! I won't let it hurt you!"

Day's curls bounced wildly as she shook her head. Her confusion must have been clear on her face as she tried to grasp why his behavior had changed so suddenly.

"No! It's a *toy*, Niv. It's just a stupid game, just something I bought to show you how much you mean to me! What is going on with you?!"

"I…I h-have to g-go. I'm so s-sorry! G-get home now, p-please…"

With that Niv turned and ran, seemingly oblivious to the tears streaming from Day's eyes as she reached out to him. Her pleas fell upon deaf ears, trembling hands dropping limply into her lap as he disappeared from view.

She stared at where Niv had been sitting, then to where the board had lain, the empty spaces mocking her like the after-image of a nightmare. A chill wind twined through the trees, the once-sunny sky darkening unnaturally fast. Within moments, broiling purple clouds, the color of a bruise, filled the sky. The first warning screeches of an approaching soulstorm split the air.

Day took a shuddering breath. She'd dismissed her servants to Crow's Cove so that she would have privacy with Niv, and she was eternally grateful that they wouldn't be outside when the storm struck. But she was too far from town to make it herself.

She spied an old fishing shack at the riverside and gasped with relief. There, she could shelter from the corrosive rain—tainted by the dark magic of a long-dead wizard—which would leech the very spirit from a person's body if it reached the skin. When Day was five years old, she had watched it happen to one of the stable hands, and she never again wished to hear someone scream in that raw, unvarnished anguish. Suffering through the wails from the souls trapped within the storm was horrific but being close enough to hear one join their unholy chorus was ten times worse.

The young noblewoman forced her shocked, cold body to move, shoving aside the food she had brought in a haphazard attempt to clear the blanket off. She draped the picnic blanket over herself, a false sense of security encircling her as the cotton settled across her trembling shoulders. Day began heading towards the hut, her petite, silk shoes wearing with every frantic step, until she was sprinting in thin rags.

She skidded to a halt, indecision bubbling. She turned from the hut, only a few steps away. She had to make sure Niv was safe.

He had run off in such a state of distress that he may not have noticed the Soulstorm was coming, and if he was not headed straight back to town…

No…

Day shook the macabre thought from her head. He could not have gotten too far ahead of her, and she would reach him before the rain broke. They would find shelter together, and everything would be alright. Even thick trees were enough to absorb the effects of the rain, so she was confident they could find enough cover to survive.

She was going to save the man she loved, no matter the risk.

Run fasta, stupid boy. The storm's a comin', an' you don' wanna be no corpse now, do ya?

Niv wanted to throw his hands over his ears—anything to drown out the voice of the crotchety, old lady in his head—but his hands were still clamped around the folded game board.

What had woken the spirit in the board? Their skin upon the pieces? The conclusion of their game? Maybe when he'd read the prophecy to Day, like some kind of magic spell? He should have left the game alone, the second he felt the unmistakable grit of bone beneath his fingertips. He'd assumed it was some kind of ivory, but he'd been wrong.

Real, human bones had been used to make that game.

He should never have touched the cursed object,

never agreed to play with Day.

Stop ya bellyachin', boy. Better you wake me than ya girlie. She knows no magic, so talkin' ta me woulda made her battier than a bear cave.

"I don't know magic."

That what ya think? Aye, I see it now. Buried it deep, so you have. All that fear o' magic, from back in the day when a mage was the worst o' them all. Yeh've lived a lie. Yer parents and yer parents' parents.

"Shut up! By the Circle, can you stop talking for even just one heartbeat?! Please, leave me in peace…"

I just be soooooo bored! Three hundred years in a tiny, little box, bones rattling around inside me. He used to think the future was a game. Prophecy was something he could dodge with just the right move. Didn't believe what the Great Madame Victoria told him. Then I told him he'd get caught, that they'd all know. Didn't like that. So here I am. Just a game now.

"Who? Who did all that?"

Ain't you listening? Lestrange, dummy! Why, I remember he said—

Niv ignored her stream of incessant babbling, but he felt a twinge of sympathy. He needed to let her chatter as she saw fit. He had no idea what he was going to do with the Tenes board, but burning it sounded like the best idea. Maybe he'd release her from it that way.

He didn't want to be used again. When she'd taken control of his body, her voice tearing from his throat as if he were no more than a puppet, Niv had been helpless. She hadn't been able to dominate his mind for long, but he had no desire to experience that sensation again. Getting rid of the board was absolutely his priority.

Right after surviving the soulstorm.

He turned his head, gauging the state of the clouds piling up behind him. They were still purple, and the soulstorm's screaming was far enough away that he could barely make it out over the thudding of his heart and pounding of his footsteps, so he had a few minutes to find shelter. The trees by the riverside were so thin and widespread that Niv feared they would fail to offer sufficient protection, and he knew he was still too far from the outskirts of Crow's Cove to make it inside a building.

Nature had gone silent, the birds ceasing to sing as the storm approached. His eyes darted left-to-right in a frantic swing as he searched for cover.

As the minutes ticked by, panic began to rise within him. There was no cover, no thick trees or buildings, not even a burrow he could dig into, and the once-blue sky was all but devoured by the purple clouds.

Over there, dummy.

As if an invisible string connected Niv to Victoria, his eyes were jerked to the left, where a few semi-rotted planks were leaning against a thin birch.

Use ya brain, while ya still got one. If ya get caught in that storm, ya be as good as dead. Just a mindless zombie. No thoughts, no soul, just hunger. Happens ta all the folk the rain captures. Seen it countless times.

"They're all mindless? So, they're basically just animated bodies?"

All of 'em. No recognizin' those they love, nothin' of their self left inside. Just a walkin' husk that you be familiar with. Now go! Get under that shelter! No time...

112

"Yes!"

Niv ran to the crude shelter, squeezing himself into the tiny wedge of space between the tree and the planks. It was cramped, and there were beetle larva wriggling in the grooves of the planks, but none of that mattered.

He was safe. He hoped.

The wailing soulstorm was growing closer, the sound of the trapped spirits within crying out in eternal anguish as they were forced to relive the worst moments of their lives in a constant loop, a cruel parody of the Unbroken Circle. Niv shuddered, tucking himself even further into his tiny triangle of safety. The rain wouldn't fall until the clouds had morphed completely from purple to green, and the—

She followed ya.

"What?"

The girlie. She be a-comin'!

"Day?!"

Without hesitating Niv squeezed himself out from under the planks, the Tenes board still cradled under his arm.

"Where is she? Where is she right now?!"

Ya ain't gonna make it, boy.

"I have to try."

Well, I'm already dead. Knock yaself out. She's left. Go left, back by the stream, where ya came from. Watch out for the rain. I ain't got skin no more, but you sure do.

"Day! Dayyyyyy!"

He ran, tuning out Victoria and screaming for his friend. His stomach knotted, sweat dripping from his brow as he held back the urge to vomit. He had to find her. He could not let the woman he loved die. She was only following him because of how strangely he'd acted. He would find her. He ignored the way his heart banged against his ribs when he thought about the size of the shelter, but that was secondary; he would deal with that once Day was in his arms.

Niv pelted down the trail, not pausing until he could see Day. She was making her way towards him, fighting against the ever-growing wind. The gale tore away the blanket she was clutching, fabric ripping from her hands and spiraling up into the green-tinged clouds. She tried to grab it back, but the storm was too fast. It was gone, and she was more exposed than ever. She bowed her head, continuing her slow trudge against the windy onslaught.

"Day!"

The call made her head shoot up, her eyes widening when she saw him. She waved her arms frantically, signaling for Niv to follow her.

"This way! There's a fishing hut back here!"

His heart leapt. So much better than the rickety lean-to he'd found. "Alright!"

"Niv, please hurry! The clouds are so thick, I think they're going to—"

He closed the gap between them, nearly getting within arm's reach, just as the storm morphed to the next stage of its macabre color dance. Day cut off mid-sentence, face twisting in fear as she threw her arms protectively over her head.

Drip.

The tainted rain began to plop down, speckling gently onto everything it touched.

Drip.

Drip.

Drip.

Everything, and everyone.

Drip.

Drip.

Drip.

Drip.

Niv tried to get to Day, to throw his body over hers if that was what it took to save her, but he was too late. She began to scream, the drops sizzling on her skin as they washed over her. Her flesh was not just dissolving; that would nearly have been a mercy. With each drop, a little bit of her soul escaped her body. White wisps of spirit gathered above her head, forming into a bright, slowly rotating ball of light. As more and more of Day's soul was siphoned from her convulsing body, she sank to her knees, head lolling skyward as the rain tore away the very thing that made her Day. The rain even got into her mouth, the smell of burning flesh growing stronger as her insides liquefied.

When looking back on that moment, Niv could never recall if he or Day was screaming louder.

His frozen limbs refused to obey him. He wanted to scoop her up in her arms, to cradle her to his chest until she woke up, to hold her until she returned to normal, but this was no mere illness. The orb that was her soul finished collecting its pieces, then began to rise, swiftly engulfed by the whirling mass of cloud. Niv lost sight of it, the green clouds devouring his beloved's spirit.

He stood there, eyes fixated on the sky, the rain soaking into his shirt and pants until they stuck to his skin.

It took him several more strained heartbeats to realize that he was unhurt.

The rain, while falling on him just as steadily as on Day, was having no effect. The Tenes board—long-since forgotten—glowed with a soft, blue light that encompassed Niv's body like a shield. When Day finally stopped moving, about ten minutes after the downpour started, her body released a final, strangled gurgle. She crumpled to the ground; limbs splayed haphazardly, but even then Niv was unable to bring himself to go to her. His screams had stopped at some point, but that barely even registered.

"Day…?"

The heartbroken whisper was drowned out by the pattering rain, the world uncaring that another victim had been claimed by a soulstorm.

Sorry, boy.

Victoria's voice, softer than before, seemed to be almost apologetic as it echoed in his mind. Niv took a moment to respond, throat hoarse as he forced the words past his tongue.

"Could you have saved her too, if I had reached her sooner?"

No, it woulda made no difference. I barely helped you as is, wasn't sure I coulda at all. I've been trapped, grown weak. We're bonded now, so even her holdin' the board woulda been useless.

"Thank you."

His reply was automatic, a generic response which was the only thing Niv could think of to say in that moment. With a primordial scream, fueled by white-hot rage, he lifted the Tenes board over his head and hurled it at the ground. Thin wood splintered, painted tiles cracking as they scattered across the path. The blue glow refused to fade, and the tingle that indicated Victoria was in his mind remained, but Niv heard no rebuke. He felt numb, void of all the happiness and determination that marked his normal self, and inside was a looming pit that threatened to overwhelm him.

Everything had happened so fast, so confusingly, that he had no time to process any of it. What did it all mean? What good was having a seer in your head if they failed to warn you clearly about important events?

He dropped to his knees, hands sinking into the mud forming from the path's hard-packed dirt.

"How do I get rid of you?"

Silence.

Victoria, like a fly trapped in milk, was still buzzing around the confines of his mind, but she was unable, or unwilling, to surface. He howled, a sound akin to a wounded animal, and from his toes to his ears he could feel his body warming as anger spread through his veins.

"Talk!"

No response.

Niv pounded his fists into the earth again and again, screaming until his already inflamed throat was so raw that it refused to produce even a whisper. Bloody tatters of skin hung from the sides of his hands, the gashes across his knuckles bleeding profusely. The rain, still falling, continued to mock him with each drop that pitter-pattered upon his hunched back. The pawns, the fragments of Victoria's bones, spilled into the mud.

He stared at them, at the way they lay in the dirt like carelessly discarded trash. Lestrange—that son of a mule—was the one responsible for all of this. Dead for three centuries, yet the newt-eyed blaggart was still causing untold damage across Guardiana. Answers were needed.

Minutes passed, the only sound the wailing of Lestrange's captured souls. When Niv trusted his voice to work, he sat up, mud splattered across his heated skin. He rubbed his neck, trying to soothe his abused throat, but questions needed to be asked.

"Were you trying to warn us of Lestrange's return, or of something to do with him? How is that even possible? This makes no sense! He is dead, so how could he come back?! This is utter nonsense."

Not dead. Slumberin'…until…new body comes…

Victoria sounded weak, her voice fizzing in and out as it had when they first connected.

"Where?"

…castle…Queen's…

With that, the connection seemed to peter out, an exhausted Victoria retreating deeper into the far reaches of Niv's mind.

"No! Please, come back! I need you…"

Once again it was silence that greeted the inside of his mind. The perpetual wail of the soulstorm continued, though the cries were ebbing as the storm passed. Niv was left alone, Day's scarred body the only company he had left. She would need to be burned; her body completely incinerated before she could come back to life as a mindless, savage zombie like so many other soulstorm victims had.

He had no means of making a fire without going back to town, so with trembling knees, Niv hauled himself upright. He gathered the remnants of the board, along with the human pawns, fingers shaking so hard that he had to reach for each piece multiple times.

There was a flint and steel set in his hut, so even though it would take a while to retrieve, he would at least be able to put Lady Daylinia Vassanar de Minthey to rest.

Then, thanks to Victoria's warning, he would tell the Queen that Lestrange was returning.

When Day awoke, she tried to rub her eyes, thinking that she was still gripped by the remnants of a bad dream, but her sore, tired body would not obey. She was in the forest still, the memory of the day's events slowly returning to her, and she wished that she had been able to get Niv to stay with her instead of running off.

Niv!

She sat up, heart thudding painfully when she realized that she could not spot him anywhere. She remembered seeing him, watching his face twist in horror as the rain began to fall, and then everything had gone black. Knowing Niv, he must have gotten them to shelter just in time, and once the rain had ceased, he had gone off to find her servants because she had not awoken.

It made perfect sense, and Day figured she could surprise him by heading back to Crow's Cove alone. Day raised her eyes skyward, studying the surrounding area to determine the best route.

The early evening sky was unblemished; to anyone who had not just witnessed the wrath of the soulstorm, it would have looked as though nothing had happened. The roiling mass of green clouds was gone, and once again bird song and squirrel chatter drifted playfully on the dusky breeze. In the distance, Day could see a dozen columns of smoke: a typical image that tended to accompany the wake of a soulstorm. With so many funeral pyres the nearby sky seemed a vast cemetery of soot, each one a tribute to some ancient god of sun or enchantress of fire.

Even as she watched, a bleak exhalation of smoke curled up from a new pyre, darkening the sky further and putting out the few stars brave enough to have started twinkling.

No matter how many shelters people made, or how often they checked the sky, the storms always rolled in unnaturally fast. No warning was ever given, and it could take anywhere from minutes to hours before the rain fell. There was simply no way to guarantee that every person was inside, or close enough to shelter to survive, but at least she and Niv had.

Day angled her gaze towards the path, slowly hauling herself up onto exhausted feet. The rain had washed away any tracks, leaving no trace of Niv. She knew the general direction of his hut, however, and set off with staunch determination.

As Day made her way back to Crow's Cove, the sky finished darkening, but the crescent moon must have been extra bright; her eyes had no trouble adjusting to nightfall as they normally did. She kept her arms in front of her, just in case she stumbled and bumped into a jutting rock or twisting root and made her way slowly down the path. Every small jostle to her body hurt, and Day could not help but let out small, pain-filled moans whenever a particularly hard step jolted her protesting muscles.

Finally, after a walk that should have only taken twenty minutes, but took closer to an hour, Day could see the outskirts of Crow's Cove. The lights of the huts and hovels gleamed through the gathering dark, and the rebuking twinge of her facial muscles told her that she'd tried to smile. She stumbled down one of the outer paths, her feet familiar with the twists and turns leading to Niv's cabin. At one point, she passed a side alley where a drunken man was leaning sloppily against a wall, singing softly to himself. Day halted, common courtesy dictating that she greet him.

"Helloooooooo…"

As Day swayed in place, parched throat trying to form a cohesive greeting, the stranger let out a screech. He backpedaled, knocking over a crate of empty milk pails, the clatter echoing about the alley.

"G-get back, evil thing! Oh C-Circle, spare me!"

Before Day could respond, the man turned, doing the best imitation of a sprint his inebriated limbs would allow. She watched him go, her brows knitted together as she tried to call after him.

"Waaaaaaaait…"

Her voice was more of a croak, the sound grating even to her own ears. After a moment, she gave a little half-shrug, shaking her head as she continued to Niv's cabin. Maybe she was covered in dirt and grass, or her red, often untamed mane of hair had been mistaken for a monster's fur? The man had clearly been drinking, so Day pushed the odd encounter from her mind to focus on getting to the one person she wanted to see more than anything in the world.

She was close, so close, and within a few moments she would be at his door.

At one point, she nearly stumbled, her arms stretching out once more to help catch her if she fell, and she moaned as every muscle tightened in agony.

Finally!

There was Niv's door, outlined by the moon's cool light. She was hardly a handful of steps from it, teeth bared happily, when Niv came barreling out. He nearly slammed into her, barely catching himself as he swerved to avoid colliding with her. His eyes, so wide in the moonlight, were fixated on her.

"Niiiiiiiiiiiiiiiiiiv…"

Damn her dry throat!

Day began coughing, body spasming, arms flailing wildly with the force of her laboured breathing. She nearly whacked Niv in the chest, but he dodged her unintended swing. She stepped back, putting some distance between them until she had better control of her body, but she failed to see what was behind her. The gently-shining lights of Crow's Cove had been replaced with a bobbing sea of torches, loud, angry yells swelling like a wave.

"Kill the beast!"

"How did we miss one?"

"Who cares? Bring her down!"

"They must all be destroyed, before they turn the rest of us!"

"BURN IT! BURN IT! BURN IT!"

Day turned back to face Niv, tears threatening to spill down her cheeks.

"Niiiiiiiv?"

Something was wrong.

His face was hard, a grimace curling up the corner of his normally smiling lips. He bent and picked up a large rock

"Niiiiiiiv?!"

"Get back, monster! You are but a husk, an empty puppet, and I shall avenge Day!"

She scrabbled frantically at her throat with dirty fingers. Why were her words so garbled? What was wrong with her? She needed to make Niv understand that she was still her, and that there was some sort of misunderstanding.

She reached for him as she always had, palm outstretched, but his only response was to pull away in disgust. The stone smashed into her chest. She lurched back, arms wrapping around herself in a weak defense. Niv sidestepped as she dropped to the cobbles.

He used to catch her when she stumbled, not be the reason she fell.

The voices behind her were growing closer, their

bloodlust-filled hollering and whoops reaching a crescendo. Like hounds after a fox, they bayed, giving chase to that which they could not understand. Day, tears finally breaking free from dry eyes, tried to stand.

A swift kick to her ribs kept her floored, and as she was bathed in the fiery glow of torchlight, she looked up at Niv one final time. His eyes were pained, but resolute. Filled with pity and resignation. He snatched her under the arm and turned towards the mob.

"I have it! Here it is!"

Interlude Two

Pawns of Fate

S.O. Green

After the swell of deprivation and misery that was Kingsgate, and the barren, grey peaks of the Range, Blue Haven was a breath of very literal fresh air. Under its expansive canopy, in the humid embrace of its dense undergrowth, and on the shores of its lakes and rivers, streams and pools, there was life. Real, natural life in all its beauty and barbarism, its magnificence and mystery.

Maybe it was just because this had been home, before the palace, for as long as she could remember. They said she'd been carried ashore from a long-distance cargo freighter, swaddled in the arms of a burly First Mate, whom Lyssa had called 'Mama' for the first few years of her life, and then 'Ma'am' for the rest. No one remembered where the ship had come from or how she'd gotten aboard, but they remembered her setting fire to a boy's breeches for pulling her hair, and freezing the pond in the middle of summer so she could skate.

Long story short, when no one else had been able to deal with her, they'd packed her off to the palace and she'd ended up as a mage-in-training, understudy to a man whose power was only a fraction of hers, and spent her days sneaking out to see all the seedy shit Kingsgate had to offer and stealing rich people food from the kitchens. She'd dreamed of escape, the power to fly away, discover her past, shape her own future. Until she'd seen the beautiful and kindly princess walking in the garden, and then leaving had been out and staying had become the thing to do.

She wondered, as she rode back through the tangle of teal, that blue tint that gave the Haven its name, if Ma'am was still alive, or even still on the continent. She also wondered what it would take to convince Camelia to come skating in summer.

You're not sight-seeing, Lyssa. You're investigating soulstorms, remember?

They were getting worse. She remembered the days, during a good season, when you could go about your business and never see a storm. Now they were dropping all over Guardiana, barely a few days apart, and sucking up souls like they were going out of fashion.

She couldn't help but think of Lestrange's study, the objects, now out there in the world. Were they the reason? What was the connection?

"Your Magisty," Merrick grunted.

He pointed out the pyres as they rounded the corner. A dozen of them, all told, smoking faintly in the crisp, morning air. The bodies were already gone. The blackened bones were watched by the people who loved them most overnight, then buried respectfully come first light.

Crow's Cove—at least, that's what the sign said—had been hit hard by the latest storms. So many loved ones lost, and Lyssa found herself wondering, once again, what she was going to do about it all.

One of the pyres must have been for the town sweetheart. The people had put out a portrait of her—dazzling smile and gorgeous, lace dress—and the floral tributes overwhelmed the stack of blackened wood where she'd been burned. One of the people who'd watched over her was still there, perched on a wooden stool, head in hands. As Lyssa dismounted, his head snapped up, eyes narrowed.

"Howdy, neighbour," she called. "Lyssa, Grand Mage to the Crown of Guardiana. Seems like you folk are having a rough few day. Anything we can do to help?"

"Grand Mage?" he asked, looking bewildered. "No, not him. A woman this time. Things have changed since your day. Maybe she's different. Maybe she'll end up the same."

"You okay? You seem a little out of it."

The stranger shook his head and rose off his stool. His eyes seemed to clear up a little. "I'm fine. You were right. It's been rough. I lost someone. Someone very important."

Lyssa nodded and tried not to look at the smile in the portrait. It made her think of Camelia, how she'd behave if anything happened to her queen. Circle, it didn't bear thinking about.

"Would you like to come inside? Drink some tea? Maybe play a game?"

Lyssa's nod was more hesitant than she liked. She wanted to help and refusing to do the one thing she'd been asked was a sizeable dick move, but there was something off about this man and she couldn't place it.

She might have been more worried if she couldn't incinerate him with a wave of her hand.

"Sure. What kind of game?"

"Tenes," he said, and laughed. She didn't know what the joke was.

The stranger's home was like the shack she'd lived in as a kid, warm and comfortable, if not entirely secure. He put a kettle on a pot-bellied stove and Lyssa sat at the table. Merrick stood by the door, hand on sword hilt.

While they waited on tea, the man set up the Tenes board.

"Nice craftsmanship," Lyssa said.

"I made it myself. To replace one that got damaged."

"Are the pawns ivory?"

"Yes," he said, turning away to pour them both a cup.

The tea was a bitter, foreign blend that reminded Lyssa of sitting in Ma'am's kitchen after seeing all the dead fish had made her cry. Ma'am couldn't comfort her worth a damn, but she'd been able to make a good cup of tea. The steam around her nostrils felt like a hug.

"You go first," the man said, pushing the coloured sticks across the table to her.

She did as he suggested, and it didn't take her long to get caught up in the game. She always played to win and Camelia called her a sore loser, but she'd never once set fire to the palace in defeat, so she thought she was actually pretty restrained.

Some of her moves were hesitant though. The tiles she landed on gave her pause.

Faith

Torment

Madness

Murder

Unborn

Theft

Was it a coincidence? She'd visited the Brothers of the Perpetual Journey and they'd told her of a madwoman with bad intentions. The woman in the tavern had told her about her employer's plan to steal a dragon egg. It wasn't a premonition, but how would this man have known about any of it?

And then, as the game progressed…

Music

Trapped

Villain

Justice

Growth

Loss

Searching

Faceless

Love

Lies

Loyalty

Killers

Power

Tragedy

The last moves sent a prickle crawling over Lyssa's flesh.

Crown

Death

"Seriously, what the fuck is going on here?"

"They say a Tenes board can be used to tell the future. It reveals omens. But it's up to the player to interpret them correctly."

Lyssa stared down at the board, at the final move that had won her the game. Every tile could be read differently based on which symbols were hidden or revealed, and hers could just as easily have read 'life' or 'change'. One wrong move. That was all it took for fate to turn for the worse.

"Who are you?"

"Just a man who lost something precious. A man who doesn't want the same thing to happen to anyone else. But I can only reveal the future. I can't change it."

"And you think I can?"

"Which would you prefer? Sight or power? Would you rather be able to see what was going to happen and know there's nothing you can do to stop it?"

"Your Magisty..."

Merrick leaned over Lyssa's shoulder, clutching the scroll of sales from Camelia's auction, which she never went anywhere without these days. He pointed to one entry, halfway down the list. A 'game board', purchased by someone whose address was listed in Crow's Cove.

"Well, shit."

"This isn't that board," the man said. He didn't even flinch when Lyssa rose from the table. "The original was destroyed, but… It just made us blind."

"What about the soul?"

"You don't need to worry about her anymore."

Lyssa pinched the bridge of her nose and gestured for Merrick to sheathe his blade. "Fine. But if I find out you were fucking with me…"

"I keep playing the game over," the stranger said, sagging in his seat. "To see if things would have turned out differently, but I always land on the same tile. Always the same tile."

He reached out and touched Lyssa's final pawn.
Death

"I hope you work it out," he said. "I really do."

A tear dripped off his chin and plinked into his tea cup. Lyssa, feeling ridiculously awkward, managed a stiff bow.

"Thank you for your hospitality. Sorry for your loss."

He didn't answer, just reset the pawns for the beginning of a new game. Lyssa excused herself and Merrick, and the two of them retreated outside.

"We should burn the place down," Merrick muttered.

"Would you stop? I think there have been enough pyres around here for one day."

She walked back to her horse, the captain in tow, and tried to shake the feeling that there would be more pyres—many, many more—before this was all said and done.

THE WRITING ON THE WALL

MARCUS BINES

Peshwin sighed. It was a long walk across town to her slitherback, Karzu. She hoped he hadn't eaten anyone while waiting for her.

As she strolled through the near-deserted streets, the approaching dusk sending Kingsgate's residents scuttling into their homes, Peshwin Flitbacke, Queen of Bandits, checked the leather satchel slung over her shoulder. Not much remained of the haul she'd swiped from the Sanctuary of Elders that morning. There hadn't been especially rich pickings to begin with; she'd been visiting her grandfather once a month for the past year and never left without a few mementoes. She'd already cleaned out anything of value from all the rooms adjacent to his, even the one belonging to Blind Bilzo, whose hearing was so good he could sense an intruder breathing at ten paces while asleep. It was amazing what a simple paralysis draft could do for a Bandit Queen's purse though.

She'd hawked the small ceramic vase with the Queen's portrait on it pretty easily in the market, and the bottles of grog she'd found under a snoring resident's bed had been a useful extra bet in the taverna at lunchtime.

Her grandfather's book of Old Faith prayers had been a relic when he'd been gifted it as a youth, that was clear. She'd felt a tiny twinge of guilt at taking it off his rickety shelf, but knew he'd never really miss it. She also knew there were novices who would pay handsomely to dig into the ancient theology between those battered covers.

It hadn't taken her long to find one, sitting on the steps of the abbey, looking forlorn.

"What ails you, sister?" Peshwin had asked, sitting next to the young woman.

She must have been in her mid-twenties, about ten years younger than Peshwin. Pretty, but Peshwin had tried wooing novices before. It wasn't worth the extra effort just for a clumsy fumble with the inexperienced.

She told her some sob story about being sent home by her Faithmother—Peshwin tried hard to pay attention—but her eyes lit up at the sight of the book.

"This is Old Faith!" she declared, a little too loudly for Peshwin's liking. "Where did you get it?"

"Never mind that," said Peshwin. "Can I interest you in a sale?"

The girl pulled the cover back and the book fell open almost in the middle, where a small, narrow piece of chalk was sitting between the pages. Peshwin wondered if it had been hidden deliberately.

"Maybe," said the nun. "But I guess you'll be wanting this back."

She dropped the chalk into Peshwin's palm, who looked it over for a moment before transferring it to her bag.

"This is worth all I have! Wait there!"

And she ran off towards what Peshwin presumed was a cloister somewhere, returning ten minutes later with a bundle of silversheets and pressing them all into Peshwin's hands. It was one of the most surprising transactions she'd ever experienced, but boy, did she love it when a day worked out exactly as planned.

Now, as Peshwin approached Karzu—sleeping peacefully in a sheltered corner between a smithy's and a dried-up well—she ran her fingers over the money inside her bag. She dared not take it out for fear of some miscreant spying her ill-gotten gains. They'd jump her for it in a heartbeat, and she knew it because she'd do the same. Her fingertips brushed against the chalk, and she pulled her hand out slowly, blowing away the white dust. She couldn't quite get rid of every trace of it, and when she woke Karzu with a gentle scratch behind the ear-holes, a tiny, white smudge appeared on one of the lizard's scales. It would be gone or covered in dust by the time they got back to Coparsna.

She mounted the beast and roused it into movement.

It took an hour to get home, and the sun had fully set by the time Peshwin pushed open the heavy, wooden door to her abode. She collapsed into bed, dropped her bag on the floor, and didn't even care that the chalk and some of the silversheets tumbled out.

bbb

When Peshwin opened her eyes, the first and only thing she saw was the message, scrawled on the grey stone wall of her house in giant, white letters:

FIVE DAYS.

She pushed her auburn hair out of her eyes and stared at it, not sure what she was seeing. There was no mistaking it though.

Five days. What happens in five days?

Something else had been written underneath, too, but it didn't make any sense to her.

MEDALLION ON A CANE? INSANE…

The Bandit Queen got up and put her fingers to the white lettering. It smudged and faded as she touched it. She went over to her clothes chest, found an old shirt she never wore, and rubbed the letters away. They disappeared, but the thought of them didn't.

Peshwin lit a fire and boiled a pan of water; she needed to wash, eat, and drink. Someone had come into her home during the night—without even waking her— and written on her wall. The silversheets were still on the floor, so they hadn't tried to rob her, or kill her for that matter.

They just wanted to communicate with her.

But why not make it clearer? And why hadn't her watchmen done their job? She paid them handsomely to make sure she was left undisturbed each night, but somehow this creepy message-writer had snuck through. She'd have to speak to Kek about it.

But today wasn't a business day. It was an eat-drink-and-be-merry day; a day for reading in the sun, smoking in the shade, drinking over some cards in the tavern and maybe finding a dick to ride. A day for wearing that fabulous, long leather coat over the white shirt and waistcoat that fit her perfectly and sent just the right message as she walked down the main street. The wide-brimmed hat topped the outfit off perfectly, and she always enjoyed looking up from underneath it.

She wasn't the town marshal, but she might as well have been; nobody dared cross Peshwin Flitbacke, Queen of Bandits.

After breakfast, she grabbed her book—'The Woe of King Aldric', the elven ruler who couldn't keep his poor kingdom together, comedy gold—and strolled into town. The sun was high and hot already, with barely a wisp of cloud cover. Raggedy kids were out in the streets, playing games of chase or scratching in the dirt with broken sticks.

A pair of them were throwing rocks, until Peshwin passed. They stood and stared, so she did the polite thing and tipped her hat.

"Nillo! You come away from her and don't be staring!" called a mother from a doorway. Peshwin glanced over at the protective parent, who looked away before their eyes met. "G-g-good morning, ma'am."

"It is a good one, isn't it?" said Peshwin, watching the woman squirm.

"Y-yes," she responded. "Nillo! C'mon now!"

The little boy ran over to his mother. His friend followed suit and Peshwin walked on, aiming for the Fire

Tree at the end of the street. Approaching it, she saw that her seat—no more than a smoothed section of root, really—was occupied by a girl, maybe about sixteen years old. Next to her was a young man trying to get romantic. His face was close to hers, and one hand was on her thigh, moving in such a way as to gradually shift her dress upwards. He was at least three years older than her.

Peshwin stood with hands on hips, watching the pair from a distance. There was something about the scene she didn't like, and it wasn't just that they were in her reading spot.

The girl noticed her first, and flicked her eyes from the boy to Peshwin, telling him to look.

He did. He sneered. "So what? She can stare for all I care."

The girl gently pushed his hand away and smoothed down her dress. "Fiki, stop now."

"What if I don't wanna stop?" the boy said, putting his hand back where it was, more forcefully now. "You're beautiful, and I wanna touch ya."

"Boy," Peshwin said calmly but clearly. He turned to face her. "The young lady asked you to stop."

"What's it to you, anyway?" said Fiki, standing. His erection couldn't be hidden by his loose fabric trousers, and Peshwin spotted it.

Peshwin stepped forward and changed her tone. "Oh, hey. You're beautiful. What was your name? Fiki?" She paced slowly towards him, raising her hat so he could see her face. She undid one button on her shirt. "That's a lovely name. Fiki…"

The boy stood his ground but glanced nervously

round at the girl. By the time he looked back, Peshwin was right in front of him. He shifted away from her, hesitant.

"Hey, don't go away, I wanna touch ya," Peshwin said, mimicking his tone. She put her hands on his shoulders, then moved them down to his chest.

"What if I don't want ya to?" he asked but didn't stop her.

She grabbed him by the dick, yanked him close and yelled in his face. "Didn't stop you touching her, now, did it?"

"Agh! Get off me!" he shouted, pushing at her with both hands.

With her free hand, she caught one of his and twisted his wrist, forcing him onto his knees. She didn't stop until she heard a pop and a crunch.

"Now, listen good, Mr Fiki," Peshwin said quietly, right into his ear. "If I catch you molesting girls around here again, it won't be your hand I crush, got it?"

She gave his penis another good tug. A gesture was worth a thousand words.

"Aah! I got it! I got it!"

Peshwin released both body parts and the boy fell to his knees, clutching his injured hand to his chest, and his other injury in his other hand. She pushed her coat back to make sure he saw the knife at her belt, then turned to the young lady. "Now, please could I sit there to read?"

The girl nodded and shot to her feet.

"And if anyone tries to treat you that way again, you just come see me, okay?"

"I certainly will, Miss…?"

Peshwin sat beneath the tree, crossed her legs, looked up from under her hat and smiled. "Peshwin Flitbacke, Queen of Bandits, at your service."

Peshwin lost herself in her book for a couple of hours, before Kek and three of the others turned up. He had no answer for her about the message on the wall, but she trusted him; if he said the guards hadn't seen anyone around her house, then they hadn't.

Once that meeting was over, and her men had realised there would be no thievery today—they weren't the brightest, but they could follow orders, and sometimes even that was a blessing from the Embrace—they left her alone. She turned back to her book but couldn't focus for long. Her stomach was telling her it was tavern time.

Walking into the dingy inn, she headed straight for the bar. Bubba Knox, the moustachioed barman, was wiping tankards. He looked up at her and a nervous flicker crossed his face.

"Hey there, Ms Flitbacke. What can I do for you?"

"Now, Bub, don't look so nervous. You know me," Peshwin said, grinning. "I'm just here to eat, drink and play some Tack. Now, what's wrong with that?"

"Well, ma'am, you and Tack… Don't always go so well, do it?"

"I don't know what you mean… Tack always ends well for me, especially if I find the right man to play with," she said, winking at Bubba Knox.

"And if you don't, it don't end well for my tables

and chairs!"

She ignored his complaint. "I'll have your finest chumpsteak please, with all the extras, over there at my favourite table. I'll take a bottle of Unholy Duchess now, and bring another two with my food, will you?"

"Three Duchesses? You aimin' to sleep here tonight or summin'?" laughed Bubba.

"Just want to be at my best for the game. I've heard Jadam's in town and I'm looking to…beat him sore, shall we say."

"Qalakti Jadam is a mighty fine-lookin' man, I'll give you that," said Bubba, stifling a cough. "I'll get your steak."

The rest of the day passed in a blur for Peshwin. Once she'd eaten, three gentlemen travellers joined her at her table, telling stories of Red Land towns they'd passed through recently. She made a mental note of where they said they were moving on to the next day, so they could be thoroughly robbed by a team of her men, then drained her first bottle of Duchess.

Jadam and some of his friends sauntered through the door and sat on the other side of the room. Peshwin didn't know where he lived or how he earned his bread, but he was notorious in Coparsna, and the towns nearby, as a travelling lothario. It was said there wasn't a Red Land town that didn't have a child of his growing up in it. She had no intention of becoming a mother by him, but if he was as good in bed as some of the local women said, it would be worth the experience.

Besides, she didn't need him to go inside her; 'ride it, don't hide it' was her motto, and it had worked damn well for her in the past. He came as advertised: rugged features, flecks of grey in his stubble, some short but unruly hair, and what looked like a tough, lean body.

Looks resilient. Good.

As the sun went down, she got her cards out and issued a general challenge to the bar, which had filled since she took her place. She eyeballed Jadam specifically. "Tack masters required over here for a game! No chancers needed!"

They played until it was fully dark. Jadam didn't do too badly, but by the time Peshwin finished her third Duchess and ordered another, he was on a losing streak.

Bubba brought it over. "Don't let her take you for a ride now, Mr Jadam."

Jadam looked at Peshwin and grinned, a large, toothy smile. "Why, this little lady here? I'm not too sure I wouldn't mind being take for a ride," he said.

"You're too kind," said Peshwin, "But also foolish."

"She's right," said Bubba. "She may be pretty, but sure'n I'm no idiot when I say she'll clean you out if you're not careful."

"Pah," said Jadam, looking at his cards. "Less talk, more play."

"Couldn't agree more," said Peshwin, shoving her shirt sleeves up. "I'm ready."

"You owe me," Peshwin slurred.

The bar was empty except for the two of them and Knox. Both Jadam's associates and the regular customers had long since departed.

Qalakti Jadam's reddening eyes stared at her over an empty bottle of Duchess. "Miss," he began tentatively, "I got nothing left but this body and the clothes on it. I concede."

He carefully placed his hand of cards face down in front of him and sat up in his seat, moving slowly to avoid slipping off his chair.

Peshwin smiled. "I'll take them," she said.

"Take what?" asked Jadam.

"The clothes, and the body under them." There was a moment's pause, then she repeated: "You owe me. There's no conceding to be done."

Jadam smiled, looked down at himself, lolling in his chair, then back at Peshwin. "Well, alright then. But…"

She reached over and began unbuckling his belt. "No buts. Except if you mean that pretty, well-formed one back there."

"Here? I'm pretty sure the barkeep'll have something to say about that."

"No," Peshwin purred. "Not here."

She yanked at the belt, sliding it roughly out of its loops. Jadam lost his balance, but she held him up and in one swift movement had the belt round his neck and buckled it. She used it to pull him close and lowered her voice. "You owe me a ride. And I'm gonna ride you good, so don't flunk out on me, Jadam." She grabbed his crotch. "This had better work by the time we get to my place."

"Hey," he said, batting her hand away. "It'll work fine, Little Miss Bandit Queen or whatever you call yourself. Just show me where to—"

She pulled on the belt, silencing him. "Less talk, more play. Move, Jadam!"

And she led him out of the bar by the neck, his feet barely keeping up.

The next morning, Peshwin woke to find Jadam's bare arm cradling her and his open mouth far too close to her face.

"Ugh!"

She shoved him, hard, and he tumbled off her bed, naked to the ankles, where his trousers were bunched. She resettled herself under the blankets, but she wouldn't be able to get back to sleep now the sun was rising.

"Hey!" Jadam protested. Then, when he realised the state of undress he was in, he buttoned himself up and looked around for his shirt. "Nice way to start the day! What got you so sore?"

Peshwin didn't respond.

"Ooh, bad choice of words, sorry. Probably went in a bit hard, did I?"

Peshwin turned over and stared at him. "You didn't 'go in' at all! The tool of the great Qalakti Jadam, father of countless children from town to town across the Red Land, was entirely useless, Mister! It just lay there like a...like a raw bit of sausage!"

"Shh, shh!" Jadam said, eyes widening. "Listen, I'm sorry, but... I'm not as young as I used to be, you know..."

"Don't—" Peshwin started, then noticed the wall behind Jadam.

FOUR DAYS.

And then, stretchin up the wall in the same white chalk:

OPEN NOT THE POCKET WATCH, OPEN NOT THE MUSIC BOX.

But it was the first message that Peshwin stared at for a good minute, running her hand over the wall. The chalk came away, smudging on the concrete.

"What's that?" said Jadam. "I didn't notice it last night."

Peshwin turned to face him. "No, funny that. Neither did I. Because it wasn't there."

"You think I wrote it?" he said, laughing nervously. "What does it even mean?"

"You tell me!" Peshwin paused for a moment. "I'm very impressed though, getting into my house the night before without me noticing."

"What are you talking about?"

"How much is she paying you?"

"Who? What are you—"

"That little bitch from the Northern Rip. Zola."

"Which Zola? I've met quite a few Zolas in my time. The one in Platen Gulch is especially fine. Long curly hair, fantastic—"

Peshwin's mouth tightened. "Come on, Jadam. Calls herself Zola the Intrepid? Claims she controls the Rips from north to south? Don't know why; she knows I've got the Southern Rip."

Jadam started looking around for something. "Nope, never met her. Listen, did I bring my hat with me or did I leave it at the bar?"

Peshwin stepped towards him, grabbed his chin and forced him to look at her. "No, you listen to me. I'm going to kill you if you don't tell me what that message is about and why you wrote it."

Jadam smiled nervously. "I… I didn't write it. I don't know, I'm telling you."

Peshwin grabbed his hand and wrenched his arm up behind him. "Not good enough!" she growled and slammed his head onto the stone table. A couple of drops of blood from his broken nose dripped onto the map spread there.

"Aaah!"

"Tell me!"

"I don't know!"

Another slam on the table. Jadam was trying to push back against her, but his legs and knees were locked in place; she'd caught him off-guard and now his life was in her hands.

"This map cost me a pretty penny, but I will ruin it with the insides of your head if you don't tell me why you wrote that message!"

"I don't know anything about it, I swear!" he gurgled.

She thought better of spoiling the map, so she dragged him to the floor and sat on his chest, hands around his throat, pinning his arms with her knees. She was sweating now, and spittle was frothing between her lips. "You're lying! Tell me!"

His face reddened even more. His eyes widened and his mouth opened and closed like a fish. Throaty, gasping sounds emanated from it.

She released him momentarily, and he coughed while yelling, "I don't know! I'm telling you, I—"

"Liar!" she roared and started throttling him again. His face turned red, then purple, and eventually he gave up trying to breathe. His eyes continued staring at her, even as the life behind them disappeared.

Peshwin moved off him and took several deep breaths. She looked at Jadam's head, now lolling to the side, dead eyes still open. She closed the lids, then noticed the words on the wall again.

"Damn you," she said, snarling, then screamed the words. "DAMN YOU!"

It had been a while since she'd had to kill a man. Normally, one of her men did it for her.

When Kek and the others arrived, Peshwin ordered them to dispose of the body. She wasn't worried about repercussions—she had the Coparsna lawkeepers in her pocket, and Jadam's men were the kind who would find a new boss without asking too many questions—but she didn't want him in her house any longer than necessary.

Kek organised the men into grave diggers and look-outs, and he and Peshwin watched as they began shovelling. The ground was cracked and dusty in the spot they found just outside town, by the abandoned mine.

"I'm glad that's over," Peshwin said, as they sat on the rusting mine cart, toppled onto its side by the mouth of the shaft.

"What?" asked Kek.

"The messages."

Kek looked confused. "Messages? You mean there was another one?"

"Yes, but I killed the writer," Peshwin said, pointing to the body warming in the morning sun. If her men took too long, he would start to stink.

"Oh," said Kek. "That's good."

She looked at him. "What? What's that tone for?"

Kek looked at her. "No tone, I just… Are you sure it was him? He wasn't there the first night."

"He must have snuck in," Peshwin said. "Trying to freak me out. You know how people keep trying to muscle in on my territory; he must have been hired by one of them. My money's on Zola."

"Which Zola?"

Peshwin stared at Kek. She took a slow, deep breath.

"How many fucking Zolas are there in the fucking Red Lands trying to get in on my fucking operations?! What is wrong with you people?! Zola the fucking Intrepid, that bitch from the Northern Rip! You know her, Kek! Tiny woman, pinched face, ringing any bells?!"

Kek recoiled, and the diggers paused, shielding their eyes from the sun and staring at Peshwin.

"GET ON WITH IT!" she screamed at them.

They obeyed, dramatically throwing mud and dust up in the air with their shovels.

"Kek, I'm sorry, I'm just…really on edge," Peshwin said.

"It's okay," said her right-hand man. "But maybe you should take some time off? Head into the city for some fun?"

"No, I'm all right, I just need to…do something normal, and quickly. I'm itching for a robbery. It's been too long."

"Okay," said Kek. He sauntered over to the diggers and Peshwin watched as they picked up Jadam's body, threw it in the shallow hole and spread dirt on top. She wondered if any of the local dogs would smell it but wanted to get away more than she wanted to cover it up properly.

What would a corpse care if the dogs found it?

Kek set up an easy job; they rode into Osskeola on their slitherbacks, taking up the whole main street. One deafening roar from Karzu and the townsfolk were practically throwing their worldly goods in the road. The mayor stepped out of the courthouse, blunderbuss in hand. To his credit, he didn't flinch when Peshwin led Karzu right up to him and a breathy snort from the reptile's nostrils sent his hat flying. But even a mayor with a blunderbuss couldn't do much without a head, and Karzu was hungry. The man's skull made a sickening crunch between her mount's back molars, but hey, if he didn't take precautions against giant desert lizards, that was more his fault than Peshwin's.

They returned to Coparsna with a stack of sheets—copper and silver—as well as documents from the courthouse that might be useful in the future. She'd been thinking that a more strategic plan might suit her better, rather than lurching from one job to the next to fund her lifestyle.

She needed to think of the future; it was already exhausting to rob people who didn't want to be robbed, and she wasn't getting any younger. Maybe blackmail would prove lucrative and give her more time to read in the sun.

Sooner or later, she wouldn't be Queen of Bandits anymore, but there was no succession plan. She wasn't ready to give up the reins yet, and Circle help them when that day came.

It was dark by the time they got back, so she left Kek to share out the loot with the others and went to bed.

THREE DAYS. THE PAINTING WILL FLAKE, THE SENET WILL BREAK. PROBABLY.

Peshwin woke to find the message right above her, and the rage headache took hold instantly.

"What do you mean, three days?!" she yelled at the wall. "What's all this rubbish about paintings, and me-dallions, and watches? And where the FUCK did you come from?!"

She stormed around her room, throwing clothes around until she'd put on an outfit that matched her feel-ings—all black—and was on her way out the door when her foot knocked against something on the floor. She looked down.

The piece of chalk from her grandfather's sanctuary was sitting in the patch of sunlight that crossed the room each morning. She picked it up.

"Huh," she said. Someone must have been using it while she slept.

She put it on her table, grabbed one of her biggest books from the shelf and smashed it down on the chalk, adding a shout of anger for good measure. When she pulled the book away, the chalk was still intact. In fact, she couldn't even see any crumbs on the table.

"Okay," she said to it, and placed it carefully on the concrete floor.

She brought her booted heel down on it, hard.

It wouldn't break.

That was when Kekurangan appeared at the door. Peshwin looked up, wondering whether he'd heard her speaking to a piece of chalk.

"Look at this!" she said, gesturing to the wall. "Someone's still doing it, Kek, and I'm damned if I don't kill that person today. They're nearby; I know it."

She picked up her hat, leaving the chalk on the floor. Kek wouldn't understand it being unbreakable. He'd just think she was crazy and losing control. She couldn't have that.

Peshwin tore up Coparsna that day. She and her men stalked the wide streets and narrow alleys of the town, finding anyone who looked suspicious. Men and women were interrogated, beaten, and abandoned, trapped and traumatized into confessing anything they could. She heard about husbandly infidelities, thefts of all sorts, even murders, but nobody knew a damn thing about her piece of chalk. She left one man without a hand, one without a testicle and one without a mistress. Peshwin didn't feel bad, though; the girl she saved him from— Sephena the Snitch—was aptly named. For the right price, she'd give you the information you wanted or a venereal disease you didn't.

But even Sephena didn't know who'd been leaving

those fucking messages.

Peshwin eventually returned home, exhausted but none the wiser about her tormentor. She sent her men away, except for Kekurangan.

"Listen, Kek. I need you to stay here tonight."

He looked surprised.

"It's not like that, it's just… These messages. Someone needs to stay up and watch how they're happening. Fifty coppers?"

"You don't have to pay me to stay awake."

"I'm paying you to do a job, Kek. That's perfectly normal."

"Okay. But I'm cooking dinner."

Peshwin smiled. She was glad of the offer and napped while he made it so she could take the first watch.

Kek woke her with a bowl of stew and a spoon. He'd filled her small home with the most amazing aromas and seemed to have distilled them all into the bowl she now scoffed from. How did people manage this? Her stew was always sludgy, brown mess.

He made one of her chairs as comfy as possible to sleep in while she sat up on the bed; he wouldn't hear of taking her only comfort. Within ten minutes, he was snoring, and Peshwin lit a candle and began to read.

The night was quiet. The candle flickered, throwing shifting shadows on the wall where the last message had been. Her eyes darted over to the unbreakable chalk, lying there innocently on the table.

Her nap had given her what she needed to stay awake, but Kek's stew was trying to do the opposite.

She yawned.

Kek was fast asleep in the chair when Peshwin opened her eyes.

It was her fault. She'd fallen asleep before waking him, she knew it.

She reached for an itch on her leg and looked around the walls. Sure enough, the chalk had done its work overnight.

TWO DAYS. IT'S COMING.

She wanted to yell and scream at it, but Kek suddenly snored lightly, and she reined herself in. She hated being woken before the right time and assumed he must too.

Instead, she boiled a pot of water and woke her right-hand man with a mug of wheat tea. "Now, don't down it in one. This is premium blend from the Gold Plains, so enjoy it."

Kek smiled at her. "Why, thank you, Your Highness of the Red…"

His voice dropped away as he saw the message on the wall.

"I know," she said.

"Did I…?"

"No, it's my fault for not waking you. I fell asleep."

"So…" he said. "What's coming?"

Her face was grave. "I don't know, but it feels… serious."

Kek sipped his tea.

Peshwin spoke. "I'm going to Kingsgate."

"You think there's someone there who will know

what this is all about?"

Peshwin shrugged off the blanket she'd had around her shoulders—the morning was bright, but chilly—and picked up the piece of chalk that had been tormenting her for days, holding it up for Kek to see.

"This is what's been doing it." She passed it to him.

"It's just chalk," he said, after examining it for a few seconds. He took it in two hands and tried to break it. "It's hard."

"Yep," said Peshwin. "Harder than a boot, and stones, and me slamming a book onto it."

"Maybe you can soften it in boiling water," he suggested. She made an incredulous face. "You know, like vegetables."

The small fire beneath her pot of water was burning gently, so she threw some extra wood on it and dropped the chalk in the pan.

The two criminals watched in silence as the water bubbled, then roiled. The chalk sat there, among the bubbles, not doing anything.

After a few minutes of intense heat, Peshwin took the pot off the flames and put it on the floor between them. The chalk seemed completely intact. They stared at it for a few seconds, until Peshwin picked up the pot and stepped outside.

She tipped the water out onto a flat rock. The chalk tumbled out and sat there. It felt like it was taunting her somehow. She lifted the cast iron pot and brought it down hard.

"I see what you mean," said Kek when he saw the chalk, totally unharmed. "But why go to the city?"

"That's where I got it. At my grandfather's sanctuary."

"You think he knows what it's about?"

Peshwin stood and headed back inside, calling over her shoulder. "I doubt it—he doesn't know much of anything these days—but I grabbed it from his room, so what else can I do? I'm practically out of control, Kek, and you know how I get when that happens."

"Sephena the Snitch might say you've already got there," said Kek, with a wry smile.

"Thankfully for all of us, she won't be saying much of anything anymore," said Peshwin, as she stuffed things into her satchel: an empty water pouch she would fill at the stream on the way, a loaf of bread, an apple or two, her notebook with a pencil stuffed inside.

"I'll see you later. Maybe tomorrow."

On her way out, she looked down. Scrawled on the rock, beside the chalk, was another message: TAKE ME.

"Fuck you, that's what," she said, but grabbed the chalk and shoved it into her bag.

Karzu deposited Peshwin at her usual spot at the city's edge, where the shadier traders congregated in doorways and backrooms. By the time she passed the gate, she was choking on smog. People here didn't care how filthy things were; if they could earn a crust of bread each day and keep their families alive, they coped. They just never thrived. Clothes were dirty and the bodies under them diseased and scabby; children ran around the streets, unwatched, grimier by the moment; adults bought and sold whatever they had to—food and crafted things, but also information, illicit substances, their bodies.

It was a substance-dealer Peshwin needed now, and she found her usual easily: a small, gobliny creature called Chaas Krylltessa who owned a dingy back alley emporium.

"Chaas," she said, eyeballing the creature across the counter. The shop was empty of other customers but full to the brim with bottles, jars and vials of liquid of all colours, books thick and thin, bones and body parts from all sorts of creatures, and candles ready to emit the most repulsive scents once lighted.

Chaas spoke up in its slimy voice. "It's the Bandit Queen of… Where was it again?"

"Coparsna," Peshwin said.

"Oh, right," said Chaas, shuffling something away behind the counter, over which it could hardly see. "Never heard of it."

"Haven Plague," Peshwin said, not smiling. "And no games."

"You think I have bottles of plague just sitting around?"

"I know you do," said Peshwin, pointing at the shelves behind Chaas. "There's one."

Chaas looked up and spotted the tiny vial filled with opaque bluish-green liquid. "Oh Peshwin, that's not—"

Peshwin leaned over the counter and grabbed Chaas by the shirt, pulling it onto its stunted tiptoes. Her voice was calm. "Chaas, I said no games. I'm not in the mood, no matter how much you enjoy my beautiful company in your scuzzy, little shop. One bottle of Haven Plague and one vial of antidote. Now."

Chaas' face reddened.

"Give me the lizard blood or lose your head, it's as simple as that."

She released the creature and it stumbled backwards. "Twenty," it said, coughing and rearranging its clothing.

"Pfft," said Peshwin. "Those tiny bottles are worth ten and you know it. But here's fifteen so I can get out of here."

"Fine," said Chaas, scrunching Peshwin's silver-sheets into a hidden pocket and handing over what she needed.

"Miss you already, Chaas," Peshwin said, as she ducked out of the door.

It was a short walk to the Sanctuary of Elders through the bustling, blackened streets of Kingsgate. Peshwin wanted to blast through the crowds, shove people out of her way, but her habit was to avoid drawing attention when away from her turf. A reputation like hers was only so useful this far from the Rip. She couldn't let her mood get the better of her.

The Sanctuary was quiet. Peshwin slipped inside, ignoring the protest of one of the nosier nurses, and headed straight for her grandfather's room. The man was persistent, and trotted along the dirty corridor behind Peshwin, badgering her to leave until she could stand it no longer. She turned and grabbed him by the shoulders and slammed his head into the wall. He stopped bothering her then.

"Gramps," she said as she stepped into her grandfather's room. It smelled bad, like shit and rotting meat. He was lying in bed, eyes open, but didn't respond. "Gramps."

They'd let him die. Maybe that was why the nurse had been so keen on her leaving. They'd never really been that close, but he was her only surviving family. Now he wasn't even that.

Damn it, now she had no way to ask him about the chalk!

Peshwin's anger had driven her to buy Haven Plague—maybe the thought of death by one of the most hideous diseases Guardiana had ever seen would loosen some tongues—but now she had another reason to use it. If they were just going to let Gramps die, leave him here to stink up the place without the benefit of a proper pyre, they could join him.

All of them. Residents and carers alike.

Peshwin walked out into the corridor and stumbled into the unconscious nurse. She opened his mouth and tipped a drop of Plague into it. Within seconds, he was convulsing and foaming at the mouth. She stared as the poison did its nasty work, dissolving his lower jaw then his whole body. It was slow though. There was an elderly resident behind each door, and she could go room to room, but it would take a while.

That was when she remembered the water barrels in the lobby.

Half a bottle of Plague in each should be fine. The water would speed up the effects too. It was why the Blue Haven had been hit so hard, why it had given the disease its name.

Nobody saw her multiple murder. None of the victims would know it was her. Normally, she would feel some sense of vindication at an act of vengeance like this, but today… Something was wrong. Her mind was a maelstrom, and nothing she did could soothe it.

Peshwin heard the clanging of the Abbey bells calling the believers to worship.

She pulled the chalk out of her bag and stared at it. So small, so simple. A child's writing tool. Yet it had unsettled her very soul within a few hours of coming home with her. How could something like this send her spiralling out of control?

The bells made her look up. The short, squat tower of the Abbey rose above the nearest row of houses, and Peshwin headed for it. The Faithmothers and Faithfathers claimed to understand the mysteries of time, creation, the destiny of the soul; maybe they had answers to this mystery too.

Upon entering the Abbey, Peshwin saw the novice to whom she'd sold her grandfather's Old Faith prayer book. She stood just inside the heavy, wooden doors, welcoming the faithful to the service, pretty under her dark blue veil.

She spoke in an excited whisper. "It's you!"

"Yes, hi, good to see you too," said Peshwin, scoping out the abbey's nave. It was dingy, candle-lit and sparsely populated. The paltry three-person choir at the front looked bored. A few congregants sat on the stone benches with their heads down, the murmurings of the robed priest at the front inaudible to their ears. He was a short, fat man with a bulbous red nose, intoning something into one of his many chins.

Peshwin leaned towards the nun. "That's the priest in charge today?"

"Yes, Father Temperance. Closer to the Centre than any of us."

"Temperance. Ha!" she muttered. "Listen, there's a man outside who has fallen on the floor and hit his head. He's bleeding."

"Oh no!" said the nun, and she hitched up her skirts and hurried outside.

Peshwin smiled. That girl was eminently predictable, and Peshwin didn't want her witnessing what she was about to do. She might try to stop her, and things could get ugly.

The Bandit Queen strode up the central aisle and stood right in front of the priest, who was shuffling a selection of holy gold and silver artefacts around on an altar covered with an ornate red cloth. Peshwin had no idea what any of them meant.

"Father Temperance?" she said.

The priest didn't look up, but continued praying, turned in a circle, mumbled something else into his hands and moved one of the items from the middle of the table to the outside. It looked like a silver funnel, and the man seemed to be in some kind of trance. His eyes kept flickering open and closed, and he didn't seem to know she was there at all.

That would have to change.

Peshwin moved to the end of the altar, grabbed the two corners of the red cloth and yanked hard. The worship items clattered to the floor and a few heads in the pews looked up. The priest was still going through the motions, and only when his hand reached out and touched nothing did he look around.

Peshwin was already behind him, forcing his arm up his back. "You're coming with me, Father."

She pushed him towards a side door, not caring about the interrupted service or that the novice at the door might be disciplined for allowing the priest to be abducted in the middle of midday prayer. Temperance was slow to get moving, and heavy—the trance state made that unsurprising—but by the time they reached the door they had built up momentum across the smooth, stone floor.

"What… What's happening?" the priest wailed as the door to the antechamber shut behind him. He wasn't quite steady on his feet.

Peshwin glanced around the room. A barred window admitted bright, noon light. A selection of robes hung on the wall, and there were several small barrels stacked in a corner; the opposite corner housed a bunch of crates. She sat on one.

"I have a problem, Father, and I need—"

"My child, this isn't where we confess, or how. You need to—"

"No, not that." Peshwin was surprised at the nervousness in his voice, but then this probably wasn't an everyday occurrence for him. She brandished the chalk. "This."

Father Temperance looked at it from a distance, then moved slightly closer. "That's a piece of chalk," he said, confused.

"You'd think so, wouldn't you?" Peshwin said. "But this one has a mind of its own. Watch."

She put the chalk on the floor. "Go on, do your thing."

The chalk rolled from the middle of a flagstone to its edge and sat in the space between two stones but did nothing else.

"It's been writing me messages," explained Peshwin, "when I'm asleep."

Temperance stared at it. "What kind of messages?"

"Warnings, with a countdown. Five days, four days, you know. But it won't tell me what it's counting down to or what to do about it."

"Hmm…"

"The last one said, 'Two days. It's coming.' It's driving me crazy," said Peshwin, picking up one of the barrels. "Look, you can't even break it," she said, and brought the barrel smashing down on the chalk.

"Careful, that's sanctified wine!"

The barrel was fine, as was the chalk.

"You're lucky," he said. "That costs fifty sheets per barrel."

Peshwin just looked at him with disdain. "Father, I'm out of control because of this fucking piece of chalk. I need help. I need answers. People have died because of this."

Father Temperance took a deep breath and puffed out his cheeks. "Okay, listen, my profane child. We've been hearing…stories. Weird things happening all over the Kingdom with little…items. Objects causing…problems. But that's all it is—hearsay and rumours, mutterings in taverns and back alleys, gossip."

"Lovely to know our Faithfathers spend time in taverns and back alleys," said Peshwin.

"Yes, well… If the abbey stays empty when we call for worship, sometimes we must go where the people are… Anyway, that's not the only thing people are saying. The Sensers have been making a lot more noise than usual."

"Sensers?"

"Stormsensers," the priest said. "They say they can predict soulstorms. Usually, they clamour for royal audiences, insist they should be paid for their…dubious prophetic ability. Pretty sure it's a scam, but—"

Peshwin rolled her eyes. "People in this city… How can they 'predict soulstorms'? They just appear out of nowhere."

"They do…" said the priest, "but maybe they don't exactly. Maybe your little chalk-friend here knows something we don't. Either way you'd better be under shelter when its countdown stops, or you'll be done for." Father Temperance picked up the object that had caused Peshwin such distress. "You're not going to be helpful, are you?"

"I suspect not," Peshwin said, grabbing it out of his chubby hand and replacing it in her bag. This was taking too long, and someone might have seen her go from the Elders' Sanctuary to the Abbey. When her murders were discovered, she couldn't be in the city.

"Thank you, Father, you've been very helpful," she said.

"You're welcome, Miss…?"

"Miss will do," she said. "I'm taking this wine, by the way. If you try to stop me, I'll hit you on the head with it."

The priest opened the door for her and smiled. "I like my head. I need it for all sorts of things, like eating and drinking."

Peshwin looked out into the nave. The few faithful who had come to pray had now left, as had the choir. The novice was at the door, calling for the missing priest.

"Oh, bless her Eternal Circles," Temperance said. "She's a bit too keen, that one. I'll get her away from the door."

He hurried over to the nun, who looked intensely relieved to see him. Peshwin waited until he'd led her out of the huge, wooden doors, then made her own exit.

She awoke in Coparsna, in her own home, half-dressed, thankfully alone. Karzu's calm and skilful slithering had meant she could remove the plug from the barrel while riding home, and the wine had gone down nice and smooth. She remembered that, but not much else.

She must have eaten something when she got back. Some bread, she supposed, by the crumbs on her crumpled shirt. When she swung her feet off the bed and they connected with the barrel, she could tell she'd emptied it.

But wine usually gave her a headache. Where was it? She felt unusually lucid. Maybe when you drank holy wine, things weren't so bad the next morning.

No message on the walls. She checked for anything

hidden low down, or on the floor, but no. There was nothing.

Had she somehow stopped the countdown?

A wave of relief passed over her, but it was mixed with a strange sadness too; she'd hated being out of control, at the mercy of this tiny object, but she'd expected something…bigger. Life-changing. For a while, it had felt like the old days again, when she'd been carving—sometimes literally—her name in the Rip. When danger lurked in every shadow and people were out for her blood. Threats in the night, a conspiracy to unravel. It had *almost* been an adventure.

Her leather bag lay on the floor by her bed. Peshwin reached over and picked it up, and the flap cover fell open to reveal a message chalked indistinctly on the inside of the leather.

It said: TODAY. SORRY.

"What?!" Peshwin yelled into her bag, and the sound of her own voice thumped her like a prize-fighter. There was that headache. "You got the *day* wrong?!"

She ran out to look at the sky, not caring that she didn't have trousers on. No sign of a storm yet. Returning inside, the chalk was on the floor where she'd dropped it, writing on the flagstones.

"Will I die?" she asked, but it had already started another message.

MAKE SURE I'M OUTSIDE.

"Okay," she said forcefully, "But will I die?"

It responded with a question mark. Could it hear her? It didn't have any ears, but seemed to know what she was asking…

"Great. Do we have to be out there all day?"

Another question mark.

"How can you know the day, but not the time?"

This time the chalk didn't move at all.

"Whatever," said Peshwin, and stripped off to wash and dress. "At least you don't have eyes."

All day, Peshwin waited. Bubba Knox didn't protest when she dragged one of his saloon tables out to the street and ordered herself food and drink to be served in the open air. If she had to be outside the whole day, she could at least enjoy herself while she waited. Still, she reasoned, she'd better not have too many Duchesses. Having her wits about her would be vital when the time came.

The sun dipped in the sky and clouds began to gather. Peshwin suddenly recalled the priest's words about being under shelter when the storm came.

But the chalk wanted to be outside—how could she do both?

The only place she could think of that was both inside and outside, and felt safe enough, was the abandoned mine shaft outside of town, near where they'd buried Qalakti Jadam.

She ran there now, leaving her tab unpaid.

The glare of the sun faded into a deep, fiery orange. From somewhere, a green glow crept across the sky, and Peshwin knew she only had a few minutes. She'd seen a soulstorm once before, in the city. She'd watched from behind a door as a soldier—one of the Queen's own guards, by the looks of his uniform—had turned from alive to dead to somewhere between the two in a matter of seconds.

She ran as fast as she could, leather bag hitting her backside. All she could think of was getting into the shaft, but she had to leave the chalk out in the open first.

She rounded a corner and spied the overturned cart she'd sat on a few days earlier. Glancing over to Jadam's burial site, she saw what she thought might be a foot sticking out of the sand. Maybe the dogs had got to the body after all.

The sound of the storm was closing in, wailing like a thousand lost souls trying to reclaim their existence. A sickly, green light bathed everything around her in dulled shades of lime and emerald.

She raced for the shaft entrance and dug her hand in her bag for the chalk.

"Do your thing, whatever it is," she said to it, breathing heavily to get the words out, and dropped it in the sand next to the cart. In seconds, she was inside the shaft, tripping over the wooden slats on the floor between the rails.

Peshwin fell, and the sound of the storm outside echoed around her. She pushed her face into the dirt. Maybe if she didn't look, the storm would leave her alone.

She hoped.

"Faith help me!" she screamed into the ground, as the shrieks of the soulstorm reached their peak volume, then died away almost instantly.

She turned her head. The green light was gone, as

were the clouds. Night had fallen as the storm raged, like it had stolen the fading daylight. The sky was full of stars, blinking peacefully at her, just as they always did out here in the Red Land.

She made her way to the open air, just in time to see the stick of chalk fall to the ground in a spiral motion. It landed on a rock and turned to dust.

"Oh," Peshwin said, and stared at it.

Then she heard a noise, like cracking and groaning.

A man a short distance away was trying to stand, but his body seemed awkward, his limbs stiff and unnaturally twisted. He looked familiar somehow, but also…very wrong. His face was too grey, and it looked like one of his arms was about to fall off.

Somewhere between alive and dead.

"Oh, Faith," she said, and wanted to run but couldn't tear her eyes away.

"Pshwaah," he said, croaking the sounds out as if every part of his voice was out of practice.

She recoiled, almost falling over the cart.

"Jadam?" she asked, incredulous.

The man worked his jaw a little as he stumbled towards her, massaging it with his hands. His skin was all wrong; it looked greasy and blotchy, and seemed not to be fully attached to the muscle and bone underneath.

"Jadam, is that you?" Peshwin said quietly.

"Who'shsh'adam?" the man said.

As he approached, Peshwin became convinced it was the dead card player.

"Stop right there."

The man obeyed.

"You're dead."

He looked down at himself and held his arms out to examine them. "Don't lork well, d'w'I?"

His speech improved with every attempt. Peshwin, on the other hand, was stunned into silence.

"But'm not Shadam."

"You're in his body," Peshwin pointed out, and felt so stupid about the next thing she had to say. "You're… the chalk, aren't you?"

"Baddum Lay… Lake… Lako, at your service," Jadam's face said, when he pushed his lower jaw into the right position to speak. "And yesh, I'mchalk."

"Baddum Lako?"

"Shcribe."

"Huh," said Peshwin. "Whose scribe? We don't use scribes in the Red Lands."

"King's scribe, 'course. Called me 'scrivener,' all fancy, but scribe is good for me. Where was this body, by the way?"

"Um… Buried. Badly. In the sand. Sorry."

"That explains the sand in every single hole. Going to need a new one. Coming with me?"

"What? No, but…" Peshwin had so many questions. "Why were you in the chalk? Wait… Coming where?"

"Lestrange put me in the chalk. Said it served me right for writing about his weird experiments. I think he thought it would be funny to make a writer become the worst writing implement ever. I bet someone else got to be a quill. Something really magnificent too."

Baddum Lako—in Qalakti Jadam's dishevelled, distended body, with Qalakti Jadam's clothes hanging off it—started walking towards Coparsna.

"Who's Lestrange? And where are you going?"

"Kingsgate. Told you—need a better body. Only Lestrange will be able to do it for me, so I have to find him."

"Who in the Void is Lestrange?"

"King's Mage."

"We don't…have a King anymore," said Peshwin, and Lako responded with silence. "Not for years. And that's not the way to Kingsgate. Do you even know where you are? Or how long you've been in that chalk?"

Lako's face turned thoughtful. "I guess, when you're a stick of chalk lying around, days become meaningless. And months. And years, apparently."

He took a deep breath, then coughed. Something green came out of him.

"Ugh," he said. "These lungs don't work very well."

Peshwin looked at the man, reborn in someone else's body—currently doubled over in a coughing fit—and wondered what that felt like, beyond being completely disorientating. And yet, within a few minutes, he had decided to risk going straight back where he came from, with no plan beyond 'get a new body'. How he thought that would happen, she had no idea. Was that a service you could get in some hidden corners of Kingsgate? A chance to start life over from the beginning?

Now *that* would be an adventure.

"Look…" started Peshwin, "you obviously don't know where you're going. You could use help, right? Someone to show you what's what?"

And, frankly, he owed her an adventure after the shit

he'd put her through.

"I guess I'm not going to get far like this on my own, am I? And I can trust you, can't I?"

Peshwin nodded. For now, he most certainly could trust her. Silence fell as she hesitated, then made her final decision. She whistled for Karzu.

She'd been Queen of Bandits for too long. It had stopped being fun years ago, when she'd gone from clawing her way to the top to seeing off other eager hopefuls who always reminded her too much of herself. If this worked out, she could become someone else, do it all over again from the beginning.

Void, she could do it over and over and over again.

Maybe the Faith had it right after all.

The Face Inside the Box

Holley Cornetto

Delia raced to the door as the jingle of her father's cart drifted through the window. He was early, which meant it had been a good day. He sold trinkets and did minor repairs from his wagon, but for bigger projects, he needed his shop. Bigger projects, Delia had learned, meant better pay. She stood on the stoop of their modest hut, watching as their mule, Benny, pulled the cart home.

Their home, though not impressive, was tidy and well-appointed. Since her mother's passing three years prior, Delia had taken on the task of keeping the house tidy and caring for her father, who more often than not was content to work until the wee hours of the morning in his shop, where he made magic happen.

He was a necromancer, bringing dead machinery back to life, or combining parts from broken things to create something new. Most children in the city coveted these small treasures—wind-up soldiers that marched or clockwork butterflies with wings of silk that really flew. Delia didn't know how the magic worked, but her father's creations never ceased to amaze her.

He led Benny into the yard and tethered him to a large tree. Delia ran out and jumped into his arms.

"Papa! Welcome home!"

He buried his face in her hair, hugging her tight against him. "It's good to see you too."

"Supper's not ready yet. I didn't expect you 'til later."

He shook his head and opened the wagon's hatch with a grin. "Never mind that right now. Why don't you help me unload? I have some repairs to make."

Delia stared, wide-eyed, at the items her father uncovered. Treasures from the city's wealthy families. She spied a few copper pots and a large clock, but her eyes were drawn to a small, unremarkable wooden box.

"Papa, what's this?" she asked, picking it up.

He crouched down and ran a hand over the rough wood. "Doesn't look like much, does it?" He raised a delicate-looking latch on one side and lifted the lid. "But looks can be deceiving."

Delia gasped. If the outside of the box had looked simple and plain, the inside was anything but. It was lined with black velvet and pearls. The centerpiece featured two swans—one carved from obsidian, the other from opal—sitting atop a mother-of-pearl lake.

Delia ran a finger over the neck of the obsidian swan. "It's beautiful. What is it?"

"Right now, it is just a beautifully decorated box. What it once was, and will be again, is a music box. The swans are meant to twirl and dance across the lake."

"How? I don't see any springs or gears."

He winked. "Magic, they say."

Delia grinned, then glanced back at the swans. The box was exquisite, and she knew without asking that it was the most valuable thing her father had ever brought home. The craftsmanship alone was unlike anything she'd ever seen.

"When I have this working again, Dee, we'll be rich beyond our wildest dreams. You'll have new dresses and music lessons, and Benny will get fat eating grains." Her father closed the lid and flipped the latch back into place. "Go and put this on my bench. I'll need to get a good look at the inner workings."

Delia tucked the box under her arm and walked around the vegetable patch beside the house to the tiny workshop in the backyard. The workshop was barely larger than the wagon. It was kept tidy, with tools hung from pegs that lined the walls. In the corners lurked boxes full of springs and spare parts. The room smelled of grease and sweat: the scent of magic. Her favorite place in the world.

Rays of sunshine filtered in through the skylight, illuminating dust motes that drifted through the air. She placed the box on the table in the center of the room and sat on her father's stool to examine it. The outside was rough wood. It was a thing that could easily be overlooked or mistaken for rubbish. She traced a finger along the edges, mindful of splinters. Towards the bottom of the box was a small crank. When she twisted the crank a full rotation, the box began to vibrate.

The sound of her father's heavy steps made her jump from the stool. The box was expensive, and she knew he wouldn't approve of her fiddling with it.

Papa entered the workshop and patted Delia on the head. "Would you bring my toolbox, Dee?"

She walked over to the bench that spanned the length of the far wall and grabbed Papa's toolset. He had a tool for every job, he'd often said, but these were his favorites, the ones he always started with. There was comfort in the routine.

"Papa, can you make the music box turn on at all?"

He shook his head. "No, not so much as a ping."

She glanced down at the box, which had stopped vibrating as soon as she'd taken her hand away. "Did you wind it up all the way?"

He glanced up from his tools. "Dee…"

"I wasn't messing with it, I swear! I thought I felt it move when I put it on the table."

He gave her a skeptical glance, then slid his fingers along the back of the box. She watched as he pushed the crank with his fingertips. "Nope, nothing."

Her brow furrowed. For a moment, she thought she should tell him about the humming, but what if she'd imagined it? He might get angry at her for touching it. A cold sensation started in her fingertips and traveled up her arm. She shivered and took a step towards the door.

"You aren't going to stay and watch for a while?"

Papa asked.

"No…" she said, eyeing the box. "I should start making supper."

Papa grunted, already hunched over the box, tools in hand.

It was just before sunrise when, from her pallet beside the stove, Delia heard the hinges of the door squeal shut behind Papa. She lifted her head, wiping the crust of sleep from her eyes.

He shook his head and muttered, grabbing some bread and dried fruit from the cupboard and wrapping them in cloth.

"Papa?"

He jumped, startled by the sound of her voice. "Yes, little one?"

"Are you leaving?"

"I need a few more tools to fix the music box," he said, exhaustion evident in his voice. "I got a small advance from the owner, so I'm going into town to collect what I need."

"Can I make you some breakfast?" Delia asked, rising from her pallet.

"No need. You go back to sleep." He winked at her. "I'll need you to be strong and well-rested so you can take care of me when I get home."

Delia lay back on her pallet. Sleep returned easily and brought dreams.

In her dream, Delia found herself surrounded by beauty and opulence she'd never known could exist.

Tapestries sewn with golden thread and inlaid with precious stones hung from the walls of a room larger than her entire house.

She glanced down at herself. She was wearing a gown so delicate that it might have been woven from pure starlight. Rings with stones larger than her eyes adorned her fingers.

A harp rested on the floor beside her chaise.

Touch it.

The words overwhelmed her thoughts, but the voice that spoke was not her own. She glanced around to see who might have spoken, but she was alone.

Play it.

She ran a tentative finger across the strings, and the harp answered with a soft chord. It felt like coming back to an old friend.

Again.

She crouched, studying the structure of the instrument. A pair of dancing swans were carved into the wood along the side.

Delia slid her fingers across the strings and the harp sang. In her waking life, she'd never played an instrument. She didn't have the time, nor did Papa have the money to spend on such frivolous lessons. But, in her dream, she played like a master.

It was well into the afternoon when Delia woke. Her hands were raw, as if she had spent hours playing, rather than simply dreaming it. She rubbed her sore fingertips and kicked off her blankets. She'd overslept. There were chores to be done.

Delia headed to the garden with a basket and hoe. She hadn't weeded it in a week, and a crop of dandelions tried to choke out the rows of beans and vegetables. She pulled the greens and placed them on one side of the basket for Benny. As she worked, she found herself humming the tune from her dream. Perhaps she'd heard it before, but she couldn't place it, and if the song had words, she didn't know them.

By the time her basket was overflowing with sprouts, sweat streamed down the back of her neck. She pulled the handkerchief from the front pocket of her apron and wiped her forehead. She stood in the shade of the giant elm and admired her handiwork. Though she'd stopped humming, the song still played in her mind.

Delia glanced around the yard. Papa wouldn't likely be home until sunset. She still had time, and besides, she told herself, she just wanted to check on the music box. If it were as valuable as Papa said, surely, he'd want her to keep an eye on it. She left her basket on the ground and crossed the yard to the workshop.

She stood before the door and inhaled a deep breath. She'd gone in and out of the workshop countless times over the years. Sometimes she went to clean, or to fetch something for Papa. Other times she'd gone inside for the simple joy of being surrounded by things that reminded her of him, like the scent of grease and rust, or the tools scattered over his table that he couldn't be bothered to put away. They were all little pieces of him.

But, this time, Delia hesitated.

He didn't tell me not to go in. She reached for the handle. *I just want to look at it again.*

The box lay in the center of the table surrounded by Papa's tools.

Touch it.

The same voice from her dream.

She needed to see if the box would turn on again, if she'd only imagined what had happened. She slid her tiny fingers along the box to the wind-up mechanism on the back. As her fingers turned the crank, the box hummed to life. She jumped and jerked her hand away, but the box continued to vibrate.

She hadn't imagined it after all. Before she could talk herself out of it, she flipped the latch and lifted the lid. Inside, the swans sprang to life, twirling across their pearly lake. Delia held her breath, afraid that if she moved, the magic would end.

Music spilled from the box in elegant notes she hadn't expected. She'd learned from Papa that most music boxes were limited in the number of notes they could play, but this one was different. The notes ranged in complexity, the pitch and duration of each beyond the simple mechanism inside. The melody was familiar. The song from her dream.

Her fingers, still cramped from her dream, twitched along as the notes echoed off the shop walls. The swans continued to dance and spin hypnotically as the music filled the room. Shadow and light reflected on the miniature pond. Delia thought she could see the image of a woman's face coalescing among the shadows, but that was silly.

The air in the room thickened, the inside of the shop suddenly claustrophobic. Delia snapped the lid back down on the music box and backed out the door. Papa would be home soon, and she hadn't finished her chores.

Supper was made, and the last light of the sun was vanishing on the horizon when Delia finally heard the jingle of Papa's cart outside. She picked up the birch broom from the corner and swept the kitchen to keep herself from running out to the yard. Tonight, she wouldn't meet him at the door. She feared he would somehow figure out what she'd done. She'd never been good at keeping secrets.

After what felt like a lifetime, the door swung open and Papa's heavy steps crossed the room. "Dee?"

"Welcome home, Papa."

He bent down and kissed her forehead. "Hard at work, I see."

"Yes, Sir." She propped the broom handle against the wall and leaned into his embrace.

"I have a gift for you."

Her stomach churned. She'd snuck into his shop and tampered with his work. The most important job he'd ever had, and she'd been out playing with it, like a child. She didn't deserve a gift; she deserved to be punished.

"Well, come on," Papa said, taking her hand in his.

He led her around the house to his workshop. Delia could feel her heart in her throat. What if he knew? What if he knew, and this was just some trick to get her out so he could confront her?

Her body trembled as he pulled open the door and stepped inside.

"Open your eyes, Dee."

Standing in the corner of Papa's workshop was a large, cherry frame. She knew without asking what this was. A harp frame. She stepped forward and held out her hand.

She could hear the smile in Papa's voice. "Go ahead. Touch it."

Goosebumps rose on her arms at the familiar words. She ran a hand over the wood's surface. "How?" Her voice cracked.

"It was a funny thing, really. Some aristocrat or other was tossing it out. It had been in their family for years, but no one played anymore. So wasteful, those people." Papa rubbed his beard thoughtfully. "That's what's wrong with being a tinker these days. No one wants to repair things; they just toss the broken things out and replace them."

Delia smiled to herself. She'd heard the speech a thousand times. "But I've asked before... You always said we couldn't afford it."

"I had a little extra from the advance on the music box," he said. "The frame and tuning pins seem intact. I only need to clean it up and restring it. You'll be playing in no time."

Delia ran a hand over the wooden surface, leaving a trail through the years of dust and grime. She wondered how much of the advance he'd spent. Her finger snagged on a crevice in the wood. Not a place that was broken, but something smoothed over and intentional. She leaned in closer, lifting her apron to wipe away a layer of dust. Along the side of the frame was carved a pair of dancing swans.

Her face felt hot. The room started to spin.

She sat on the chaise in the oversized hall, but this time the ballroom was full as she plucked the harp's delicate strings. Ladies in high-necked gowns with jewels in their hair twirled around her, complimenting her songs and the gown she wore. The gentlemen, some dancing, others simply watching her play, gave her looks she didn't yet understand.

She knew the songs intuitively, without ever having heard them before.

You could be someone, the voice reminded her.

I want to be someone, she replied.

Delia opened her eyes to see Mrs. Carlotta leaning down over her, dabbing her face with a wet cloth.

"Oh, child! Thanks be to the gods!" the woman said, wringing her hands.

"Mrs. Carlotta, what are you doing here?" Delia asked.

"Shh…" The older woman placed the back of her hand against Delia's forehead. "You've been ill, my dear. Your father had to go out for work, and he asked me to sit with you while he was away."

"Ill?" Delia asked. She'd felt as if she'd been sleeping, lost in the most beautiful of dreams. Her hands were chapped and raw. "How long?"

Mrs. Carlotta brushed a strand of hair from the girl's face. "It's been a few days. Your papa said you were standing in his workshop one moment, and the next you'd fainted dead away. Why, I told him that workshop was no place for a fragile thing like you. You should be spinning or weaving, not out in all that…" She waved her hand instead of finishing the sentence.

Delia bolted upright. "My harp!"

"Now, now. There will be time for all that later."

Delia brushed the old woman's hands away. "I appreciate you checking in and taking care of me, but really, I feel fine now."

"You need your rest."

"I've been resting," Delia said, pushing back her heavy quilt.

Her whole body ached, but her hands most of all. She flexed her fingers. She needed to see the harp again. Without even changing her clothes, Delia left Mrs. Carlotta sitting beside the pallet, and headed out back to Papa's workshop.

A new scent lingered in the air of the shop; something familiar that Delia couldn't quite distinguish beneath the layers of grease and adhesive.

The sun filtered in through the skylight, lighting up the harp in the corner. Papa had restrung it and polished the wood. He'd brought it back to life.

The music box sat on the table still, looking untouched. Perhaps Papa had decided to fix her harp first. Maybe he'd felt guilty that she was sick. The swans began their graceful dance across the lake as soon as she lifted the latch. She hadn't even had to wind the crank this time. She pulled Papa's stool over to the harp and sat, stretching her weary, aching fingers toward the strings, and began to play along with the melody of the music box.

The sunlight faded to dusk, then dark, but still she played. Everything around her blurred into nothingness except for the harp, the melody, and the music box. When the workshop door creaked open, she jumped from the stool, startled back to reality.

"You're a natural talent," Papa said, hanging his lamp on a hook beside the door.

"I can explain…"

Delia glanced over her shoulder to the music box. It sat there, closed. But, hadn't she just…?

Papa laughed. "I take it this means you like your present? I was hoping I'd be able to show it to you myself when you were feeling better."

She smiled but kept a wary eye on the music box. She could have sworn she'd opened it. "Papa, did you fix the music box?"

"As a matter of fact, I did."

He walked past her to the table and lifted the latch. The same way she could have sworn she'd done hours before. He turned the crank, and the box began to play. The song it played was basic. It was nothing like the elegant chords and soft melodies it had played for her. No, not for her.

With her.

She stepped forward and peered into the box. The light from the lamp cast shadows on the pond, and Delia saw that face again. "But the music isn't right."

Papa's brow furrowed. "What do you mean?"

"It's supposed to be…more."

She couldn't capture the feeling in words. How could she describe something so transcendent that it made her lost? Or to describe the impossible place where the melody became the only thing that existed?

A shadow passed over his face as he took Delia's hands in his and turned them over. Her fingertips were raw and bleeding. She hadn't noticed. "How did this happen, Dee?"

"I don't know. I was playing the song from the music box. I lost track of time."

"The song from the music box?"

"Yes, but it was different. Here, let me show you." She sat once again at the stool and raised her chapped and bloody fingers to the strings. She tried to pluck out a melody, but the strings replied only with discordant pings.

Papa placed a hand on her arm. "You have to let your fingers heal. You're making a mess of your hands, and your harp."

Delia's gaze fell to the spattering of blood on the floor beneath the harp. Her hands began to ache again.

Although she'd sworn to Papa that she wouldn't, Delia found herself in his workshop the next morning as soon as he'd set off for town. The music box still lay on the table. He'd told her he'd be returning it to its owner later in the week and collecting his sum.

She knew something wasn't right. Her dreams, the music box and the harp were all related somehow, but it seemed to be something only she could sense. Yet, when she'd tried to play in front of Papa, the notes hadn't come. It was as if she'd forgotten how.

But had she ever really known?

She'd been sick, and she'd been dreaming strange dreams. That was why she'd had to come back to the workshop. She had to know for sure if any of it had been real.

Delia lifted the lid with heavily bandaged fingers. Swans and shadows danced across the mother-of-pearl lake, forming the same face she'd seen before. She swallowed. "Are you real?"

The voice that answered was the same voice she'd heard in her dreams. The one that had urged her to play the harp. The one that had told her she could be more than a tinker's daughter.

Next, you must learn to sing.

"I can't sing."

Yet.

"But I—"

Try.

Delia rubbed her eyes. The face in the lake didn't move; there was no indication it was speaking at all. But she could hear it, and it could hear her. This was madness. She must still be sick.

Try.

The voice was more insistent this time. Desperate.

Delia closed her eyes and tried to think of a song, any song that she knew the words to. Her mind blanked, and then it came to her, a lullaby Papa used to sing when she was little. She closed her eyes and began to softly sing:

Night's approaching,
Dreams come to take you away,
There I'll find you,
And chase all the bad things away.
Stop! the voice barked. *That won't do at all.*

Delia's cheeks burned, and she turned away from the face in the box. She felt like a disappointment. Maybe the voice would realize it had made a mistake and refuse to teach her.

The music box began to play, and lyrics filled Delia's head. She began to sing again, the words in a language she didn't understand.

She sang for hours, until her voice was cracked and hoarse, never understanding a word.

Good. You will come every day. You will play and you will sing.

"I…I can't."

You will.

"You aren't mine. Papa has to return you."

You must not let that happen. You want to be famous, don't you? Wealthy? Adored? I can give you things your papa could only dream of. You will perform for kings and queens.

Delia nodded with barely concealed excitement and closed the lid on the box, tucking it under her apron. Papa would be home soon, and she needed to find a place to hide the music box.

Papa banged the door open in a frenzy. He pushed through the kitchen into the back room, and then returned to the kitchen again. He turned toward Delia, expression frantic and frightening. "Where is it?"

"Where is what, Papa?" she asked, already knowing the answer.

"The music box, Dee. I went to the workshop after I tied Benny up, and it wasn't there. Have you been out there today?"

"No, Papa. I promised I wouldn't." She felt a pang of guilt at how easily the lie came.

"Has anyone else been here?"

Delia shook her head. "Here, Papa. Sit, have some supper." She placed a steaming bowl of stew in front of his seat at the table.

"I can't, Dee. I told Lady Carlisle I'd deliver her music box tomorrow. I have to find it."

He leaned down and searched beneath the table, as though he might find the box there.

"Can't you just tell her it isn't ready yet?"

He ran a trembling hand through his hair. "The box is more valuable than you can imagine. She is anxious to see it returned."

Delia chewed her bottom lip. She wanted to tell Papa the truth, but if what the face inside the box said was true, Delia could make enough gold to pay for it several times over.

Papa rummaged through the house late into the evening. He went in and out, emptying his workshop, then putting everything back inside. He cleaned out the kitchen cabinets, and even went so far as to search Delia's pallet. He muttered to himself the entire time about how he should've known better, should've kept something so valuable more safe. Words like 'thief' and 'stolen' opened a pit in Delia's stomach.

Papa eventually fell asleep in a chair at the table, and Delia covered him with a quilt. She hugged her knees to her chest and wept. It was the first time she could remember ever lying to Papa.

When Delia woke the next morning, Papa was gone. She had dreamed again, that familiar dream which promised all the things she wanted. The things she was willing to lie and steal for.

In the days that followed, Delia left the house each morning and went to the corner of the vegetable garden to uncover the canvas sack containing the music box that she'd buried there, then crept into the workshop.

The routine had become familiar by now. The swans glided around the lake, and the shadows pooled together to form the face in the box.

Begin, the voice commanded each time, without hesitation.

Delia would dutifully begin to play or sing along with the music box each time, until the healing wounds on her hands broke open and bled, or until her voice was gone.

Each day, Papa returned home looking more haggard than before. He barely slept and hardly ate. He cast wary glances at the bandages on her hands, perpetually stained with fresh blood.

Then, Papa returned from town with his leg in a splint and a crutch under his arm.

Delia had been waiting for his return, worried that each day might be the one where he confronted her about the music box, or worse, he didn't return at all.

She ran out into the yard to meet him. "Papa! Are you alright?"

He paused, taking shallow breaths. He held a hand against his side. From here, she could see fresh bruises on his face, and a swollen lip.

"What happened?

"Lady Carlisle," he wheezed, "believes I've stolen her music box."

Delia felt like she'd been punched in the gut.

"She has given me until the end of the week to return it…" He paused and collected his breath. "Or I will be thrown into debtor's prison."

Delia gasped and wrapped her arms around him. He grunted in pain, looking down at her bloody bandages, not returning her embrace.

"I have to give you back to Papa," Delia said to the face in the music box. "He'll be thrown in jail if I don't."

Someday you will be able to buy his freedom. You will play for nobles and royalty.

"Thank you for teaching me, but what I've learned will have to be enough."

Tears spilled down her cheeks. Before the music box, she'd only ever cried when Mama died.

You were nothing without me. You will be nothing once again.

Delia wiped away a tear.

Sing one last time for me.

The first notes of the music box began and Delia opened her mouth, but only a croak escaped. She grabbed her throat. "What did you do?"

The face inside the box began to laugh.

Delia ran over to the harp and plucked the strings. She was met with a barrage of discordant notes.

You are nothing.

Delia slammed the lid down on the music box and fled the workshop, weeping.

That night, when Delia dreamed, she sat upon the chaise, and though she plucked at the harp, there was no music. The people around her in the hall stopped dancing and stared. Then, the laughter began. The men and women who'd once crowded around to hear her play now circled, laughing and jeering, tugging at her jewelry, ripping her dress to shreds.

She woke up screaming.

Papa jolted upright and hobbled to her side. "Delia, what is it?"

Even though the foggy veil of sleep had not completely lifted, she recognized that Papa had called her Delia. He'd never done that before.

"I'm sorry, I didn't mean to startle you. It was a dream."

"Delia… If there is something you need to tell me…"

"No," she answered, a little too quickly. She'd hoped to figure out a way to 'find' the music box without arousing Papa's suspicion. After all she'd put him through, she still couldn't bear to tell him the truth and see the look of disappointment on his face. "I mean, I don't think so."

He nodded and winced as he rose and hobbled back to his chair.

Delia settled back on her pallet, but she couldn't sleep.

With his busted leg, Papa had not gone back to town. He mentioned that he had no reason to on one of Mrs. Carlotta's many visits to check in on him. He didn't speak to Delia anymore.

Delia snuck into the shop and opened the lid on the music box. She knew she had to return it to Papa, but she needed to look at it one last time before she did. This time, the swans didn't move, and no face appeared.

"Hello?" Delia asked.

She felt a bit silly for talking to a box. It was different when the face lit the lake, like talking to a person, but now there was no sign of it.

"Please?"

The word hung in the air, and just as Delia was about to close the lid, the swans began to move, and the face materialized.

"How long will it take to make me good enough… so that those things I dream about can happen? So that I can become rich and take care of Papa and Benny?"

There is a way.

"How?"

Let me in.

Delia stared down at the box. She wasn't sure what it meant, but the tone was enough to give her pause. "What do you mean?"

It would take a lifetime for you to become my equal or better, but if you let me in… Give me a body, and I can play through you.

"You want to be me?"

Long ago I was trapped inside this box. I no longer have a body of my own, but if you let me in, I can become a part of you.

Delia's brow furrowed. She didn't believe in magic. At least not beyond the type of magic her father made in this shop, but there was, after all, a music box talking to her at this very moment. "But then I wouldn't be me anymore."

I'll only come out when it is time to perform. You won't even know I'm there. Think about your poor papa and how proud he'd be of you.

"How do I let you in?"

Keep playing.

Delia sat beside the harp and plucked the strings. The music had come back to her. She could feel it pulsing in her blood. The harp felt like it had become part of her body.

She glanced at the music box on the table. A dense white fog lifted from the surface of the lake and began to drift across the room, plunging itself inside Delia's ears and nostrils.

She played on.

The fog grew thicker. Delia felt the music drawing

inside her and filling her up, but then, she felt something different. She felt incorporeal, as though she were being pulled outside herself. She tried to take her fingers from the harp strings and stop playing, but her hands refused to cooperate. It was as though someone else now controlled her body.

Delia felt that last moment when her consciousness completely severed from the rest of her. The music stopped. She blinked, staring up from a mother-of-pearl lake.

She watched her own hand close the lid of the box.

The box lid popped open, and the faces of two women appeared above her. It was hard to see with the swans dancing in and out of her field of vision.

"So, the tinker was able work his magic, I see," one of the women said.

"Oh yes," the second woman answered, "but not without trouble. His little girl took a liking to the box and hid it from him while she learned to play its melodies. She's quite the musical prodigy. She's only just began playing, and already she's been invited to perform at the palace."

"What do you intend to do with the music box now that it's been repaired?" the first woman asked.

"I will gift it to Queen Camelia, naturally. A trinket like this belongs in the palace."

She closed the lid, sealing Delia in darkness.

Interlude Three

Imprisonment

S.O. Green

They'd put the woman in a cell, but it didn't seem to faze her. She reclined on the rough, wooden bench, smoking from a pipe she shouldn't have had, while the other prisoners cowered in the opposite corner, trying not to draw her attention.

Lyssa wasn't especially impressed, and she wouldn't have made an extra effort to visit the cells over this particular criminal, except that she'd been arrested trying to enter the city with what the official report had described as 'obviously a zombie'. That, at least, had earned a raised eyebrow.

"And you are?" she demanded, eyeing the lady with the long legs and fashionable doublet stained with Red

Land dirt.

"Peshwin Flitbacke," she said, and Lyssa thought she might have practiced that nonchalance. "Queen of Bandits."

"Never heard of you."

"Don't be cruel, sweetheart. Besides, I wouldn't have expected the high and mighty Grand Mage of all Guardiana to take notice of us peons living out our tiny, little lives down here in the dirt anyway."

Lyssa scowled, but she didn't rise to it. She did notice, and that was why she was here. If she'd been like all the others in the queen's court, she'd have just stayed home. Fuck the poor people.

"Tell me about the zombie."

"You mean, Baddum Lako, Scribe to the King of Guardiana?"

"Queen Camelia doesn't have a scribe and Guardiana hasn't had a king since her daddy passed."

Good riddance…

"That's what I said. Only it turns out he was scribe to the king about three hundred years ago."

"And he was wandering through the Miners' District with you in a body that didn't belong to him?"

"We had an adventure, he and I. He was trapped in a stick of chalk I found in a book about the Old Faith. Kept leaving me cryptic bloody messages on my wall. Five days, four days, yadda-yadda. Then he made me wait through a soulstorm while he jumped into another body. He might have known a little something about your mysterious necromancer, Lestrange, but…"

But the guards had cut his head off and burned him

to ashes. If he'd known something, it had gone to the pyre with him.

"For the love of…"

"Has it been one of those weeks?" Peshwin asked, and there was an abiding sympathy in her tone and in her eyes.

Lyssa wondered how many silly, young girls from the town Peshwin controlled had fallen into bed with her after a comment just like that.

"You said you found him in an Old Faith book. Like the one that was sold by Queen Camelia recently? The one that Lord Hargraves gifted to his elderly grandmother, and which was missing from the sanctuary where she was living? I say 'was living' because someone gave the lot of them Haven Plague just recently, so they were all dead when we got there."

Peshwin said nothing. They'd located the book at a temple nearby, in the possession of an eager and easily confused Faithsister, who'd praised the name of the kind soul who'd let her buy it at such a low, low price. 'A gift from within the Circle', she'd said. Lyssa had wondered why the book had no soul trapped inside, but if it had been concealing another object…

"You can't prove I had anything to do with that," Peshwin said, sucking rather too aggressively at her pipe.

"Actually, I can. There are only so many alchemists dealing in things like Haven Plague, and only a handful who'd be unscrupulous enough to sell it to someone like you. And they rolled on you the moment we stepped through the door. Didn't even need to threaten them."

The Bandit Queen lapsed back into silence. She

seemed to be considering whether this was a very well-constructed bluff. It wasn't. The guard had done their duty, investigated and collected evidence, and there was enough to weave a rope for Peshwin Flitbacke's slender neck.

Personally, Lyssa thought there was no place in a civilised society for the death penalty, but the courts listened to her about as much as the merchant guilds did, so she was going to swing.

"The sad thing is, if it wasn't for this mess with Lestrange's objects, you'd probably have gotten away with it."

"If it hadn't been for Lestrange's bloody objects, it never would have happened!" Peshwin roared. Everyone in the cell block, except Lyssa, flinched.

She set her pipe aside, rose gracefully from the bench, and stalked over to the bars so that they were face-to-face. Lyssa made sure she was standing out of stabbing range. The guards should have searched her for concealed weapons, but then they should also have confiscated her fucking pipe.

"Can I ask a favour?"

Lyssa scoffed. "Wow, for a woman, you've got some balls."

"It won't cost you anything. But my grandfather was a resident at that sanctuary. The only family I had left and they let him die and rot in his room. I want you to strike his name from my list of crimes. If I'm going to hang, I don't want it to be for a crime I didn't commit. I wasn't much of a granddaughter, but I'd never have hurt him."

Lyssa rolled her eyes. "The Bandit Queen with a heart of gold. Now I've heard it all. Alright, fine. I'll make sure the very long list of charges they read out before you drop doesn't include that one murder."

"Much obliged."

Peshwin smirked, tipped a hat that wasn't there, and returned to her bench.

"You said he told you about Lestrange," Lyssa said. "The scribe. So, he was able to talk to you. Operate like a normal human instead of a soulstorm zombie. Did he have any idea how that happened?"

"Your guess is probably better than mine, sweetheart. But it's funny, isn't it? Soulstorms, doing things that only old Lestrange could do. Almost like part of him's still here with us, don't you think?"

"Yeah," Lyssa said, and turned to leave. "Real funny."

Over the years, Lyssa had perfected a walk through the halls of the palace that made her robes billow and courtiers scurry out of her way. Camelia called it 'the warpath'. It wasn't entirely inaccurate.

She'd planned to give her full account of the 'Flitbacke issue' to the queen, and then chew out Merrick for the way his guards had killed literally the only witness they'd had thus far to Lestrange's experiments. Instead, she stopped in the doorway when she realised the queen had company.

Lady Carlisle stood before the throne in full, courtly regalia—all the fashionable gowns were modelled on

Camelia's these days, but no one could pull it off the same way—while one of her servants presented the queen with an ornate music box on a silk cushion.

"It has come to our attention," Lady Carlisle announced, loud enough for everyone to hear, "that the Crown wishes the return of the objects that were sold at auction. Therefore, we are here to do our duty, as a concerned citizen of Guardiana, and return the item purchased by our estate. And the Queen may rest assured that we seek no remuneration for this act. We are simply doing what any true subject of Her Majesty should do."

"We?" Lyssa muttered. "Give me a break."

"That is very kind of you, Lady Carlisle," Camelia said, and Lyssa wondered how she managed to stay so diplomatic about the whole thing. "I will entrust the object to my Grand Mage, so that we can determine if it is safe."

Lyssa strode to Camelia's side, plucked the box off its cushion and stuffed it in her robes. "Yeah, thanks."

Lady Carlisle flicked a glance at Lyssa like she was something she'd tried to avoid stepping in on the way out of her carriage. Then, she curtseyed floridly, summoned her entourage with a wave of her hand and departed.

"No remuneration. What a crock of shit. That bill's going to come due sooner rather than later. Believe that. Bloody snake-lady."

"You're probably right," Camelia sighed. Then her expression brightened, and she gestured to Lyssa's robes. "But we got one of the objects back. That's good, isn't it?"

Lyssa nodded and pulled the box back out to examine it. A music box, if she wasn't mistaken. She could feel the press of a confined soul, trying to reach out from its prison. Probably waiting for some poor idiot to open it and cause all kinds of havoc.

It turned out the souls weren't as bound to their objects as she'd first thought. The scribe seemed like he'd been benign, but some of them would be dangerous. Three hundred years could change people for the worse.

"What are you going to do with it?" Camelia asked, staring at the box pensively.

"What I should have done from the start," she muttered. "Burn it."

Mirror Shard

Aaron P. Hansen

The cart came to a halt smack in the middle of the busiest market Bergsen had ever seen. He sat, nestled between what he assumed were burlap bags of potatoes, and watched more people than he could count move through stalls of food, fabric and finery.

Beside the cart, a woman, with two boys in tow wrestling for possession of what looked like a rock, was haggling with a merchant. Bergsen could see their mouths moving, but whatever they were saying was absorbed into the roar of every other haggling shopper and screaming kid. The tableau repeated across the square.

"Oi, Father!" The farmer who drove the cart looked over the back of the bench, arm embracing the backrest for leverage. "This is yer stop, ya? We ain't goin' no further."

Bergsen clutched his pack to his chest and considered staying right where he was. This was not the Violet Range, and this was definitely not the monastery. Hiding behind sacks of potatoes couldn't be the worst plan, could it?

The farmer's son appeared in front of Bergsen. The youth was large as any farmer's boy would be expected and would be an even bigger man when he was done growing.

"Come on now, Faithfather Bergsen," the boy said, grinning. "It ain't so bad once you get used to it. An' if you just stand tall, most folk will leave ya be."

To emphasise his point, the boy straightened his back and puffed his chest out to stand nearly two meters in height.

Bergsen sighed and gave in. There was no way he could let the boy show him up. He scooted to the edge of the cart and placed his legs on the ground. He did as the boy said and stood at his full height, staring over the crowd.

"Yessir," the boy said, looking up at Bergsen. "Just like that and you'll be fine."

Bergsen rubbed his head, feeling the prickle of the new growth. People eddied around him and colours swirled in rivulets of magic. Despite himself, he felt himself grinning. Where life as a Brother of the Perpetual Journey had been austere and disciplined, this was vibrant and magical. He missed his little room in the monastery a little less.

"Thank you," he rumbled to the farmer and his son,

as they unloaded the cart. "Continue on this path and you will find yourself within the Unbroken Circle."

"Aye," the farmer said, eyeing Bergsen with a smirk. "If ya ever need yerself some honest work, come find me and you can pull me carts."

"If the Circle wills it, then I will pull your carts and your horses," Bergsen laughed.

"I believe you," the farmer said, hoisting a bag over his shoulder. "Off with ya now, before I put ye te work unloading me potatoes."

"May the Circle guide you within," Bergsen said to them, placing a hand around each of their shoulders.

With that, he left them to their task. They were good and honest men, but he had his own task which had brought him all this way from his research. But first, there was something he had to attend to.

He placed his hands on his hips, causing traffic to give him a wide berth. Seeing what he was looking for, he barked out a laugh that caused more than one person to squawk in surprise.

The vendor looked up as he heard the swish and rustle of Bergsen's dark robes and grinned. Mostly a toothless grin, but genuine all the same.

"Ah, bless me, my good Father," the beer vendor said, and began pouring a draught into a wooden mug. "You are a man a long way from home and in desperate need."

"Sir, you have marked me well," Bergsen said. "But you will need to give me more than a thimbleful of your water."

"Water!" the vendor sputtered but handed the mug to

another patron. "You are not from Kingsgate, are you?"

Bergsen shook his head.

"Ah," the vendor murmured, understanding.

The vendor put a finger in the air, signalling Bergsen to wait, then wandered to the far side of his cart.

"You'll like this," the vendor called. "It ain't the Violet Range swill you drink, but it'll give you something to think about, it will."

The vendor rounded the cart, using both hands to carry a stein filled with dark amber liquid. Bergsen smacked his lips and reached for the stein. He took a most unholy pull, letting the beer cool his throat.

It was crisp and sharp, with flavours unlike the black and chocolaty beers of his home. This was bright and full of life, like the city itself.

Bergsen wiped the foam from his lip with his sleeve.

"This…" he breathed, "…is mighty delicious."

Bergsen drained the rest without taking a breath.

"Another!"

The vendor shook his head but left to refill Bergsen's stein.

"Easy now, Father!" A labourer in dusty overalls laughed as he sidled next to Bergsen. "That stuff is thick as tar and will muddle your brains before you've finished your second."

Bergsen looked down at the man as another dusty companion joined him.

"Are you…" Bergsen rumbled, hands on his hips, "…challenging my ability to hold my beer?"

"Yes," the second labourer said, giving his friend a slight shove. "Yes, he is."

"Ah! No! I am most definitely not!" the first man shouted, throwing his hands in the air in surrender. "The last time I did that, I was hung over for two days straight. My wife nearly threw me out because I was too sick to work."

Bergsen placed his hands on his hips and leaned back with a bellowing laugh. "You are a wise man that learns well."

The second labourer snorted his beer and doubled over, alternating his fit between coughing and laughing.

"Shut up, Ster."

Ster straightened and wiped his tears away, shaking his head.

"It seems to be there's a story that needs told," Bergsen said. "I will buy you a round of the vendor's finest and you will tell me."

"Deal," Ster said.

"I hate you a little bit," his friend said.

Some time, and a few too many beers, later, Bergsen found his way to the Abbey. His new friends left him at the gate and stumbled off, waving their goodbyes. Bergsen used the wall that led up to the entrance of the Abbey for support while the pathway changed directions and tilted in unpredictable ways. He stopped and puffed out his cheeks, willing the world to stop swaying. A good lie down was all he needed.

He walked around a black carriage, ignoring the chatter of people. Bergsen puffed out his cheeks, happy to be close to a bed.

"You," she said. Her voice carried the whip-like tone of a woman who suffered no dissent. Bergsen towered over her like she was little more than a child, but she carried herself like she was a giant.

"Circle preserve me," Bergsen muttered, as he realized she was the Abbess.

She folded her hands behind her back, appraising Bergsen's dishevelled, travel-worn, and slightly drunk appearance. Bergsen weighed the likelihood he could find his new friends and hide in the city.

"You're late," she snapped. "Primarch Leonardo sent word of your arrival yesterday. You were supposed to arrive this morning. Instead, you've been out drinking like a tavern rat with the local heathens."

"I have been among the common folk, hearing their confessions and bestowing forgiveness. No investigation can be successful without the goodwill of the people."

The Abbess scoffed. "The Primarch insisted you were his best. Show me. You will accompany Mowatt the Healer to the…latest scene."

She pointed to the carriage with a ramrod arm.

Bergsen started to mumble something about having just gotten into the city and perhaps taking a moment to freshen up. The Abbess arched an eyebrow, but otherwise didn't move.

He didn't even consider arguing further. He had been down that path before. One didn't argue with an Abbess. Bergsen pulled himself into the coach, causing the thing to lean to one side. Once he took his seat, a man in blue and silver robes sat across from him.

"Mowatt the healer, I presume," Bergsen grumbled.

"Yes, I am," the healer laughed, then paused to study Bergsen. "Who might you be and why are you in my carriage?"

"One doesn't argue with an Abbess," Bergsen mumbled, then added, "Faithfather Bergsen, at you service. I was sent by the Primarch to be the Faith's eyes in these… matters."

"It seems odd to me, to send a Faithfather for something like this."

"Hmm…"

Bergsen leaned back, feeling his eyes get heavy as the carriage rocked its way through the city streets, out of the worker's district, away from the slums, towards the palace and its hub of walled manors and sprawling gardens. Mowatt had questions, but he needed a nap. He watched through the window, struggling to keep his eyes open, as they rolled over cobbles and past magical, iron lamps. The Healer said something, but it was background noise as Bergsen closed his eyes. The tug of sleep was pulling with the added weight of too much beer.

His fatigue drained away suddenly. He snapped his eyes open and scowled at the other man.

"What did you do," Bergsen growled.

Mowatt the healer rolled his eyes and wiggled his fingers. "I need you awake if you're coming with me." Mowatt crossed his arms. "And why *are* you coming with me? This is healer's work. I don't think the victim is particularly faithful. Not judging by the size of his house."

"The men," Bergsen said, feeling his prickly scalp. "The ones who are mutilating their faces. I am studying them. I think I have a pattern. Primarch Leonardo assigned me personally."

Mowatt's eyebrow arched again.

"What makes you think they are doing it to themselves and this is not the work of some deranged killer?"

Bergsen rummaged through his bag to pull out his notebook. Licking a finger, he leafed through the pages.

"At first glance," Bergsen said, "it's easy to believe they are targeted. They are all men of some wealth or minor importance. But there is more going on, I think. The man we are going to now, he is also like this?"

Mowatt nodded. "That's correct," he said, looking out the coach window as it rounded a corner and passed through the gates to a large estate. "Duke Dolamore. He's a duke with some minor holdings in the Gold Plains but has done well enough to keep a residence in the city."

"It's easy for a rich man to make enemies."

"No more than any other rich person."

"These attacks are so savage. Who does that to a person's face?" Bergsen rubbed his scalp, "but these aren't the only people to have behaved strangely since they came into contact with…certain objects."

"Are you talking about the Lestrange auction?"

Bergsen didn't answer. The coachman opened the door, letting bright light spill into the compartment. Bergsen squinted and gave his head a shake.

They were met by a young woman with bloodshot eyes. She led them through the halls while she sniffled into a white handkerchief. She neither looked at nor spoke to them as she gestured for them to enter the Duke's bedroom, lit only by a few candles.

In the low light, Bergsen saw an older woman sitting on the bed, holding the hand of someone he couldn't see, but assumed was the Duke. That would make the woman the Duchess Dolamore. She did not look up as he and Mowatt took tentative steps into the room. Neither wanted to interrupt her grieving.

It was only as they stepped into the room that they saw the man's face. Or the blood-soaked bandages that covered it. Bergsen froze, shocked by the butchery. Only a slit for a single eye and his mouth were not bound in the red-stained, inkblot silk dressing. Bergsen had read every report, but he was not prepared for this savagery.

Mowatt rushed to the man's side, ignoring the Duchess. Bergsen watched a gentle, yellow glow, like sunlight, form an aura around Mowatt that flowed down his arms, into his hands, and coalesced around the Duke's face. The light flowed like water, eddying and pooling, before being sucked into the black space that surrounded the Duke.

Bergsen had read of the inverted aura, the result of evil that left a hole in a person but had never seen it. That darkness belonged in the past, with the long-dead necromancer, Lestrange. He murmured a prayer to the Unbroken Circle.

The Duchess clutched her husband's hand and pulled it to her heart. Mowatt cast a glance at her, then to Bergsen, tilting his head to the woman.

Taking his cue, Bergsen knelt in front of the Duchess Dolamore. Had the bed not been so high, he would have been looking directly into her eyes.

"My lady," Bergsen said, in a soft rumble as he took her hand. "We must let Mowatt do his work now. The Circle will guide him."

He stood, guiding her up. He was deliberate and slow, careful to be no more than a suggestion to her slight frame. The Duchess raised her chin and narrowed her eyes as she took him in. She studied his robes and her shoulders slumped.

"Father," she sobbed, as she sought shelter in his robes.

He led her to the small couch on the other side of the room and held her hands in his. The Duchess pulled a cloth from her sleeve and dabbed her eyes. For a moment, she sat still, slowing her breathing, forcing the composure she could not have felt.

Bergsen waited for her. He itched to interview the staff, to ask them what they had seen. This was his first opportunity to learn firsthand what had happened, and he was eager to fill his notebook.

Instead, he looked around the room, bored by its wealth. He wondered what it would be like to be so burdened by possessions. Not for the first time in his life, he was grateful that most of what he owned fit in the satchel he carried. There had always been freedom in that.

But, over her shoulder and in the corner of the room, he saw what he believed to be the Duke's cane. It was propped against a small table, as if forgotten.

Yet, the golden lion's head, with its intricately carved mane that flowed into the cane's handle, stared back at him. Bergsen could almost feel the ebony and gold in his hand. Even in the low light, he saw the twin strands of red spiralling elegantly through the ebony. He had the vague impression he had seen it before.

A cane wasn't really a possession. It was practical,

useful. Even an expensive and beautiful one like that wouldn't break his vow of poverty.

"We have not been the most devout followers since we moved to Kingsgate," the Duchess said, folding her hands together and looking at the ground between them.

"That is of no consequence," he murmured, forcing himself back into the moment. "The Faith does not preach adherence, only that you lead your best lives."

The Duchess nodded, and brought a hand to her face, suppressing her tears. He looked around the room, wondering if a candle had gone out.

"Why did this happen?" she asked, her voice on the edge of breaking. "He is a good man."

Bergsen hesitated, weighing his desire to investigate and his duties to the Faith.

"That's why I am here, my lady," he said.

She snapped her eyes on him and set her jaw.

"I don't think it was entirely him who did this," he continued, before she carried on with whatever thoughts she was ready to fight. "Tell me, what was his behaviour like recently?"

Her expression shifted as she was taken aback by his question.

"You said he is a good man. Did you notice anything unusual in the past little while?"

He didn't need her to speak to see the truth, but he did not interrupt.

The Duchess took a shuddering breath and gripped the cushions of the couch, but she squared her shoulders and sat tall.

"I don't know when it first started, but lately…" She

paused. "Lately, he seemed more…"

She waved a hand around, trying to conjure the word she was looking for. Bergsen saw the fine suit hanging from the dressing screen, the oils and tinctures arrayed around the mirror. The cane.

"Vain?" Bergsen suggested.

"Yes," she whispered, bringing the hand to her mouth. "That's it."

Bergsen nodded. Everyone had been the same.

"He never used to worry over much about his clothes or how he looked," she said. "He's a handsome man, in his own way, but he was never dashing."

"But it was more than just vanity, wasn't it?" Bergsen said.

"The other day, he was making fun of one of the staff. A young man just coming of age. Henry was relentless and wouldn't stop teasing the boy about his looks. It was almost like he was jealous of the boy. Sounds crazy, now that I say it."

Bergsen shook his head.

"Henry had become jealous and vain," she confirmed. "And, well, just mean."

"This is the same story surrounding every one of the victims," he said to her. "Then, each of them ends up doing the same thing."

"But why?" she pleaded, grabbing his hand. "Why did this happen?"

"I think…" Bergsen hesitated, thinking maybe it was better to keep the information to himself. "I think the men come into possession of some object that carries evil in it. I used to believe it was the knife they used, but each man uses something different. A sword. A dagger. A kitchen knife. No, I think it's something we would see every day and ignore."

She began to look around the room, hunting for the trespassing object.

"Is there anything new in here? Something you don't recognize?"

She shook her head, but continued scanning.

"Do you think the object is in here?" Mowatt asked, as he walked over to them.

Bergsen and the Duchess looked up at him in surprise. His shoulders were slumped, and he had bags under his eyes that Bergsen hadn't noticed before.

"What? I can still hear you talking from over there," Mowatt said. "Anyway, I want to take the Duke back to the Abbey. I need to rest; his wounds are…resisting me. But I think, with some help, he can make a good recovery."

Neither of them asked what a good recovery meant, but Bergsen didn't hold a lot of hope.

"If the object is in here," Mowatt continued, "what do you think about taking everything back to the Abbey so it can be examined?"

Bergsen smiled grimly. He'd been about to suggest the same thing. They looked at the Duchess, seeking her approval.

"Yes, yes," she said. "I don't care about what's in this room, just please take care of my husband."

"My Lady," Mowatt said. "You have my word on it."

Bergsen used the time it took the Duke's staff to

get organized to look around the room for the object. He knew it was his imagination, but he felt as though he knew its presence. He peered into a case that had a row of gold and silver medallions. He made a note in his book to give these special attention but added a question mark since they were behind glass.

After the Duke was placed into a cot and carried off to the waiting carriage, a few staff were directed into the room. They began the process of packing everything in the room into crates.

Bergsen stood vigilant, watching them work. If any-one was carrying something from the room, Bergsen would spot it as the likely item trying to make its escape to find its next victim. Or so he hoped.

As he left the room, lingering at the door. He cast a last look back, eyes sliding over the small table that was next to the bed. For a moment, he felt like there was something about that table he was missing. The thought tugged at his brain. What was special about that table?

With a shrug, he left the room and closed the door. The thought would return to him in its own time.

Bergsen sat in front of the endless assortment of items that had been pulled from the Duke's room and sighed.

A week later and nothing. None of the trinkets gave any indication that they had any power at all. An assortment of magic users had tested each item under his supervision. He didn't want to believe this had been a waste of time, but the thought intruded and wouldn't be chased off.

He rubbed his eyes until he saw stars and yawned so wide his jaw cracked. Whatever it was that had been the Duke's misfortune had grown legs and marched off. Bergsen had a vision of a golden lion sauntering through the tall grasses of his range. Proud, the king of his domain, not to be caged.

He smiled at the thought and reached to stroke its mane.

That was enough for today. There was nothing left to be done with the stuff lying about here. He left the room and gave the word to Mowatt's staff that everything could be returned to the Duchess. That done, Bergsen stood in front of the mirror he'd purchased at market for his sparse room and admired his robes, looking for dust and wrinkles that would ruin his look. He'd had new robes made to replace his old, road-worn ones.

Satisfied, he sauntered off to find Mowatt, whom he found glowing next to the Duke. Mowatt had been trying daily to heal the man's face. The best he'd been able to do was encourage the scars to heal over without splitting open anymore. Duke Dolamore would never again be a handsome man. He would be scarred and disfigured despite paying an immense amount for the healer's service.

Mowatt's efforts were a pathetic joke. Bergsen tried not to chuckle.

"Ah, Bergsen," Mowatt said, glancing up from his efforts. "I'm glad you're here."

As Mowatt's glow receded, Bergsen noted the medallion hanging around his neck. Gold and inset with jewels, dangling from a red silk ribbon. It spoke of wealth beyond what was plausible for a simple healer, even after his payment for this job.

Bergsen didn't recall seeing it on the manifest of items from the Duke's room, but he couldn't help but wonder if it had been one of the medallions he had seen in the case. Had Mowatt helped himself before Bergsen had a chance to study it?

Or had it been a gift from the Duchess? The thought settled into Bergsen's mind, fitting like a puzzle piece. He would have to watch Mowatt carefully.

"What can I do for you?" Bergsen made his voice even and welcoming. There was no need to tip his hand yet.

"I was able to speak to the Duke earlier today," Mowatt flexed his hands, working his fingers as if shaking out the evil that lay within the sleeping Duke.

"He was awake?" Bergsen was genuinely curious.

"Very little, unfortunately. He seemed mostly confused about where he was and kept asking for a mirror. He said he needed to make sure he was himself, whatever that means."

"You didn't give him one, did you?"

"Of course not," Mowatt said, taken aback. "I told him it was best he waited a while."

"When do you think he will be awake again?" Bergsen asked. "I have so many questions."

Mowatt shrugged. "I honestly don't know. I've never seen anything like this. His body just refuses to heal." Mowatt looked down at the Duke, face still bandaged, but not in its entirety anymore. "I can't even be sure I'm helping or if he's just living on his own accord, or if there's something else I'm not seeing. There's some kind of…taint lingering in him, but the worst of it seems gone already."

"I think the thing that did this to him has moved on," Bergsen said.

"Yeah, maybe," Mowatt yawned.

"Perhaps you should rest a bit," Bergsen said. "I will sit with the Duke and pray to the Circle for guidance."

"Thank you, Bergsen," Mowatt put a hand on Bergsen's shoulder as he walked past. "You're a good man and I appreciate your help here."

Bergsen sat on the stool next to the bed and found he could not look at the man's face, even bandaged as it was. He was too hideous, too destroyed for Bergsen to rest his eyes on.

There was nothing to be done for the man, really. He had let himself go and become weak. If he really had been as strong as the lion, he would not have had to cut himself.

Disgusted with the Duke, Bergsen left the room in search of something more pleasant to surround himself with. He left the Abbey to wander the streets. He was in search of something but wouldn't have been able to say what it was if he'd been asked.

As usual, the streets were full of people, jostling and going about their business. This section of the city was busy with merchants and vendors and people buying their wares. None of what he saw interested Bergsen, and the persistent presence of the unwashed wore on him.

There had to be something better than this. He deserved better.

Bergsen lay in his bed, staring at the ceiling. He kicked off his blankets, looking for some reprieve from their heat, but immediately pulled them back against the cooler air. He rolled to his side, arm hanging off his bed.

"This is ridiculous," he muttered, and shifted to plant his feet on the floor.

He sat on his bed, head in his hands. He wished he could sleep. The thought that Mowatt had curried favour with the Duchess ran through his head, a mantra that kept him awake into the night.

He needed to walk and clear the fog in his head. There was a part of him that questioned why he was so irritated by Mowatt's wealth. It had never been something that bothered him before.

It really just came down to the effort Bergsen had put in. He wasn't just trying to fix the Duke; he was trying to solve the mystery. His efforts could save all of Kingsgate, maybe even Guardiana itself. If anyone had deserved a reward, it was Bergsen.

He pulled his new robe from its hanger and paused, feeling the smooth fabric between his fingers. The tailor had done a fine job, crafting this robe from the pattern of his formal robes, but had used silk and embroidered the sleeves with fine, silver patterns that ran up into the shoulders, then spread like whispery veins across the chest. The effect was subtle, but stunning.

No one would see that if he wore it in the dead of night. Instead, he chose a simpler, black robe with a deep red sash around his waist. While it wouldn't be as dramatic in the night, at least it would be noticeable. He stood before his mirror and adjusted the sash, making it even and straight.

It was a good night for a walk. A good night to prowl.

The streets were quieter at night, but not without activity. Enough people trickled past that he didn't have to be concerned with being accosted or recognised. Nonetheless, he avoided some of the darker alleys. It wouldn't do to put himself in harm's way.

The people on the streets worked to ignore him. Although they saw him, they shifted their eyes to look sidelong, but never directly at him. At first, Bergsen was perplexed by their behaviour. People were usually quick to speak to him. Then, he realized he wasn't wearing his robes of the Faith. To them, he was another wealthy patron they need not bother.

Bergsen pouted, missing the attention. But it's just as well, he thought, who has time for peasants?

For a while, he wandered. He was in no rush. He wanted Mowatt to leave his head. He wished he could think of anything else besides how unfairly he had been treated. He could not.

When he found himself in front of Mowatt's home, he was almost surprised. Bergsen stood in front of the gate, contemplating returning to his bed.

He pushed open the gate. It wasn't locked; it never was. A healer was always ready to be disturbed by whoever was ready to pay for his services. Bergsen didn't like the opportunistic nature but had grudging respect for Mowatt's business sense.

A light from the entrance betrayed the attendant on

duty. Bergsen slipped into the shadows and skirted the building to the side door. He could have walked straight in, but tonight felt like a night not to be seen.

Bergsen shook his head. Why was he here? He stopped with his hand on the door, considering what had brought him here. His stomach clenched as he forced back a wave of nausea. He needed to go home. He needed to stop this nonsense.

Except Mowatt owed him, didn't he? Mowatt was getting the favour of the Duchess and Bergsen deserved some of that wealth.

He rolled his shoulders back and stood tall. No, he was not going to let Mowatt use him like this. Bergsen leaned into the door, opening it slowly. Inside, it was dark. He was in a storeroom that smelled of linen. Bergsen let his fingers drag along the soft cotton of the sheets.

He was on the main floor of the building, with its narrow halls unlit. The dim light of a single candle drifted from the main entrance, carried by the clerk passing through the corridor. Bergsen pressed himself close to the wall, letting the shadows swallow him. He remained unseen as the clerk went up the stairs.

Waiting a few breaths, Bergsen followed. His soft shoes were nearly noiseless on the stone, their slight swish masked by the heavier footsteps ahead. With a rattle of a key in a lock and the creak of a door, Bergsen was cast into the dark.

An edge of thrill ran up his arms and tickled his sides. He was invisible and ephemeral.

At the far end of the hall, a soft glow illuminated

the bottom edge of Mowatt's door. Until that moment, Bergsen hadn't known what he needed to do. Now, it was obvious. He strode down the centre of the hall, hands outstretched, feeling the texture of the stone and doors with his fingertips as it alternated between cool and smooth to rough-hewn wood.

Head bowed, he paced his steps, placing each step in the direct centre of the hall.

Tonight, the lion hunted.

He placed his forehead on the door and listened. Bergsen stood like that, with his eyes closed and hands braced on the door frame, until his breath slowed.

No noise came from within.

When he tried the handle, Bergsen found it was unlocked. As he had expected.

Wrapping his hands around the door as he opened it, he slid in through the barest margin.

Compared to the darkness of the hallway, the room was a shock to Bergsen's eyes, although only a single candle burned low on the table. Asleep, with his head on his arms, was Mowatt, his breath a whisper onto the pages of the book that lay under his head.

Bergsen stood motionless, watching the man sleep. His back and legs tensed as the urge to club Mowatt's head where it lay crept through him. The simplicity and finality of the action tempted him. Bergsen clenched his fist, coiling muscle to strike, and stopped when he saw the gold of the medallion hanging from a hook on the wall.

It hung among others, similar, but none so tauntingly perfect. Bergsen's muscles relaxed, the taut anticipation oozing away. The medallion beckoned him closer. Begged him to remove it from its place among its unequal neighbours.

And why shouldn't he? Bergsen deserved it more than anyone else. The lion deserved his trophy.

He cupped his hands under the trophy and brought it to his lips.

"Hello, my beauty," he whispered into the cold metal. "It's time to come home."

As he lifted the silk from the hook, he froze. His body reacting before his brain registered the noise.

Mowatt was awake.

He jumped up, knocking the chair over in the process. A flicker of glowing light created an aura around him as he healed away his fatigue.

"Bergsen," he said, through his confusion. "What are you doing here, man?"

Bergsen turned to face him, medallion in his hands. He didn't know what to say. The words he had practiced died on his lips and he could only stand there, staring his hatred back.

Mowatt flicked his eyes to Bergsen's hand and registered the shock.

"Bergsen!" Mowatt was nearly panicked, the fear in his voice coming out choked. "It's you! Do you see what you have?"

"The medallion is mine now," Bergsen sneered. "I deserve it, not you!"

"What? That thing? It's yours." Mowatt shuffled around the table to stand in front of him. "The lion, Bergsen? Don't you see?"

Mowatt reached for Bergsen's hand, trying to take away his prize. The trophy he deserved.

Black enveloped Bergsen. His sight dimmed into a narrow tunnel and the rest of the room evaporated into the shadow of his rage.

He leaned on his cane, trying to catch his breath. What had he done? Mowatt's blood stained his robes, glistening on the black. He clutched the medallion close to his chest, as if that would solve his problem. At least he had it now. But at what cost?

The lion kills.

Of course it does, he thought. It is its nature to hunt and kill its prey. Was he not the lion?

He stroked the lion's mane with his thumb, feeling the gold figure under his hand.

Bergsen froze.

He didn't breathe. He didn't move.

The air around him seemed to stand still. There was no sound but the thumping of his heartbeat bashing at his temples.

The warm metal of the carved lion was almost alive in his hand. He could feel the lines of its jaw and the points of its teeth with his thumb. His fingers rested on the mane that flowed down its back.

He tasted the coppery fear in his mouth and his vision wavered.

"By the Unbroken Circle, what have I done?"

His arm felt as though all the muscles had atrophied to nothing more than mere wisps as he lifted the lion to his face. It stared back at him with ruby eyes as he inspected it.

If he could have thrown it, he would have hurled it from the rooftops into the night and into oblivion. But he was transfixed. His arm wasn't his to move anymore.

"Oh…"

He was never the lion. He was the prey.

Baldwin awoke to the noon sun beaming through his window. His head ached. Around him were several bottles of wine that he did not recall drinking. Around those were several more bottles he did recall. Those had been delicious, at least. As had been his company, wherever they had gotten off to.

What he needed now was a bath to clear his fuzzy head. Leaving his room, he looked about for a moment. His apartments had a bath chamber, did they not? They always had. Yet, as he looked about, none of it seemed familiar to him. While he recalled living here, it seemed foreign and wrong to him.

"Must be the bloody wine," he muttered to himself. "Fine. If I must quit this drab place for a decent bath, so I shall!"

He walked back into the room and began rifling through the robes in the closet, tossing much of it aside in disdain.

"What is this?" He held up a robe of the Circle then threw it on the bed while counting the number of wine bottles on the floor. "Where have I ended up?"

In the end, he found a passable robe which would do

until he found his own clothes, but not before having a bath and getting the awful taste from his mouth.

He considered donning the medallion he found on the dressing table, but thought it was rather plain, so left it where it lay.

"The lion doesn't wear such trinkets, does he?"

He slipped into the robe and walked before the mirror. The mirror was small and tended to fog in some places, so he had to lean in to see himself.

He jumped back when he saw his face in the reflection. For a moment, he stood back, seeing only a fuzzy version of himself. Fingers attached to hands that were the wrong colour probed his lips and cheeks. The man in the mirror was too light. Even standing back, he knew the face was wrong. It wasn't his.

"No, no, no…" he groaned.

He took a step closer, daring to see the face staring back at him.

"No," he breathed. "Not again."

"This is not my face!" The face in the mirror distorted with rage.

"This is not my face!" He screamed, clawing at his face, leaving raw flesh behind.

He bent in two and screamed a wordless roar of animal pain, raking his face. Blind with rage, he threw over the dressing table, scattering its contents and spilling its drawers.

He could not go through this again. It wasn't fair.

"I am Baldwin of Kingsgate!" he screamed into the room. "I am the Lion!"

He scooped up his cane from the floor and wielded

it like a sword to the mirror.

"You cannot do this to me!"

Spittle landed on the mirror as he threatened the face on the other side.

"You won't have me this time."

He swung the cane into the glass, shattering it. Jagged shards fell to the floor. Large pieces stuck out invitingly.

He stood taller and slowed his breathing.

"Fine," he whispered. "If this is the way you want it."

He strode to the mirror, ignoring the glass in his feet, ignoring the pain that shot through his body.

In his head, a voice raged silently. An echo of a wind lost to the fury of the hunter. If he'd listened, he would have heard that voice cry out in agony, pleading for him to stop.

Begging him to put the broken glass down.

Crying for him to stop cutting his face.

SEED

JOEL HUNT

Dunn pressed his fingers to the old bear's nose. He liked to imagine that its fur still held Ella's scent and the warmth of her touch. In truth, all traces of his daughter had long since faded from the ragged thing.

The portrait looked nothing like her either. After Ella passed, Lord Maisley had offered to send his court artist to immortalise her, explaining that she would need access to Ella's body to capture her features with accuracy. Dunn had refused. He couldn't think of anything worse than seeing his daughter's dead face every time he stepped into the room. If there was to be a painting, Dunn wanted it to be of Ella as she was in life, bright and beaming.

It was only after the burial that he'd changed his mind, and by then it was too late. The artist had done her best with a description, but the girl staring back from Ella's memorial was a stranger. She had Ella's hair, but not her eyes, her skin, but not her freckles, her mouth, but not her smile.

Years later, all Dunn truly had left of Ella was the voice he heard in his dreams.

"Are you okay, Papa?"

Dunn turned. Pate was watching him with curiosity, as though he were an injured bird. Dunn grunted and ruffled the boy's mop of hair.

"Just thinking of your sister," he said.

Pate turned to the portrait, then the stuffed bear, then Dunn. He frowned.

"Why?"

"Don't bother your father," said Cilla. "He's had a busy day. Leave him be."

"I worked too!" Pate said. "I helped with the chickens!"

Across the room, his two sisters finished cutting the vegetables. Grutta handed hers to Lina, who tipped them into their mother's pot.

"He fed them in the morning and then spent the whole afternoon petting them," said Lina.

"That's helping!" Pate insisted, with a stomp of his foot. "They like being petted."

"Enough," said Cilla, stepping between them before fists flew. "Off to your room, the lot of you. The lord's coming soon."

Pate's looming tantrum disappeared like a mouse spotting a cat. He bounced on his feet and tugged at Cilla's apron.

"Can we meet him?"

"You *have* met him," said Lina. "He was at Ella's funeral, remember?"

Pate shook his head.

"He's really fat," said Grutta, giggling as she waddled around the kitchen with imaginary pudge. Pate laughed and joined her, until Cilla clipped them both on the shoulder and shepherded them out of the room.

"You'll welcome him to our home and thank him for his patronage," she said, in a tone that didn't invite debate. "No rudeness, no questions. Then, to your room. The Lord won't want pesky children bothering him over dinner."

"I'm not a child, Mama," Lina said, in her best adult voice.

Cilla smiled and squeezed her shoulder. "Of course, Lina. But we need you to watch the others and keep them out of trouble. You'll be doing a lot of that when you're a mother."

That seemed to satisfy their eldest, who set about ordering Pate and Grutta to wash their faces and brush their clothes so that they wouldn't offend Lord Maisley. With the children gone, Cilla made her way to Dunn's side, running a finger down his neck.

"He won't want to see you sad," she said. "Nor do I."

Dunn took her hand in his, squeezed her fingers and nodded.

They set the table together and, when the clop of approaching hooves announced their visitor's arrival, shouted for the children to join them. They lined up in their best clothes—the ones with no stains or holes—and did their best to look respectable. Cilla considered them, straightened Pate's tunic, then gave a huff of approval.

A soft hand rapped the door. Taking one last look at the table before nodding to Cilla, Dunn opened it. Lord Maisley filled the doorway. His fine-patterned coat barely covered his ample belly. Rings glittered on pudgy fingers, and his long, slick hair was fastened with a ruby-studded clasp. The lord's tastes had certainly become more extravagant since his latest windfall, but beneath it all he was the same man he had always been, and he walked into the meagre farmhouse as though he were returning home. He spread his hands and grinned at them both.

"Dunn! Cilla!" he said. "A pleasure to see you both looking so well."

He shook Dunn's hand and kissed Cilla on the cheek. A servant followed him into the house—a young man Dunn hadn't seen before—but Maisley didn't introduce him and Dunn didn't ask. Instead, he gestured for the lord to make himself at home.

"How was Kingsgate?" he asked.

"Dank and miserable," said Maisley, "but richer than when I found it. They won't be forgetting who helped refill their coffers any time soon, and I can swear to that."

"I've always dreamed of seeing the city," said Cilla, taking his coat.

"My dear, join me on my next visit. You'll soon see that it's a lot of fuss over nothing. I'd take good folk and country air any day."

Dunn grunted his agreement. Like Cilla, he'd never seen Kingsgate himself, but from what he'd heard, he wouldn't care to. Everything he needed was right here.

After more small talk, Cilla called over the children, and Lina gave a half-decent curtsey. Grutta and Pate attempted to copy her, with Pate holding out an imaginary dress. Though Dunn was sure the lord had never seen sloppier curtseys in his entire life, Maisley grinned at the sight, belly rippling with a chuckle.

"Good children," he said. "They'll do you proud."

"Thank you, m'lord," said Dunn, and Lina echoed him quietly. With that done, Cilla hastily shooed the children out before they could change the lord's mind.

"Now then," said Maisley, "I'm quite looking forward to your cooking, Cilla dear, but there's a small matter to attend to first."

He clicked his pudgy fingers and the servant placed a cloth-covered item on the table. From the shape of it, Dunn couldn't guess what lay beneath. Maisley must have seen the question on his face, and after dismissing the servant he patted the object and pinched the cloth.

"This," he said, "is what a crate of rubies will fetch you in the capital."

He yanked the cloth away, revealing a smooth, wooden box no larger than his hand in any direction. A bronze crank jutted from one end and a chute descended from the other. Dunn and Cilla peered closer. They were hardly wiser now.

"What is it?" asked Dunn.

"Damned if I know," said Maisley. "I was after a portrait of some old Primarch—incredible artistry, the most vibrant eyes ever put to paint—but the Faith snapped it up before I could get out my rubies. As is their right, I suppose. Anyway, I couldn't go away empty-handed, so I got stuck with this contraption."

"Does it do anything?" asked Cilla.

By way of answer, Maisley grasped the handle and wound it. Despite a squeak of protest from inside the box, the crank turned easily enough, and after three rotations, a dull, yellow seed clattered down the chute and onto the table. Dunn picked it up and examined it from all sides.

"It's no seed as I've seen before."

"Indeed?" asked Maisley. "I feared as much. Not one of us could work out what the blasted things were, but then we've never worked the fields like you. In truth, there aren't many seeds I could name. I knew this one was rare though. I could…feel it, if that makes sense?"

"Didn't they tell you at the auction what would grow from it?" asked Cilla.

"I'm afraid they hadn't a clue," said Maisley. "And since you don't either, there's only one thing for it. Empty the box, plant whatever comes out and tell me what grows from it. You can keep the produce, I'm just damnably curious. Though if it makes a good pie, I won't say no."

Cilla looked to Dunn, and he didn't need to ask what was troubling her. He'd had the same thought.

"That's very kind of you m'lord," he said, "but we've already planted the season's crop. Besides, without knowing what would spring from these seeds, I'd worry about growing them near my vegetables. They might be weeds or carry some blight or who knows what else. We just can't afford to plant them in our fields."

"About that," said Maisley. "You know Old Jemmin's patch by the stream?"

"Of course, rest his soul."

"Clear it out and sow it. It's yours."

Cilla gasped and Dunn's eyes widened. He tried and failed to speak several times, eventually managing a strained, "You honour us, m'lord."

Maisley only laughed. "Yes, quite an honour! 'I bought a trinket, now work twice as hard'. I only pray you don't honour me in kind!"

He waved away all of their attempts at gratitude and sat by his empty plate.

"Now enough of all that," he said. "I've been travelling all day and I didn't come to prattle the evening away over farmwork. Let's eat."

Maisley finished off a week's worth of meals before finally setting down his fork. The lord had always had a bountiful appetite, but it had deepened during his time on the road, and Dunn was relieved when the dinner was over. There wasn't much left in the house to serve.

After that, the three talked long into the night, laughing over old times and at the pomposity Maisley had experienced at the capital.

By the time the lord was ready to leave, darkness had swallowed the land, and Maisley had to call for his servant to bring a lantern so that he might find his way back to the carriage. Cilla's offer for him to stay the night was politely declined, but Maisley did allow Dunn to walk him to his horses.

The two men traded idle chatter as they traipsed up the lane from Dunn's farmhouse. As they reached the side of the road where Maisley's carriage was waiting, the lord paused. One finger tapped his thigh as he stared at the horizon. Even in the depths of the night, the great stone wall that shielded them from the Red Land was bathed in eternal fire, a constant artificial sunrise. Dunn followed his lord's gaze and watched the distant haze for a time. He rarely glanced at the wall these days. Strange how one could become so accustomed to something so strange, simply by being exposed to it each day.

Maisley hummed to himself.

"I see that the memorial for little Ella is still up," he said.

"Yes, m'lord."

The silence continued. Maisley placed a hand on Dunn's shoulder.

"Respect for the dead is an honourable thing," he said, "and she was a delightful girl, truly. But it's been two years. Your wife needs to move on. Heavens, you'd think she were the only mother to have ever lost a child!"

Dunn grunted. He almost corrected the man—explained that the memorial was his idea, that he prayed at it far more than Cilla ever did, that Ella visited his dreams nightly and begged him to come home—but Maisley wasn't interested in all that. Instead Dunn folded his arms and let his silence be taken as it would.

Maisley offered a supportive smile, squeezed his shoulder and then clambered into his carriage.

After he had settled inside, he leaned out and called, "Let me know what grows from those seeds". Then, as his servant closed the door behind him, he added with a grumble, "If there's any justice in the world, it'll be a ruby tree."

Jemmin's farm lay beyond a hill at the edge of Dunn's land. It was a small patch split by a stream— all that Old Jemmin could manage by the end. Since his passing, it had gone untended, too much work for the other farmers to take on, not enough to draw a new family to the region. It had been left at the mercy of pests and weeds.

Until now.

Dunn, Cilla and the children arrived at first light, a bag of tools slung over Dunn's shoulder. Tearing out the unwanted growth and getting the land ready for sowing would take days, and Dunn wanted it finished as soon as possible. They even brought the goats over to speed up the process. After all, the mystery seeds might not even be in season, and the whole venture could be a waste. Better to get it over with quickly.

For the first two days, the whole family toiled from sunrise to sunset, hacking away the largest weeds and uprooting bushes. Dunn forbade the children from handling anything thorny or poisonous, dealing with those growths himself, so by the end of each day his palms were raw and blistered. It was a relief, at noon on the third day, to look out over an empty, tilled field. He picked up Lord Maisley's strange seed box and strode to

240

the nearest corner.

"Let's get this over with," he said.

"Papa!" Pate tugged on Dunn's sleeve. "Can we plant them?"

"Do you know how?" asked Dunn.

Pate scowled. "Yes! Turn the thing and put the seed in the ground."

"And bury it after!" added Grutta.

Dunn smiled and held out the box. Pate and Grutta both grabbed for it, slapping and jostling one another for the prize. They failed to notice Lina reaching over their heads. The usual bickering followed, but despite the protests of the younger two, the children soon settled into a routine; Pate dug a hole, Lina turned the crank until a seed dropped into the dirt, then Grutta scooped the soil over it, patting the little mound as though it were a small animal.

Once he was confident they could deal with the task, Dunn left them to it, eager to tend to the rest of his land before it became too neglected.

Dusk was closing in when the children returned, Pate proudly clutching the box in both hands.

"You took your time," said Dunn. "How much of the field did it cover?"

"All of it!" Pate beamed.

Dunn grunted. He should have told them to sow the seeds closer together. He was hoping to have a decent strip of Jemmin's land left over to plant some onions in.

"How many seeds were in there?" he asked.

"We lost count," said Lina. "A few hundred, I think."

Dunn blinked.

"A few…hundred?"

Grutta and Pate nodded earnestly. Dunn took the box from them and pressed his fingers against one side; the seeds had been about the size of his thumbnail, and he tried to measure up how many could fit inside. Perhaps a hundred or so was right, but only if the box was empty. Surely the crank's mechanism must have taken up some room. The weight of the thing, too, had hardly changed since that morning.

Dunn grunted and placed the box aside. He nodded to Lina, though he knew they had to be mistaken.

"Good work," he said. "Who's ready for dinner?"

The next morning, as Cilla returned from milking the goats, she gestured to their paddock.

"One of the goats got out," she said.

"Blasted things," grumbled Dunn. "You see which way it went?"

Cilla shook her head. "I'll have the children check the turnip fields," she said, peering out the window and evidently finding the scenery goatless. "D'you suppose she might have gone back to Jemmin's patch? Got a taste for the weeds?"

"Could be," Dunn grunted. "I'll go."

He pulled on his boots and strode along the beaten footpath, casting his eyes all over for any sign of the stray goat. His legs led him automatically, so that he was almost on top of Jemmin's field before he realised it.

Even when he did, he hardly recognised the place.

He froze, rubbed his eyes, checked again.

Hundreds of leafy bulbs dotted the field, deep green fists punching their way out of the dirt. Each was the size of a full-grown cabbage. A whole season's worth of growth in a single night.

He marched back to the farmhouse to fetch Cilla. She'd think he'd gone mad. Perhaps he had. As he walked through the door, he almost doubted his own memory, and only managed a husky, "Come see Jemmin's field" before turning and marching out again.

Cilla knew better than to pepper him with questions. He'd never been one for practical jokes or tricks—he didn't have the imagination for it—so she dutifully followed.

The pair arrived at the edge of the field, and Dunn found the crops to be as big, if not bigger, than he had left them. Cilla pressed into his arm as they took in the sight.

"They've never grown already," she breathed.

"You saw this field yesterday," said Dunn. "Nothing but dirt."

"Do you know what they are?"

"No."

"Does anything grow this fast?"

"No."

Silence, broken only by the rustling of the leaves in the wind.

"This must be why the box was so costly," said Cilla. "Perhaps the seeds are magical."

Dunn bristled. "Never trusted magic."

After that, they watched in silence, waiting for some sign of supernatural influence. As they looked on, the bulbs shifted ever so slightly, a ripple across a lake of green. It was hard to tell if the leaves were fluttering in the breeze or growing before their eyes.

Dunn shook his head. "Let's find that damned goat."

They spotted her on the walk home, munching at the hedgerow. Despite a few bleats, she put up little protest as they guided her back, and she rejoined the others happily enough. The same couldn't be said for Dunn, who passed the day in a haze, wondering what might come of the unusual bulbs. The day passed before he knew it, and he found himself preparing for bed without knowing what he'd done that afternoon.

Only the bristling of his neck hairs shook him from his thoughts. A cold breeze trickled in through the window, chilling his skin and bringing with it an odd, whistling noise. The sound had a quality he hadn't heard before. He approached the window and strained to pick it out, turning his ear to the night.

fwoooooooooo

He scowled. It wasn't just the wind, he was sure of that. But what was he hearing? Some animal? An approaching storm? A traveller in distress?

It struck him most as a distant voice, but it wasn't a word he was hearing, or a scream or laugh or any other noise he'd expect from a human being. As the wind picked up, he held his breath and strained to hear it again.

"Dunn, come to bed."

He ignored Cilla, leaning out of the window and trying to peel back the layers of sound drifting on the breeze. A minute passed. Nothing. Perhaps he had imagined it after all.

"Dunn?" said Cilla, shifting in bed.

He grunted, turned from the window and joined her under the cover. She placed her hand on his chest and he wrapped his fingers around hers, but long after her breathing turned to the steady rhythm of sleep, Dunn was still fully awake, listening for any unusual sound from outside.

It was hours before he heard the sound again, just as he was drifting to sleep. Clearer. More insistent. Like a voice whispering at his window.

fwooooooooool

He woke to the excited faces of the children.

"They've grown!" shouted Pate. "They've grown, they've grown!"

"We know, Pate," Cilla said, without opening her eyes. "We saw them yesterday."

"No! They've grown more!"

At that, she opened her eyes. She and Dunn shared a cautious look.

"How much more?"

Dunn's skin turned cold as he took in the sight. The plants were now waist-high, sprouting in every direction and flooding Jemmin's field with green. The leafy bulbs that had sprung up yesterday were still visible at the top of each plant, but beneath they widened out, perhaps an arm's length across. Thick vines dangled from each side, drifting back and forth as if clawing at the dirt.

Cilla held the children back as Dunn paced the edge of the field. All this growth without a drop of rain. It wasn't natural. At this rate, the crops would outgrow the nearby woodland in a week. In a month, they'd be taller than the Red Land Wall.

In half a year, they'd pierce the sky.

Dunn pulled Cilla aside. "We need to get word to Maisley," he said. "He can see them if he must, but after that I'm cutting them down. I'll burn them if it comes to it, magic be damned."

Dunn marched the children back to the farmhouse while Cilla left to visit her cousin, who was close with one of Lord Maisley's housemaids. She'd pass the message on and Maisley would arrive in a day or two. Dunn certainly hoped it would take no longer than that.

He had the children stay nearby for the remainder of the day, mostly tending to the goats and chickens, then made them all a stew. It was, Pate explained, worse than any stew their mother had ever made. Dunn couldn't disagree.

Cilla returned after the children had gone to bed. Dunn gave her the remaining stew and sat with her while she ate.

"Well?"

"She's meeting the maid at market tomorrow," said Cilla. "She promised to pass on the message and get Maisley to come see the field, but I don't think she understood. Kept asking what it was we were worried about, if the plants were poisonous or diseased."

"Might be nothing," Dunn conceded. "Might just

grow fast. But I don't want it on our land. Not until we know what it is, and when it stops getting bigger."

"You don't need to convince me."

As she finished her meal, Cilla changed the subject, telling Dunn all about how her cousin's family were doing and what their harvest had been this year. He nodded along, but his mind never left Jemmin's field, even as they changed out of their farm clothes and climbed into bed.

Hours passed, but Dunn couldn't shake his sense of unease. His skin itched with the sensation of being watched. He lit a candle and cast his eyes around the room. Nothing out of the ordinary. Perhaps he just needed to stretch his legs.

He moved to the other room and paced back and forth, casting furtive glances at the windows but seeing nothing unusual outside. Then the candlelight caught metal and Dunn's attention turned to Maisley's box. The crank gleamed, as though seeking to be noticed.

He gave the box an experimental shake. No rattle. It must finally be out of seeds. To assure himself, he turned the handle. Just as before, it squeaked in protest, and just as before, to his surprise, a dull yellow seed rolled out.

How many more could possibly be inside?

He continued to turn the shrieking handle, and seeds continued to rattle down the chute. When the growing pile spilled over the sides of the table, he gathered them into a bowl. When that was full, he swapped it for a bucket. When there was no more room in the bucket, he started filling up a barrel.

Squeak, rattle. Squeak, rattle. Squeak, rattle.

His eyes grew heavy. His arm arched. Still the seeds came. Uncountable. Impossible.

He succumbed to sleep before the box ran out, fingers still grasping the noisy, metal handle. The squeaks followed Dunn into his dreams. He was back at Jemmin's field, sowing the seeds from a basket. Each time he plucked one from the pile, it squeaked like the box. The noise grew, seed after seed, and soon it wasn't a squeak at all.

It was a scream.

A pained, desperate, agony-fuelled scream. Dunn was causing it. With every seed torn from the pile, he added to the agony. He didn't stop though. He kept on sowing those seeds, as though it were all his soul knew.

He sowed until the whole field was screaming.

Dunn woke, hunched over the barrel, hand turning the crank. Seeds flowed onto the floor, spilling out like water. The handle still squeaked with every turn, except now it sounded to his ears exactly like the noise from his dreams: a raw, distant scream.

He jolted upright and tossed the box aside. Seeds that never ended, plants that grew a season in a day. That proved it; the damned thing was magic, and he wanted it out of his home. He gathered the seeds from the floor and tossed them into his stew bowl, ready to burn at first light.

Once again, he heard the voice-that-wasn't-a-voice drifting through the windows:

fwooooooooool

He glowered at the darkness. He still couldn't make out what, if anything, it was saying. Except now, he knew exactly where it was coming from. With a grim scowl, Dunn put on his boots, lit a lantern and set out to Jemmin's field.

He should have been ready for it, but his breath was still snatched away. Each crop now stood tall as a full-grown man. Lit only by his flickering lantern, they seemed like an army awaiting orders, twitching in anticipation of violence.

Then, in the very centre of the field, leaves shook. It wasn't the wind. Dunn raised his lantern.

"Who's there? You're on my land!"

The only reply was a whisper.

Whooooooooooool

Dunn grunted, then marched into the midst of the vegetation. The uppermost bulbs seemed to watch him pass, swaying back and forth like startled faces. Vines and twigs plucked at his clothes, or caught on the nearest crop and held there, blocking his path. The field became a labyrinth, and he cursed himself for not bringing his sickle; his free hand was soon blistered from tearing through the rough vines.

More rustling ahead. Movement. Hushed voices. Dunn's heart thumped in his chest, and he felt his lack of sickle even more keenly. He had nothing to defend himself with.

"Show yourself!" he called out, forcing his voice to remain steady.

"Whole..." came a whisper.

"Why...not...whole..." came another.

The words echoed all around him. Each time he turned to face the speaker, another voice hissed behind him. Some close, some far. The movement was everywhere now, each plant rustling and every vine shaking. Cold hands grasped him from behind. He spun, ready to strike. His hand froze mid-swing.

Standing in his path, holding his shoulders, was a man-sized plant. Its bulb-head pressed against his own. The leafy surface stretched and distorted, and in the flickering light of his lantern, the bulb split. With a wet squelch, it tore and widened, until it seemed that a mockery of a smile had been carved into the vegetation. The plant-thing pulled him close.

And screamed.

Sap flecked Dunn's face. The screech stabbed at his ears and he recoiled, clamping his hands over them. His lantern smashed against the floor, spilling oil and catching ablaze. Another scream came from the plant-creature as it released him, sending him tumbling to the dirt. Its fellow creatures echoed the monstrous sound, lurching away from the fire in a flurry of movement and rustling leaves.

Dunn took his chance, scrambling onto his knees and crawling as fast as he could though the writhing, screeching, whispering mass. Vines lashed at his face. Roots stamped on his fingers. Leaves reached for his back, his ears, his mouth. All the while, the inhuman chanting continued.

"Whole... Whole... Whole..."

Scrambling between two of the creatures, Dunn caught sight of the stars. He kicked off from the ground and leapt out of the writhing mass, landing painfully on torn-up mounds of dirt. He didn't stop to check for pursuers. He staggered upright and ran.

The whispering never stopped, but as Dunn stumbled across the field, it got more distant. He risked a glance behind. What he saw made him stumble to a halt. He fell back into the dirt and traced a circle around his heart.

"By the Faith..."

The plants hadn't followed him. In fact, they seemed to be fighting amongst themselves, wrapping around one another, tugging and grasping at anything that moved.

But it wasn't a fight. It was a union. Even as Dunn watched, it became impossible to tell one plant-creature from the other. Even their whispers mingled together, until they spoke with one terrible voice.

"Want...be...whole... Need...be...whole..."

The monster—as now Dunn could only see it as a single being—rose two plants high. Three. Five. It towered larger than any building he'd ever seen, rippling and shifting like trees in a storm.

Then it began to walk.

Despite being a single mass, each twisted crop moved independently, unified in their horrible and unfathomable purpose. Each time the beast lurched forwards, a dozen of the living plants lunged out and half-burrowed into the dirt, as if they had been expelled from the greater mass. The moment they landed, the remainder screeched in unholy pain and clawed their way along the new extremity, engulfing once again those that had pushed forwards. In this way, the monster moved unerringly forwards, never changing from its path.

Without knowing how, Dunn was certain of where the beast was heading. He forced himself to his feet and charged ahead of it, running like a whipped stallion to his farmhouse, where the barrel of seeds lay waiting. Whether faith or fear spurred him on, he arrived sooner than expected, well ahead of the monster that lurched through the dark. Its haunting whispers followed him and he knew it would catch up soon.

"Must…be…whole…"

"Cilla!" he cried, as he barged through the door. "Cilla!"

He didn't wait for her response. He lunged for the barrel and wrapped both arms around it, hauling it up and staggering back towards the door. Cilla appeared moments later, rubbing her eyes.

"Dunn, what's happening?"

"Wake the children! They need to be ready to run!"

"What's happening?"

He ignored her, straining under the weight of the full barrel and grimacing at the rattle of seeds hitting the floor with every step. They rolled under his feet, spreading over every corner of the room. Dozens, hundreds of them. He was nearly at the door when he lost his footing and dropped the barrel. Yellow seeds scattered everywhere. A second later, screams echoed in the distance like a peal of thunder. A familiar voice followed.

"Need…be…whole…"

Dunn's heart froze. There was no time.

"Out!" he cried, leaving the barrel and storming to the back of the house. "Everyone out!"

Cilla bundled the children out of their room, half-dressed, panic on their faces. Dunn gestured for them to leave, then paused, turned, and ran back to Ella's memorial. He grabbed her bear, hesitating over the portrait. The shaking floorboards made his decision for him, and he abandoned the painting along with everything else in the house. Cilla and the children were waiting for him outside.

"Pate," he said, "look after Ella's bear for me."

The boy turned large, watery eyes towards his father, holding out what was already in his hands. The seed box. Dunn shuddered at the sight of it.

"Why do you have that?"

Pate clutched the thing close, shielding it with his arms. "I... I like it," he stammered.

Dunn hissed through his teeth, then passed the bear to Grutta.

"Look after it," he repeated. She nodded.

With that, Dunn spread his arms and half-pushed, half-dragged his children away from their home. Away from the monster. They got to the next field before Grutta stumbled, causing Lina to turn.

"What is that?" she cried, pointing to the writhing mass of vegetation shambling towards their home.

"Magic," growled Dunn.

He grabbed the girls and continued to flee. Seconds later, the beast collided with their home. A shattering boom echoed through the night. Walls crumbled. The roof collapsed. Pate and Grutta wailed as everything the family owned was smashed under the onslaught of the unholy creature. Debris hurled through the air as it searched, spreading like moss over the stone and splintered wood.

"Be…whole… Be…whole…"

From the wreckage, the monster rose, barrel held aloft on a dozen grasping branches. A ripple ran the length of the beast, tearing the barrel to splinters and causing seeds to fall like rain. The monster swallowed them with a hundred mouths, then lapped at the farmhouse floor, sucking up every seed it found. At last, it seemed to have consumed them all. But it wasn't soothed. It clambered from the remains of the house and, though it had no eyes, Dunn knew its attention turned to his family.

"Keep running!" he barked.

"Papa!"

Dunn turned. Pate was splayed across the dirt, foot sunk into a rabbit hole. His wide, desperate eyes were locked onto his father, and in the distance, the monster shambled closer.

"Take the girls!" Dunn called to Cilla.

As she led them away, he ran back for Pate. The boy was weeping, struggling to free his foot from the ground. Dunn grasped his shoulders, hauled him upright and pushed him in the direction of his mother. The ground trembled as an avalanche of screeches drew near.

"Must…be…whole!"

"Run, boy!" Dunn screamed.

"But Papa…"

"Run!"

Pate turned his pale face to the approaching monster, clutched his box close, and ran. Dunn took a deep breath as his son scrambled to safety. He faced the beast, spread his arms and cried into the night.

"It's me you want, demon! I filled the barrel! I own the field! Do what you will!"

The writhing, screaming mass of vegetation hurtled closer. Absorbing the seeds had given it fresh strength and it moved unstoppably, flinging plants ahead and wrenching after them. Dunn grimaced, heart pounding. He would give everything if it slowed the monster down, even for a moment. He braced as it bore down on him. Vines lashed out, wrapping around his body. He strained against them, but the monster didn't falter. He was lifted off his feet and hurled aside, crashing to the dirt with a heavy grunt.

His head spun. His eyes stung with soil. As he blinked and wiped the dirt away, he saw the back of the beast. It was catching up with Pate, stretching spindly limbs towards him.

"No!"

Before Dunn could stagger upright, the vines and branches consumed Pate's legs. The boy cried out as he collapsed, and in seconds he was engulfed, disappearing entirely under the swell of leaves and bulbs. Dunn roared and charged. The monster did nothing to evade him, and he ran into it full pelt, tearing at anything he could reach.

It was useless. Each time he made some hole, more vegetation slithered into its place. Beyond it, a muffled cry penetrated the urgent whispers of the torn plant-mouths all around him. Then, from the centre of the writhing mass came a sickening crunch of what might have been wood.

Or bone.

"Pate!" Dunn screamed.

The churning of the beast slowed, the whispers faded. As Dunn tore more vines away, they no longer replenished themselves. Every bulb gave a deep, soulful sigh, as though a great weight had been lifted.

"Whole... again..."

The beast rocked, sending Dunn stumbling back. A thousand shimmering wisps coiled out from the leaves, eerie green in colour, rising like smoke from a dying fire. They drew together as they danced through the air, forming the outline of a human body. The apparition rose higher and higher, head turned to the sky as it slipped free from the vines below. Dunn blinked. Rubbed his eyes.

It was gone.

A moment of pure silence followed, before a shudder rippled from the centre of the beast. Then the vegetation sloughed to the ground like rotten skin off bone. It formed a pile greater than a year's harvest, and nothing in that pile moved.

Dunn shook the wonder from his head and waded in.

"Pate? Pate!"

A voice replied from a great distance.

"Papa, what's happening?"

Dunn's heart fluttered. He lunged towards his son's voice, hurling mounds of dead plant aside.

"I'm coming, Pate!"

"Where am I?" asked the boy.

He'd travelled even further away, so faint that the rustling leaves in Dunn's hands threatened to silence him. Dunn halted, straining his ears for the source of Pate's call.

"Come to me, son!" he bellowed. "Come to my voice!"

When Pate replied, it carried the strangest echo. He seemed to be speaking from the bottom of a well, far from the field Dunn stood in.

"Papa! Papa, help!"

The rest of the boy's cries were carried away by the faint night breeze.

Dunn's desperation took over. He swam through the leaves and roots, clawing for any sign of his son. Though he called out constantly, he never heard another reply. At last, after what felt like an eternity, Dunn's hand landed on a small foot. It was cold to the touch. He ripped away the plant matter and uncovered his buried child.

Pate had never seemed so small. His body was un-broken, almost untouched. If not for his eyes, the boy might have been sleeping. Yet he wouldn't wake from this. His eyes were open and still, clouded like old glass. The moment he saw them, Dunn knew his son's soul was gone.

On Pate's chest, clutched by unmoving fingers, lay the box that had started all this. Like Pate, it was undam-aged. Unlike the child, however, Dunn found the box warm to the touch. He recoiled, then returned and eased it from his son's grasp. He refused to let the cursed thing bring any further harm to his boy.

Dunn had no idea how long he stood over his son's body. An age might have passed before Cilla and the children arrived, and he watched Cilla collapse as if from a different world. She cried out and clutched Pate close, and Grutta wailed by her side.

"My boy," Cilla wept into his pale forehead. "My precious Pate."

Dunn couldn't speak. He wanted to console her, but the words, like his heart, had fallen away. He said nothing as she cried. Did nothing.

Not until she turned to him and thrust a finger at the box in his hands.

"Get rid of it!" she screamed. "Smash it! Burn it! Not one shard left!"

Dunn didn't want to take his eyes off his son. He couldn't bear to let himself forget that face like he had begun to forget Ella's. But, as Cilla's words dug into him, he nodded.

"Take him home," he rasped, gesturing to Pate. "He doesn't need to see any more violence."

He gave Cilla time to compose herself, then Lina lifted Pate into her arms and the pair set off to what remained of their farmhouse. Dunn watched them go, clutching the box until his knuckles turned white. Grutta plucked at his trouser leg, tears glistening on her cheeks.

"What are you going to do with the box?" she asked.

Dunn looked down at her. He wasn't yet sure. He only knew that it needed to be taken far from their home.

"Don't worry," he whispered. "You'll never see it again. Now follow your mother."

Grutta sniffled, hugged her father's leg tight, then wiped her nose and ran after the others. Dunn waited until they were all out of sight before turning in the opposite direction. He had no idea where he was heading, but let his numb legs carry him away.

He hit the stream at the edge of Jemmin's field, waded through it and crossed the woodland on the other side. He came out to a well-travelled dirt lane, picked a direction at random and continued walking.

He was halfway down it when he fell to his knees and wept.

Pate was gone, just like Ella, and it was the damned box's fault. His fingernails gouged scars into its wood. With a roar, he hurled it down the lane. It bounced and skidded across the stones and beaten dirt, bronze crank juddering against the earth. As the box came to rest upside down, the crank twitched and slowly sank down, as though letting out a long-held breath. A squeaking cry came from inside.

A familiar cry.

Dunn scrambled along the path to snatch the box back up. He must have been mistaken. Surely?

Trembling fingers wrapped around the handle. He turned the crank in a full, steady rotation. The box cried out again, in the hushed voice of his own son. It was underscored by a twang, and from within the cursed box there rolled a single, dull seed. It fell to the dirt, where it lay unmoving.

With trembling fingers, he picked it up. It was warm. Like a living child.

Dunn roared. He raised the box and smashed it down, again and again and again. When the wood split and buckled, he beat it with raw, splintered fists, stopping only when the thing was in total ruins.

His breath caught in his throat. He eased himself

back. Spectral green slivers emerged from the shattered device, just as they had done from the monster of Jemmin's field. Again they twisted through the air and formed the shape of a human being; not an adult this time, but the smaller, slimmer shape of a child. Its features were shimmering and indistinct, but Dunn thought it was a boy with an unruly mop of hair atop his head.

He swallowed and watched it rise.

"Pate?"

The spirit flickered. Looked down. Reached for his hand.

Then disappeared.

Dunn remained on the spot until darkness swallowed him, and the chirps and hoots of night creatures drifted through the air. He made a fire and burnt the splintered remains of the box and used its flickering light to bury the chute and handle in a nearby ditch. All that was left was the fresh seed clutched in his palm.

Dunn turned to the horizon.

And slipped the seed into his pocket.

They never sowed Jemmin's field again. After three summers, it was nothing more than a patch of wild grasses and weeds, used only as a plot for the goats to graze on. At the far end, however, hidden behind a ring of overgrown bushes, Dunn had erected a shack no larger than a carriage. Sturdy and windowless, it had a single entrance, barred and chained against all but himself.

Today, the children were tending to the chickens, and Cilla was looking after their new-born. Dunn had made his excuses, slipped away and now marched across the patch, Ella's bear in hand. Ducking behind the bushes, he hauled the wooden beam aside and unlocked the chain. The door creaked open as he slipped inside.

The shack was bare, little more than tools and a chair. Occupying the seat, however, bound by rope and wood, was a writhing, thrashing mass of vegetation. A fleshy bulb made its head, split by a wet tear along the front. Vine-like arms spread from its leafy torso, and two coils of roots bound it to the ground just beneath the chair. In all, the creature was the size of a human child.

Dunn approached and rubbed the top of its head. It twisted to bite him, but he didn't flinch, knowing it couldn't reach. He inspected its arms and noted a number of rips and tears.

"You've hurt yourself struggling," he said. "I'll get that fixed up for you."

Ignoring its screams, Dunn crouched in the corner and gathered some new rope, using it to reinforce the old restraints. Once the thing was bound tight again, he placed Ella's bear in its lap and rubbed its head.

"Don't worry, Pate," he said. "I already lost Ella. I'm not going to lose you. Not ever."

VALIM TE

K. B. ELIJAH

"Any more bidders for this fine and mysterious book? Don't worry about its sealed binding. I'm sure one of you enterprising souls out there can figure out a way past that lock! It even comes in an original Kaizae chest! No? Going…going…and gone! Lot 27 sold to the elf in the blue cloak!"

The auctioneer slammed down her gavel with a nod at Myrin. She barely took a breath before launching back into her frenetic spiel for the next item, a collection of hand-crafted wands that drew considerably more interest than the book.

But Myrin had no care for wands, even those owned by a supposed mage, if this Capricorn was everything the auction pamphlet had boasted. He slipped through the crowd to the battered desk at the entrance to the hall and caught the clerk's attention with an impolite cough.

"Lot 27," Myrin said. "I'd like to pay and collect, please."

The clerk blinked at him. "I've barely just recorded the sale, sir. If you could wait—"

"I've already waited three fucking centuries," Myrin snarled, slamming his fist on the desk.

He regretted the outburst as the young man—a child by elven standards—paled beneath his neatly slicked hair. Myrin cursed under his breath when he realised making a scene could get him kicked out of there…without the book.

And there was no way in hell he would let that happen.

Myrin smoothed his features into the semblance of a smile. "Apologies, it's been a long day. My carriage is waiting, and I must get going. I'm obviously happy to pay the *priority fee* for fast processing."

The clerk returned the fake smile with a sly one of his own. "The priority fee. Of course, sir. I believe twenty per cent of the item's value is the *usual* rate."

Weaselly little shit, thought Myrin.

They both knew there was no such fee, but he nodded brusquely to confirm the arrangement and began counting out the silversheets. It wasn't that money was no object to him: nearly ninety per cent of his metalworking business profits went to that snollygoster Zhoren each month, and as an elf, a lifespan of nearly five hundred years didn't so much mean more savings to Myrin as it did more costs and a hell of a lot of inflation. A silver didn't buy what it used to anymore.

But for this book—Jassin's book—there was no price too high.

And as he scrawled his signature in the clerk's ledger underneath the words 'The Estate of the late Dwellt Capricorn (Certified Mage): Lot 27', Myrin felt hot and cold all at once, an exhilaration of gut-wrenching heartache and hope that he hadn't experienced in a very long time.

Myrin nudged the door open with the toe of his boot, shuffling into the rented room on the top floor of the inn with his arms wrapped tight around the wooden chest. He, and all of the other bidders at the amateur mage's estate auction, had been correctly sceptical of the auctioneer's claim that it was a true Kaizae—the hinges were too plain, and the wood didn't have the distinctive sheen of the artisan's usual work. Myrin could only be glad it was such a shoddy knock-off, or else he might have had actual competition for the sale.

Not bothering to shed his heavy cloak or scarf, Myrin placed the chest reverentially on the bed and knelt before it. If he'd had any doubts as to the book's authenticity when he first bid on the lot, they had been eviscerated with the soft but wretched cries that had reached his ears on the carriage trip through the streets of Kingsgate.

Help me, the book whimpered, the sharp stings of pain blunting the usual melodic voice Myrin knew so well. *Myrin, please!*

And the elf had urged the driver to move quicker, tears flowing freely down his cheeks as he laid a gloved hand on the chest, his thoughts resting on the book inside.

Jassin, my love. I have you. And I will not lose you again.

Now Myrin took a breath, flicking the clasp of the chest and lifting its lid to reveal the tome lying inside. Covered with worn, brown leather, stamped with the image of a thistle, the edges of its pages were spotted with age. Yet the metal banding around the book, two silvery circumscriptions that looked thin enough to be snapped, held both as firm and burnished as the day he'd set them in place to protect Jassin's work from prying eyes. There were faint indentations that suggested someone had tried to break it open—that amateur mage who'd found it in his possession perhaps, or else the auctioneering team— but the pages were still clamped firmly shut.

Tears found Myrin's eyes again and he wiped them away roughly before pulling out a silver key from his pocket. The day he'd found it in Jassin's abandoned chambers at the palace, he'd thought he'd never see the book again. His only comfort was knowing that, without the key, no one would be able to open it. At the time that had been an idle thought, an unimportant musing intended to distract himself from Jassin's death.

He hadn't known then what it had taken him three hundred years to discover: that Jassin's book, his vade mecum, would prove to be the only thing that mattered in the whole of fucking Guardiana.

Running his pale fingers reverentially along the book's spine, Myrin pressed the key to the lock. He barely dared to breathe as it clicked into place and he turned it, a quarter revolution, a half…

Stop!

Myrin flinched at the sudden scream that erupted around him, echoing in the chilly confines of the room.

"Jassin?"

A sob burst from his chest as the book responded in a breathless whisper. *Myrin, is that really you?*

"Yes! Jas just hold on a little longer. I've got you, I've got you—"

No, Myrin, you mustn't open the book!

Myrin stilled, pale fingers wrapped around the key. "I don't understand. Isn't it…? I've been tracking bespelled objects belonging to that bastard Grand Mage for centuries, and I thought… Jassin, your soul is in this book. Isn't it?"

Despair filled him. Could it be that after all this time he might have gotten it wrong, that the whisper of his lover's voice was nothing more than the imaginings of an elf steadily losing himself to the insanity of time?

A soft laugh filled the air. It was Jassin but it wasn't. A warped echo turned inside out and upside down. *Myrin, valim te.*

Myrin closed his eyes, the elvish words stealing his breath with their bittersweet remembrances. *My heart.*

I'm in here, Jassin confirmed. *But if you open it, it will destroy me.* A wry chuckle danced around the cramped room. *I'm assuming that if you've waited this long, you had rather more grandiose plans in mind for us.*

With a choked noise, Myrin turned the key in the opposite direction, firmly locking the bindings once more,

266

before dropping it back into his pocket. He wrapped his arms around the book and slid down the wall, fighting back tears as he clutched Jassin's soul close, tucking his knees up to prevent anyone—*anyone*—from taking him away again.

"I thought you dead," he whispered to the empty room. "The day that palace cart pulled up outside my shop was the worst day of my life. It was meant to be a fucking botany research job, Jas; why did you have to get involved with necromancy?"

He couldn't help the anger that bit through his words, mixing with regret and grief and guilt and that sheer, endless horror that had twisted his heart through the decades at the thought of Jassin gone. When all the light in the world had dimmed, the colours muted, for what could possibly have meaning or matter if his heart had been ripped from his chest?

Jassin sighed. *I tried to keep my head down just as I promised you. I spent my days in the palace greenhouse studying and recording the King's collection of flora. I hardly ever left the grounds. The anti-elvish sentiment whispered among the courtiers was enough to keep me from attempting to mingle with anyone beyond the other botanists. You're in Kingsgate: even three centuries later, you must have seen how much worse the city can be compared to Craydon.*

Myrin gave a small smile at the name of their hometown. Or at least, as much home as anywhere in Guardiana had been for them. Neither he nor Jassin had ever set foot in the homeland of the elves, its forests razed and polluted long before they had been born.

"And Lestrange?" he asked, when Jassin fell silent. "Tell me how the Grand Mage featured in this. Tell me why that cart dumped your lifeless body at my feet, and the palace ignored my pleas for answers? Tell me why, after centuries of silence, I suddenly start hearing about cursed objects, souls trapped in everything from quills to pieces of chalk, and an extremely familiar-sounding vade mecum? How did your book end up in his laboratory, Jassin? How did *you*?"

Myrin squeezed the ancient tome so tightly he feared it would break and had to force himself to loosen his grip before he accidentally squished his lover into oblivion.

A lot of questions, Jassin whispered. *But I fear the answer is far simpler that the conspiracy you portray it to be.*

"I'm not saying it's a conspira—"

I made a mistake.

Silence.

"Jassin, please just tell me."

I'm tired, his lover's voice said, coming from everywhere and nowhere at once. *Take me home, Myrin.*

Myrin nodded, swallowing back tears. He'd never expected their reunion to be easy, but he hadn't thought it would be this: pressing his face to a worn book in a lonely inn, his lover seeming more distant than even his lack of corporeal presence could account for.

He couldn't lose him. He *wouldn't* lose him. They had time, and he had patience. He'd restore Jassin to the world, and they would find their way back to each other. In time.

🜄🜄🜄

It took two days to return to Craydon. Myrin's old mule stubbornly refused to pull the small cart any faster than her trademark snail's pace, despite his various threats, bribes and cajolements. As the beast's hooves clacked rhythmically down the road, Myrin filled the awkward tension between him and Jassin with mindless chatter, babbling away to the book tucked safely back in its chest in the depths of the cart.

He spoke about everything he could remember of the last three hundred years: the good, the bad, and the downright boring—which was most of it, as Myrin hadn't exactly been living life to its fullest when he'd believed Jassin dead. He told him of his metalworking shop, and its steady stream of customers, most of them descendants of the families Jassin had met when they lived together. He told him of the great plague that swept through the small villages around Kingsgate a hundred and fifty years ago, decimating their populations and livestock, and the hardships that followed. Of the treaty signed with the elves a scant handful of decades past, already accused of being a farce. Of the scandal that rocked Craydon when the dressmaker's daughter chose the butcher's boy instead of the mayor's son she had been promised to. Of the stories Myrin had collected of the other souls trapped in Lestrange's belongings that were now starting to see the light of day.

But while Jassin had listened intently to the inane and everyday tales, he quickly grew uncomfortable whenever the conversation—if it could be called that, considering how little he spoke—strayed too close to his own fate. Myrin's natural curiosity, and his desperation to know what had happened, bubbled hot under his skin, but he had forced it down with no small degree of effort, recognising how delicate their newly-recovered relationship really was.

Centuries without a body, dead, and bound within the pages of a book. And if the rumours were true, left to rot in Lestrange's laboratory for hundreds of years after his own death.

Myrin shivered as he imagined what Jassin had endured. Isolated in the cold and the dark. Had he entertained himself by talking to the other trapped souls? Had he even been able to project his voice outside of his prison back then? Had they? Or had all of the cursed objects laid lifeless and silent on their shelves, screaming soundlessly as the world passed them by?

Myrin murmured praise to the mule as they pulled up behind his shop, although the nonchalant beast barely acknowledged it, flicking an ear as if to demand she be released from the harness after such a hard gallop home. In retaliation, he forced her to wait until he'd deposited the chest and the few belongings he'd taken with him to Kingsgate inside his house –their house—before unburdening her and giving her a quick rub down.

Then he rushed back inside, fearful to be separated from Jassin for even the scant minutes it had taken, half-expecting the chest and its contents to have disappeared, as if this had all been the wisps of his desperate mind.

He let out a half-sob as he saw the chest where he'd left it, and opening its lid, found the book tucked snugly inside.

"I'm crying too much," Myrin admitted, stroking the cover of the vade mecum reverently. To finally have it here…for Jassin to have returned home to the house they'd chosen together, decorated together, lost themselves to ecstasy together under its roof more times than he could count. "I suppose you think I've gone soft since you last saw me. It's just that…ever since that day, I've felt like Good King Aldric. My world fell apart around me and what I loved slipped through my fingers. I almost walked into the sea, just as he did."

I'm glad you didn't. Myrin, I could never think worse of you. I've cried a lot too. In…my own way.

"A tearful book," Myrin mused, latching onto the thought. "I hope you didn't get your pages wet."

Jassin laughed, and again it wasn't quite right, not really his laugh, but a good approximation of it. How else had he changed over the years? He wouldn't look different: Myrin had seen to that. Would he sound different? The voice that had emerged from the book was barely a whisper, grittier than the melodic tunes of his lover's lilting voice, and if he'd heard it anywhere else he might not have believed it him. How much had his cruel banishment to a lifeless object shredded him? Would he move differently—tentatively perhaps, as if fearing his body might be ripped from him again?

Myrin expected his own movements would mirror those. His fears certainly did.

"I wish I could open it," he said, a finger tracing the embossing on the front of the book. "I'd like to see your sketches. The peace lily, and the mint sprig. And all the new ones you made from the King's collection."

In time. We can't risk—

Myrin!

A voice cut across Jassin's words, shrill and clearly terrified, despite it only uttering one word. A voice that sounded like…Jassin?

Myrin flinched, holding the book at arm's length and staring at it. The vade mecum had vibrated with the shout, as if Jassin's soul was trying to force its way through the binding.

Myrin, Jassin said breathlessly. *Valim te, you must help me.*

"What was that? It sounded like you, but you—"

My soul is fragmenting. It's been imprisoned too long in this book, and I'm losing myself. I can't—

Myrin, it's me!

Myrin, it's happening too quickly. Help me!

Myrin gaped helplessly. "What can I do?"

Sage, Jassin forced out between laboured breaths. *Dip my book in sage water. Hurry!*

"Sage, really? Doesn't that dampen the…you know, the supernatural?"

What are you, a Mage? Just fucking do it, Myrin!

He looked around, racking his memory to recall if he had any in the house. But it had been a long time since he'd cooked anything but the barest of meals, and he kept no herbs in the kitchen. Perhaps his neighbours might have some, but it was late in the evening and it was hardly proper to go banging on doors to demand someone produce sage for him.

Jassin cried out as if in pain and Myrin made up his mind. Propriety be damned, he'd drag every single

Craydon resident into the street in their nightclothes if it meant putting an end to his lover's anguish. He barrelled out of the front door, book tucked under his arm, and made it halfway to the gate before his steps faltered, gaze flashing to a bundle of weeds in the corner of the small yard.

His elvish eyesight picked out a familiar, fuzzy leaf from the darkness, its rounded tip stirring memories in Myrin of laying upstairs with Jassin three centuries ago, their limbs tangled together in sated serenity. Myrin had been playing with the other elf's long, white hair, plaiting it absently between his fingers as Jassin scrawled a sketch into his vade mecum, one of the earlier entries of the tome when Jassin was still figuring out his art style. Myrin, tempted to pick up where they'd left off only a few minutes previously, had endeavoured to distract him from his work, pressing kisses down Jassin's collarbone, and when that hadn't worked, had moved his way lower. He'd had to push the book aside to move the elf into a position that suited them both, expecting to spy some exotic and rare flower on its page, and had scoffed indignantly when he saw nothing more than a simple garden herb.

"Jas? Are you ignoring me for parsley?" Myrin had teased, and Jassin shot him a look of despair.

"It's sage, you lummox," he'd shot back, and when he'd dared to look longingly back at the sketch, as if hoping to finish it, Myrin had finished him instead, endeavouring to prove to his studious lover that sometimes, just *sometimes*, sex really was better than plants.

Now, Myrin dove through the darkness for the tendrils of sage he'd spied in the mess that was his garden, and for once he was relieved rather than ashamed that he'd never attempted to tame its wild depths. Gardening had been Jassin's domain, and the idea of pulling out even a single weed had felt wrong. Wrong, and ever-so painful.

But the sage had blossomed in its neglect, sturdy leaves set on a thick stem, and Myrin yanked it bodily from the ground.

Myrin, I can't...

Myrin hurried back into the house, ripping a saucepan from the wall of the small kitchen and tossing it to the floor.

Hurry!

No! No, you can't!

Myrin, I'm losing myself!

It's not me!

It's not me, I'm falling, I'm fragmenting. Hurry!

You need to stop him!

I couldn't stop Lestrange, Myrin. You need to stop him, because I couldn't. Couldn't stop, couldn't stop, couldn't stop...

Myrin ripped the leaves from the muddy plant, scrunching them in his fist to release their menthol scent before dropping them into the pan. He heaved over the bucket of water he'd drawn before he left for Kingsgate and sloshed it over the herbs. He didn't have time to worry about its freshness. Jassin was dying.

"Do I just... Jas, it's going to get the book wet!"

Drop it in, now!

And Myrin obeyed, submerging the vade mecum in

the sage-infused water as the manic shouts abruptly gave way to silence.

"Jas?"

I'm here, Myrin.

Myrin's legs gave out and he slumped to his knees beside the saucepan, thankful he hadn't killed him with the dunking. Jassin's voice sounded steadier, and it didn't endeavour to contradict or shout at itself, which seemed promising. Now he just had to deal with a sodden book.

"Tell me what happened with Lestrange," Myrin whispered, knowing he shouldn't press. Knowing he needed to give his lover space, but the way he'd cried out the Grand Mage's name had Myrin clawing desperately at the wound. "Why you?"

Jassin sighed. *I don't wish to tell you, Myrin. You will think worse of me.*

"Never," Myrin said firmly.

And then coldness twisted around his heart as the paranoia took hold. Maybe the reason Jassin refused to talk, why he seemed so distant…

"Did you… Did you and he—?"

He couldn't say it. Couldn't utter those words. He leaned back and rested his face on the cold stone of the kitchen floor, twisting his fingers in his scarf.

"It doesn't matter," he mumbled into the astricted air, its weight pressing down on him like a physical thing. "If you did, I mean. I'd understand."

Actually, he didn't think he would. But he had to try, didn't he?

Myrin, it's not like that. I didn't sleep with Lestrange.

The pressure eased, and he could breathe again. "I

just thought maybe that's why you wouldn't tell me…"

Another sigh.

You're not going to let this go, are you?

"No," Myrin murmured.

You always were stubborn.

Myrin smiled at that, a chill seeping into his cheek. "You know me too well."

If I tell you, will you help me?

"Fuck you, Jas. Of course I'm going to help you, whether you tell me or not. Why would you even ask that?"

I just… I need a body, Myrin. I need to escape this prison.

Myrin shifted on his side so he could stare at the saucepan. Soft bubbles occasionally popped to the surface of the water as the book reluctantly released its last breaths of trapped air.

"I can do better than that," he promised. "There's someone I'm going to take you to see tomorrow."

A pause. *Someone?*

Myrin gave a dark and bitter laugh. "A necromancer. Calls herself Zhoren. Half-wraith, by the look of her, and the other half has got to be all highwayman, for she robs me blind each month."

Jassin let out a soft noise. *For what?*

"For keeping your body hale."

Myrin! Jassin's voice increased in volume, rough and gravelly like he'd survived a hanging, or else half a tonne of pipe tobacco. *Are you telling me you've preserved my body for three centuries?*

"Don't say I never do things for you," Myrin teased,

276

although in truth it was no light-hearted matter. Something inside him had broken the day he'd seen Jassin's corpse on the cart, pale skin waxen with death, long hair matted with dirt. He'd taken it to Zhoren the following day, more out of an unwillingness to let go than any plan to rescue Jassin. After all, he'd believed him truly dead, his soul gone from the world.

And then it had been easier to keep paying the necromancer, who'd assured him she was as immortal as he was and unlikely to fail in her task anytime soon, than it had been to give up on Jassin. The months had rolled by, years and decades, and still he'd dutifully paid her a portion of his shop's income to keep Jassin as preserved as the day he'd returned home. He'd stopped visiting after a while, only returning once he'd learned about Lestrange's cursed objects to check that his money hadn't been wasted. And for all the necromancer's creepy smiles and creepier laboratory, he had to admit she was good at her job.

A necromancer, Jassin mused. *Who would have believed it, you of all people, working with one?*

"I know. It's a foul profession."

Indeed. And that…I suppose is my cue.

Myrin waited, pressed still against the floor despite his legs starting to cramp.

There was another botanist working with me at the palace, Jassin began. *Barely a girl—a human girl—but so extraordinarily talented. She could remember a plant's properties after learning them once. Not like me, needing to keep my notes with me all the time.*

Myrin let out a fond laugh, looking back at the

saucepan. Its shadow loomed over the floor, cast by the pale moonlight filtering through the uncovered window.

Eliva. That was her name. And for all her skill, she wasn't arrogant about it. She was sweet, and polite, and...and one day I found her in the greenhouse, her heart torn from her chest.

Jassin took a haggard breath.

They all knew it was Lestrange. The whole court. They'd been whispering about the undead creatures he had at his command, and he hadn't bothered to hide the fact he'd been interested in Eliva. But none of the bastards did anything, too scared to even point a finger at him outside of whispered gossip. I thought... I thought it was up to me to do something.

Of course he did. That was so fucking Jassin.

He'd always helped others, from rescuing stray wolf pups to handing out coins to street kids who were clearly conning him. They'd only met because Jassin had saved Myrin from a gang of humans in Kingsgate who'd taken a particular dislike to an elf drinking in the same tavern as them. Neither of them had much skill in fighting off drunk xenophobes, but that hadn't stopped Jassin from launching himself into the fray. Between the two of them, they'd managed to plant enough bottles around enough heads to allow them unfettered passage from the establishment. And then Myrin had kissed him. The surprised but pleased noise that erupted from Jassin's lips told him he'd read it right, that he hadn't messed up this time, and that it really was possible to find someone who understood you so thoroughly that your heart exploded from happiness, even here, in human lands.

278

I thought if I could find damning evidence, Jassin was saying, *that the King would have no choice but to act. But Lestrange caught me snooping in his quarters. I thought he was going to kill me.*

Myrin was silent, letting him talk.

That wasn't what he had in mind. He… Fuck, Myrin. He told me he'd killed Eliva for that exact reason, to draw me in. That he'd endeavoured to get me alone for a long time, but I was such a recluse that I'd inadvertently avoided all his efforts. Myrin, she died because of me!

"No," Myrin growled into the darkness, wishing he could wrap his arms around his broken lover. Perhaps tomorrow, he could. "That's not on you. That some asshole was stalking you wasn't your fault."

His fingers itched to claw their way around Lestrange's throat, and he almost wished the necromancer was still alive so he could have the pleasure of killing him himself.

A bitter laugh echoed around him. *If I hadn't been there, she'd still be alive. I struggled, but what was a botanist to do against a goddamn Grand Mage?* Jassin sighed. *It wasn't my body he wanted, Myrin. At least, not in that way.*

Myrin let out a breath he hadn't known he'd been holding. If Lestrange had… Nothing could make what the bastard had done to him right, but it gave him a small measure of relief to know that Jassin—his sweet and innocent Jassin—had been spared from such a violation.

It was because I was an elf, Jassin whispered. *For all his experiments—*he spat the word like a curse—*he'd never had an elf before. He wanted to see how my soul* *differed from the others. So he ripped it out of me and flung it into my book, tossing my body out of his chambers for the morning staff to find as if it was a pair of muddy boots. I think he may have been disappointed in me, for he lost interest pretty quickly, leaving the vade mecum on a shelf in the laboratory as he moved onto other things. And then one day, he never returned. I think I slept, Myrin, at least for some of it. I hope I did.*

Myrin crawled over to the saucepan and fished the sodden tome from the water. Setting it on the floor beside him, he pressed a hand to its cover, and they lay there in the darkness together, sharing comfort in the silence.

They set off for Zhoren's laboratory as soon as the sun began to peek over the Violet Range. Myrin had wanted to leave the chest behind so they could travel lighter, but Jassin had insisted he bring it, explaining that it helped him feel more grounded and better able to keep himself together. A piece of familiarity, he'd claimed, although he hadn't said from where. Maybe the chest had been in the laboratory with him, although why he'd want the reminder, Myrin didn't know. But he wasn't going to deny Jassin any comfort, and so he'd dutifully hitched the cart back up to his mule and set off for the hamlet a half-hour walk from Craydon proper.

Myrin scratched the mule's head as they arrived, promising to return to her soon by way of apology for not unhitching her from the cart. He knew he should give her a name if he was going to properly introduce her to Jassin when his soul was restored, but the various beasts had blurred into each other over the years. Their fragile lifespans seemed mere seconds compared to his own, and names had not seemed important before for animals who didn't even answer to them. But now… Now there would be Jassin.

Myrin could hardly contain his excitement as he heaved the chest off the cart, flicking open its lid to check that the vade mecum was still tucked inside. Its pages were a little shrivelled on the edges, but soon it would be nothing more than the reference guide it once was. Perhaps Jassin would want to keep it, but Myrin would do his best to convince him to start again, free of any foul memories.

He banged on Zhoren's door with his elbow. The necromancer took a decidedly frustrating length of time to answer as the chest grew heavier in his arms.

"Myrin," she said distastefully, as she cracked open the door.

Her slight frame hovered just beyond the reach of the sunlight, dark eyes lidded with kohl. They should have been allies—elves and necromancers had both been abominations in the eyes of the Old Faith, violators of the Eternal Circle—but they'd despised each other from the off. Elven immortality was natural. Zhoren, like Lestrange, was a monster. They tolerated each other for the sake of their business arrangement.

"I hope you have an excellent explanation for disturbing me at such an hour."

"How about an incentive?" he offered instead. "That after today, you'll never have to see me again."

Zhoren gave him a sinister smile. "And lose your

generous monthly payments? I think not."

"Lump sum generosity can be just as beneficial. Let me in."

She sighed and snarled, but did as he said, pulling open the door to let him through. He led the way down the stairs to the basement without asking, neither caring about decorum nor wanting to indulge her propensity for turning even polite requests into laden favours.

"I have him," Myrin said, resting the chest on a bench in the basement laboratory and trying not to look at the cadaver with its chest spread open that was resting only a few feet away. "Jassin. His soul is in here."

"The chest?"

"The book," he clarified, lifting the lid and showing her. "You can restore it to his body, can't you? Like we discussed?"

Zhoren sucked on her teeth. "I can. But as we discussed, my fee for such work is not cheap."

Myrin pulled a bag of coins from his pocket and dropped it next to the chest with a heavy thud. "Everything I have," he snarled. "It's a heck of a deal for you for a single piece of magic, and you know it."

Zhoren peered inside the bag, checking it was gold rather than silversheets no doubt, and then shrugged. "Fine. Let's get you your boyfriend back. I could do with the space anyway."

She sashayed to the far wall, where a dozen tiny doors were set in a sequence. Pulling open the third from the left on the second row, the necromancer pulled out Jassin's body, her strength belied by her small stature as she heaved him over her shoulder. Long white hair fluttered down her back and Myrin winced at the insensitive treatment of his lover's corpse. But he said nothing. Angering the necromancer would only lead to further delays and demands for financial recompense.

Myrin...

Zhoren flinched as Jassin's voice cut through the air. "Your elf, I presume?" She dumped him on another bench, and Myrin moved over to him, smoothing his hair behind his pointed ears, and retrieving his hands from where they had lolled off the side of the table. She'd done a good job; no traces of decay showed on his body or his clothes, despite being in that locker three centuries. She'd preserved him in the same state he'd brought him to her all those years ago, lifeless and cold.

"Let's get this over with so I can go back to bed." Zhoren said. "Elf, this might hurt a little."

Myrin thought it a remarkably considerate comment until he noticed the necromancer's anticipatory smile. She *hoped* it would hurt. Fucking mages.

"Do it."

Zhoren closed her eyes and began to chant, one hand pressed to Jassin's chest and the other curled in the air, reaching out as if searching for something.

Myrin held his breath, his hand clutching Jassin's. Could this really be it, after all these years? He glanced up at Zhoren when the chanting turned from pseudo-elvish to words he understood.

"Elf, get your ass over here," she snapped. "You're wanted in this devilishly handsome body, and I have an appointment to keep with a few more hours of sleep."

It's working! Jassin yelled, and his voice sounded so

deep, so wrong, that it grated at Myrin's nerves.

My...rin...

Myrin flinched. That time, it had sounded more like his lover. Was Jassin's soul splintering again? Would the restoration spell work if his soul wasn't whole?

"Hold on," he breathed, staring at Jassin's face, his delicate cheekbones and pale lips. "You're almost there."

Stop him, Myrin!

"Lestrange is gone," he murmured. "You don't have to worry about him."

Not...Lestrange. Capricorn!

Myrin frowned. "Capricorn? He's dead. I bought your book from the auction of his estate, remember? Why would he matter?"

Don't listen, Myrin! That's the broken part of me. It's not making sense.

Fuck you, Capricorn! Myrin, he's been manipulating you! He's—

I'm here, Myrin, so close. Don't you want me back?

Get away from my body! Don't you dare—

Myrin froze, opening his mouth to tell Zhoren to stop. But the necromancer had already dropped her hands with a satisfied expression, and he followed her gaze to where Jassin's eyelashes were fluttering against his pale face.

"Jassin?"

Jassin heaved in a breath, sitting bolt upright on the bench so quickly that Myrin was forced to release his hand in case he broke something. Jassin cried out, clawing at his throat, and his eyes shot open.

"Jas, can you hear me?"

Jassin looked at him and cocked his head. "Myrin?"

Myrin let out a sob. "Jassin, you're back. I've missed you, Jas, so very much."

Jassin reached for Myrin as if he was going to cup his cheek in his hand, and it was such a gentle movement that Myrin almost smiled.

And then Jassin slammed Myrin's head down onto the bench, and everything flashed dark. Pain lanced through his skull and Myrin slumped to the floor, his limbs suddenly loose and disobedient. A scream ratcheted through the air and Myrin vaguely wondered if it was his.

No. It was Zhoren.

Or it had *been* Zhoren, before her head landed on the floor in front of him, lips twisting in an outraged snarl.

Myrin choked, scrambling backwards from the gruesome sight, but he couldn't work out which was back or up or right or wrong, and fucking hell, Jassin was standing over him with Zhoren's headless corpse in his arms.

The other elf dropped her and flicked his long hair over his shoulder as if it irritated him. Flexing his hands, he admired them closely, and then glanced over to Myrin with a dark smile.

"You were wonderful," he purred, stalking towards him with Jassin's elegant grace. "If Jassin hadn't interfered there at the end, I might have been tempted to see how this played out with you before I showed my hand. I bet you'd have been very generous to this body with all that time to make up for."

Myrin stared at him, a warm wetness trickling into

his eyelashes.

Jassin tsked, reaching down to wipe Myrin's forehead with his thumb. It came away bloody.

"But the bastard elf had only been getting stronger in your presence. The sage helped keep him quiet, but not for long, it seems. A pity."

"You're Capricorn," Myrin whispered. "How…? Where's Jassin?"

"Exactly where he always was, valim te," Capricorn mocked, twisting Jassin's soft features into those of cruelty. "In the book."

"But you were…"

"In the chest, of course. Did you know it's a Kaizae? It was rather inconvenient, accidentally detaching my own soul when I was endeavouring to replicate Lestrange's work. They sold my whole bloody estate around me." He lashed out without warning, kicking Myrin in the ribs to keep him down. "But what a stroke of luck, to be sold with Jassin! The soul I'd stolen so many secrets from in our time together, from details on Lestrange's experiments to your boring life together." He sighed. "Unfortunately, it all came as a package deal: plucking memories from a soul is hardly a delicate process."

That's how Capricorn had fooled him. All the little details: the pet name, Jassin's humour, his tale of what happened in the castle. All of it was Jassin, just told through the mouth of a liar, using Myrin for his own ends. Only his voice wasn't perfect, and like a fool, Myrin had overlooked that discrepancy, believing the years of imprisonment had warped him.

"Last night, when you said you were fragmented. That was him, wasn't it?"

Capricorn scowled, and then brightened. "It was. But you believed it to be madness, drowning your elf in sage so he couldn't contest me when I reached for the necromancer's tether to his body."

"I don't get how you knew this was your endgame," Myrin said, stalling. If he could get to his feet, he might be able to find a weapon. His head still swam, but he could hold off the wooziness long enough. He hoped. "How did you know I was planning on returning him to a body?"

"Because I know everything about you, dear Myrin. And Jassin knew your resourcefulness, your diligence. I'll admit I was surprised you'd managed to hold onto his body, but I knew you'd have something ready to restore his soul with."

Capricorn knelt down so they were at eye level, Jassin's yellow eyes boring into his. "You know, I'm tempted to let you live. You really have given me such a gift, Myrin. With this body, I will endure for centuries."

Myrin was silent, and Capricorn chuckled.

When he stood up again, Myrin moved, launching himself at the man's legs in a blind and reckless tackle. Capricorn came down hard, and Myrin swung a fist at his face, hoping to keep him down long enough to escape with the book. He wasn't sure he was ready to kill him, not wearing Jassin's face, but if he could—

Myrin, watch out!

Myrin cried out as he was wrenched off Capricorn, the open-chested corpse wrapping its arms around him and holding him back.

Capricorn touched a finger to his cheek and winced. "No," he snarled. "You can't provoke me that easily. You will still live. But you will watch as I do something I've wanted to do for a *very* long time."

The mage stepped towards the chest and Myrin's heart stopped.

"No! Please, don't! I'll do anything—"

The cadaver's arm closed around his throat, cutting off his words.

"Hello, Jassin," Capricorn hissed, fishing the vade mecum from the depths of the chest and glaring at the book as if it had personally offended him. "You've fucked with me for the last time, elf. I bet you thought you were awfully clever, tricking me into detaching my own soul, hmm? But your precious Myrin listened to me, not you."

Leave him alone!

Capricorn's eyes flickered to Myrin, trapped in the corpse's grip as he struggled vainly to break free. "I will. He's done nothing to me, and the magic controlling the cadaver will dissipate when I am far enough away. But you, my friend, are a thorn in my side I'm eager to be rid of."

Jassin ignored him, directing his words to Myrin instead. *Valim te, Myrin. I love you. I—*

Myrin's heart was torn apart for the second time in his life as the book burst into flames in Capricorn's hands.

The body that had once been Jassin's gave him a wink and ascended the stairs, leaving Myrin in the dark with nothing but broken bodies and the scattered pieces of his heart.

Interlude Four

Faceless

S.O. Green

66 **I**'m sorry things turned out this way. I wish I could have figured this out sooner. Then maybe…"

Lyssa trailed off. All these apologies were pointless. Bergsen couldn't even hear her anyway. According to the healers, the wounds on his face were superficial, but they couldn't wake him from his coma.

She could feel the weakness of his spirit, like something had depleted him, fed from him to sustain itself, even while it mutilated him beyond recognition. Even if he awoke, his identity would be buried under thick scar tissue until the day he died. He'd never see himself in the mirror again.

She knew it had to be one of the objects. Why else

would he have ended up like all the other poor souls he'd been sent to investigate? The problem was, there was no sign of the bloody thing anywhere. They'd found a medal in his quarters, but it had been mundane. Nothing but a trinket. Apparently, he'd killed someone to get it, but Lyssa had to believe it was the object, whatever it had been, that had made him do it.

"I should have refused Leonardo's offer of assistance," she sighed. "I should never have let anyone else get involved, but…"

They were all already involved. She knew that. Lestrange didn't just threaten her, as the Grand Mage, or Camelia. He threatened the entire realm and everyone in it. If she didn't stop him soon, what had happened to Bergsen could happen to people all across Guardiana.

There had already been reports from the Gold Plains. A farm had been destroyed by a creature made of plants—the landowner had made a purchase from the auction—and a suspected necromancer in Craydon had been found decapitated alongside a trunk belonging to an arcane dabbler.

And maybe these were just small, personal tragedies brought about by cursed items, but how many more people would die before people acknowledged this for the disaster it was?

For now, the merchants and guild halls were content to offer their thoughts and prayers and make token gestures, but they weren't actually helping. At least the Faith had sent someone to investigate under their own power.

Yeah, and look what happened to him…

Lyssa sighed. "I'll figure this out. Whatever happens, I'll fix it and make it right. I just need time."

The only problem was, she didn't know how much time she had left.

Uncommon Bonds

Jessica Chanese

A slight, dark-haired girl wove her way through the crowded streets of Kingsgate, hooded cloak pulled tight. A rangy mutt with matted, grey fur followed close at her heels. Both figures blended into the endless stream of people and animals and carts clogging the dusty lanes. The pair dodged angry mothers scolding wailing children, carriage drivers whipping stubborn workhorses, and merchants touting wares while keeping a wary eye out for would-be thieves.

As tended to happen when a young woman traversed the city unaccompanied, the girl occasionally caught the unwanted attention of unsavory men whose odor of stale ale and too many days without a bath was hardly distinguishable from the stench of manure permeating the stagnant air. It took only a rasping snarl and snap of yellowing teeth from the mutt to give pause to reaching hands and leering grins.

The girl had been named Zara by the old woman who raised her, after her drunkard father failed to return from his shift in the mines one evening, the same drunkard father who referred to his child as 'a filthy whore, like her mother' when he deigned to refer to her at all.

Zara, in turn, called the woman D'ama, Olde Gaurdiana vernacular for grandmother, despite their not being blood kin. When D'ama died, Zara buried her behind the small shack they'd shared, packed her few belongings in a rucksack and made the trek south, out of the Red Land, to Kingsgate.

She'd been in Kingsgate for nearly five years now, though she couldn't quite bring herself to call it home.

Zara resided in the city out of necessity, not preference. The vast majority of those who dwelled within its walls did so for the same reasons—as Guardiana's main population center, it offered the most opportunities to earn a living, if it could be called that.

Above-board jobs were scarce and paid scraps, though they afforded a measure of security and respectability not associated with the less seemly ways one could get by in Kingsgate.

Zara knew money was money. It meant food and a semblance of shelter, whether it came in the form of legal wages or a fistful of silversheets pushed across a backroom table by a gang boss for illicit errands run. She'd gained a reputation among the denizens of Kingsgate's underbelly as a highly effective thief.

The city was rife with children who survived by pickpocketing, but no one trusted an urchin. A doe-eyed thing like Zara, on the other hand, engendered only sympathy. They underestimated her. Or maybe they overestimated her. She'd found her ability to evoke pity in place of suspicion to be quite lucrative.

Zara moved through Kingsgate with singular focus, never taking her eyes off the road. She was anxious to arrive at her intended destination; not an unusual feeling after she'd just completed a job. Zara trusted her hound, Bones, her sole confidant in Kingsgate as D'ama had been in the Red Lands, to ward off miscreants, but she never felt fully secure until the drop had been made and the silversheets were tucked in her back pocket.

Under her cloak, Zara squeezed the brass key, wrapped in a handkerchief and clasped tight in her palm, to assure herself she hadn't dropped it. Stealing it had taken three days of surveillance—three days of sneaking through the city, trailing her target, waiting for the right moment to relieve the portly fellow of his satchel's contents. It was worth putting in the time. Del was paying top dollar for this one, for reasons Zara didn't care to know.

Other than a roughly engraved symbol—Zara had first taken it to be a mark of the Faith, but further inspection showed it was more like an ouroboros, the alchemists' mark—the key looked and felt like every other heavy brass key she'd carried.

There must have been something notable about this one though, since Del was offering up such a hefty purse for its retrieval. Either it was worth more as an object than it appeared, or it promised entry to something or somewhere of immense value.

Zara speculated it was the latter. She cared only that she'd be able to make this month's squatter's fee and have a bit leftover for a meal large enough to share with Bones once Del made good on their deal.

As long as he paid up, Del could use the key to kidnap and murder the Queen and her entire court as far as Zara was concerned.

Three hundred years earlier…

Seething. Livid. Incensed. No words could capture Barros' roiling anger at learning of Lestrange's deception.

He knew, of course, who Lestrange was a depraved, and tremendously powerful, necromancer with a penchant for boundless cruelty. Barros covered for him, anyway, allowing his heinous work to continue. Feeding it even, by teaching Lestrange how alchemy could enhance his experiments. All with the implicit understanding that Lestrange would return the favor by championing Barros' work to the King—and funneling Barros enough funds to keep his work alive.

As a master alchemist with no living equal, Barros' powers rivaled Lestrange's. But alchemy didn't garner the funds attached to the kind of inherent magic Lestrange possessed. Alchemy wasn't as mysterious or glamorous in the eyes of the populace because it could be learned, a trade anyone could perfect with enough effort.

And while this was a woefully misguided belief—mastering alchemy required a superior intellect and an exacting hand possessed by few—it was prevalent enough to influence how the King chose to spend his gold.

Lestrange had unfettered access to Kingsgate's coffers as Grand Mage. Throwing a few silversheets Barros' way every now and then was of no consequence to him, and he grudgingly recognized the value of Barros' contributions to his own work. Though Lestrange's powers knew few limitations, Barros had shown him how alchemical principles could augment and enhance his castings. The alchemist's knowledge made the Grand Mage's enchantments exponentially more potent, and power was the only currency of significance to Lestrange.

They'd kept to their arrangement for nearly a decade, both men seemingly satisfied with the mutual benefits. And here they'd finally made progress with the phylactery enchantment they'd been laboring on together for years; it was the one casting that had resisted both the Grand Mage's abilities and Barros' alchemical prowess. After many failed attempts, yielding grotesque results, they'd recently made quite promising developments.

At least part of the soul of a Palace stablehand now resided in a brass thimble sealed tight inside an apothecary jar on Lestrange's workstation.

The alchemist never fully understood why mastering the phylactery enchantment was of such great importance to Lestrange, though he harbored his suspicions.

Ultimately, it was of no consequence to Barros that fragments and slivers of a few dozen, unfortunate souls were lodged in various objects strewn about their laboratory so long as Lestrange's pursuit provided justification for his continued financial support of Barros' work.

Still, he'd taken precautions, just in case his hunch about Lestrange's true motivation for perfecting the phylactery spell proved true.

Barros knew that he and Lestrange were nothing more than begrudging business partners—neither the alchemist nor the Grand Mage had the time or stomach for anything as plebeian as friendship—but if business was good, why would Lestrange turn on him now?

The alchemist's ire boiled over when the Grand Mage returned to their laboratory and had the audacity to greet Barros casually, as if he hadn't passed off one of the alchemist's most significant achievements as his own when meeting with the King over that morning's breakfast. Barros knew he shouldn't care, knew that as long as the sheets kept flowing, it mattered very little whether or not the King had any appreciation for his work. But Barros' pride could only withstand so many insults.

"How could you?" Barros roared.

Lestrange leveled him with his cold, empty stare. "I'm merely a champion of your work, Barros. I want only to see it survive beyond the end of your miserable life."

The alchemist scowled. Such an odd remark, he thought, though speaking in cryptic riddles was per usual for Lestrange.

The Grand Mage gave Barros his back then and busied himself with a tray of steaming vials on his work station.

"I hardly think I'll need your assistance securing my

legacy," Barros finally responded.

Lestrange turned to face him, an ornate pocket watch in one hand and a vial of dark liquid in the other. The Grand Mage uncapped the vial, releasing tendrils of vapor that grew and stretched to wrap themselves around Barros.

"Sadly, you're mistaken, my friend."

The alchemist had barely registered his meaning before he was overcome by a sickening sensation; a dreadful feeling as if his innards were being wrenched, suctioned, from his body.

He heard Lestrange's dark chuckle as his soul was drawn into the pocket watch that would be his prison for centuries to come.

Zara stood in Del's darkened office, dropping her earnings into the worn leather pouch strung around her neck. It hung just below the protective talisman D'ama gifted to her as a child. She had little use for the Faith, but her talisman was her one concession to the beliefs she was raised with, if only because it was the last material tie she had to the one human who'd ever cared about her safety.

She counted silently as she placed the silversheets in the small bag, a furrow forming between her brows.

"This is less than we agreed, by half," Zara said, her tone accusatory.

Del grinned and leaned back in his chair. "You should know better than to take me at my word, little Zara. You'll learn soon enough. Integrity is overrated.

300

Honest people are paupers or dead men. And I, as you can see, am neither of the above."

Zara's nails dug into her palms as she struggled to resist the overwhelming urge to throttle her double-crossing employer. She breathed deep, willing herself to stay calm.

"I've done dozens of jobs for you, Del. I always deliver. Why short me now?"

Del shrugged. "Times are tough, my dear. And you never should've trusted me, no matter how many times I did right by you. See, this is really your own doing."

He flashed a crooked smile and the last frayed thread of Zara's control snapped. She unsheathed her dagger and lunged at Del.

"You lousy piece of— "

Thick, coarse fingers wrapped around Zara's neck as Del rose to meet her attack. All humor had disappeared from his pockmarked features, revealing the callous career criminal underneath. He was nearly two heads taller than her, and close to three times her weight. He lifted her off the ground with ease.

"You stupid child. I'll break your pretty, little neck and shit on your corpse when I'm done," he growled.

His hand crushed Zara's windpipe, causing her to gasp as she fought for air. Bones lunged at Del then, lips pulled back in a menacing snarl. Del fell backward with the force of the hound's weight, landing sprawled with the dog pinning him to the concrete floor. Alerted by the sounds of chaos, two of Del's men burst into the room.

"Get this mangy bastard off me!" Del spat.

The heavier of the two lackeys yanked Bones up by

his collar while the other grabbed Zara from where she'd landed in a heap. The hound howled and snapped his jaws until the man had enough and threw him carelessly against the wall. Zara cried out as Bones' lean body thudded against the brick. He slumped to the ground with a whimper but stayed down only a moment before returning to Zara's side.

Del stood, still shaking with rage. He glared at Zara in silence, chest heaving. The girl was certain she'd come to her end, certain she'd be seeing D'ama again soon.

I hope Bones runs, she wished to herself. *I hope he finds Yuri and Audra. They'll look after him.*

Zara entwined her fingers in Bones' rough fur and waited for Del or one of his henchmen to make their move.

"Get the fuck out of here and don't even think about coming back," he said finally.

Zara was surprised by Del's unexpected display of mercy but knew better than to question his motives. She shook herself free from the goon holding onto her and made for the doorway.

"Come on, Bones. We're done here."

Numb with anger—at Del's trickery, at her own gullibility—Zara made her way back to the makeshift encampment where she and a few dozen other street kids took shelter each night. It wasn't much, just an abandoned courtyard crowded with tarp-covered lean-tos and dotted with firepits and rickety structures built to house chamber pots. But, for a monthly fee paid to Arlyn, leader of another Kingsgate syndicate, Zara and her campmates had a reliable place to eat, sleep, and store what few belongings they had.

More importantly, the site was guarded and policed by Arlyn's people. The squatter's fee was as much a protection fee as it was rent. She was willing to pay for the chance to catch some shut-eye without fear of getting her throat slit or her silversheets stolen.

She found Yuri and Audra sitting in the dirt near her shelter. Zara knew better than to consider any person in Kingsgate a true friend, but Yuri and Audra had proven their loyalty enough that she thought of them as friend-adjacent.

Yuri looked up, catching sight of Zara's murderous expression. "Yikes, who pissed in your porridge?"

"Fucking Del shorted me," Zara grumbled.

Audra jumped to her feet. She looked ready to track Del down and cut him herself. "Lousy bastard!"

"But that means you won't have enough to pay your share of this month's fee, doesn't it?" Yuri asked.

Audra gave her younger brother a smack on the back of the head. "You don't need to remind her, dingus."

Yuri ignored his sister's reprimand. "So what're you gonna do?"

Zara led Bones past their campmates and began to rummage around her sleeping area.

"Don't know," she shrugged. "I'll have to figure something out, won't I?"

She retrieved a few scraps of leathery, dried meat from under her sleeping mat, offering one to Bones and dropping onto the dirt beside him to chew on the rest herself. The hound devoured his eagerly, then licked his owner's cheek in gratitude. Zara laid her head against the grimy stone wall at her back. She scratched behind the dog's ears absently and pondered her predicament.

Bones had been Zara's companion almost as long as she'd been in Kingsgate. After he'd scared off a gang of teenagers who'd threatened her one evening, back when she'd been too young and too small to fend them off, she'd kept the hound by her side. Sure, her belly might have been a little fuller some nights if she hadn't needed to split her meager rations with him, but the sense of safety Bones gave her was worth the hollow feeling in her stomach.

Hunger was commonplace to Zara; the security she felt with Bones curled up beside her every night was not.

"I heard the Queen emptied out the room where she'd kept that old necromancer's stuff," Yuri piped up, after a few moments. "Maybe you could get your hands on something of his and pawn it?"

"That's not gonna be easy," Audra said. "Every thief in Kingsgate probably has the same idea."

Yuri grinned. "Yeah, but only a handful of 'em are even half as good as our girl here."

Zara mustered a weak smile. "Thanks for the vote of confidence, Yuri. And that's definitely something for me to consider. But I think Bones and I have had enough excitement for one day. We'll head back out into the hellscape tomorrow and see what we can find."

Three centuries. Three hundred years of languishing

in oblivion, with only his intellect and seething hatred of Lestrange to keep him occupied. And now, he had a chance at freedom. More importantly, he could seek his revenge.

Some dimwitted royal had ordered the chambers emptied and the objects inside sold. Barros hadn't registered what had happened until the pocket watch that had been his soul's cell for so long was already outside of the palace gates, making its way to some unsuspecting noble.

In the endless days of his imprisonment, Barros had perfected the ability to cast his consciousness beyond the enchantments that bound his soul. It irked him no end that when it mattered most, his alchemical prowess couldn't best Lestrange's unnatural magic. Alchemy was a science and an art form, requiring tools and intellect. Barros considered his abilities exponentially more noble and prestigious than Lestrange's. After all, Barros studied tirelessly to perfect his craft, while a mage like Lestrange had been born into magic.

But even disembodied, he found a way to use alchemy to his benefit. He couldn't break Lestrange's spell entirely, but he could draw from the metals of his prison to partially subvert it. He could cast his mental awareness into the space around the pocket watch.

It was a trick of little use when the watch had occupied the same soundless, dusty room for hundreds of years, and Barros had grown lax in his environmental monitoring. He'd occasionally lapse into a type of stasis from the lack of stimulation, whether for days or decades he never knew.

Whenever he emerged from one of these periods, he'd cast what he'd come to think of as his mental net out of reflex to aid his acclimation to the present. How startling, how exhilarating, it had been when, this time, his net captured novel information—evidence of new surroundings—for the first time in centuries.

Now, Barros needed only to find another vessel for what remained of his soul; a new host to grant him freedom from the confines of the pocket watch, and a means to finally enact his long-formulated plans to ensure Lestrange suffered an infinitely worse fate.

The pocket watch had come to rest with an older nobleman, one whose cloak and shoes said his finances had seen better days. He must have thought the novelty of owning an object that had once belonged to the storied necromancer was more valuable than splurging on new finery. Barros personally disagreed but was grateful the gentleman's indulgence meant his soul was now traveling through Kingsgate, among hundreds of unwitting potential hosts.

The alchemist searched the crowds for the right specimen. He needed someone with certain attributes if his plan was going to work.

That one.

His projected consciousness registered a thin, unremarkable girl with a grimy mutt at her side. She had the gaunt frame and drawn expression common among the mess of interchangeable servant girls he remembered scurrying around the palace so long ago. And by the looks of her shabby clothes and dirt-stained skin, she was street trash. He'd have to clean her up a bit before entering the palace, of course, but no one would miss her if she disappeared for a while.

She'll do.

Barros waited until he sensed the noble's side brushing against the girl. He funneled his will into fusing his soul into his mental awareness. With a massive push, he cast himself, soul and mind, toward the girl.

But, instead of the sickening leeching sensation he remembered from when his soul was pulled into the pocket watch, Barros smashed into an impenetrable wall; a barrier of pure energy so intense, he felt his phantom skin burning.

His world went dark for a moment, then was quickly flooded by a wash of sounds and smells and painfully clear images. So much time had passed since he'd actually felt anything that the sensations were enormously disorienting. He had eyes again, suddenly. Ears, a nose, a mouth. Skin and bones and nerves. He'd forgotten.

His soul had obviously landed in a new body, but it didn't seem to be that of his intended target. He took stock of what he could see, of the angle at which he was looking up at the denizens of Kingsgate packing the city's streets.

Had he landed in a child's form? That would explain his short stature.

But why was everything—every sight, every odor, every sound—so very intense? Yes, it *had* been centuries since he'd experienced those feelings, but something felt off. Something felt *wrong*.

He heard a growling sound then, one that built into a crescendo of loud, rough barks and snarls. The alchemist was mortified when he realized the uncivilized sounds were coming from him.

A cur. I've landed in a blasted cur.

The indignity was nearly enough to override Barros' sudden terror that he could be trapped in yet another prison, one that alchemy may not be as well-suited to help him escape. He looked around wildly, trying to understand what had happened. Barros caught sight of the girl he'd meant to be his new host, and saw the talisman hanging from her neck, just as she grabbed for him.

The Circle unbroken. Damn the Faith.

Barros attempted to wrench his unwieldy canine body from the girl's hold but succeeded only momentarily until he felt thin but strong arms wrap around his chest.

Curse my luck, Barros thought. *And curse that bastard, Lestrange.*

Zara once again wound her way through the masses filling the streets of Kingsgate, searching for a wealthy-looking mark in the hopes she could recoup the previous day's losses. Bones had her trail as always. They'd been on the hunt for less than an hour or so when Zara felt a hard shove, strong enough to send her reeling into a fruit cart.

"Watch it!" Zara snapped, looking around for whoever or whatever had knocked into her.

It was then she spotted Bones a few arms lengths away, running in circles while barking frantically. She hurried over to him and he jumped on her immediately, clawing at her talisman. The hound's normally vacant eyes held fear and panic, emotions Zara had never seen in them before. She grabbed him by his scruff and was shocked when he twisted out of her grasp. Bones never tried to get away from her.

Zara lunged and quickly wrapped her arms around the dog's middle. She dragged him, whining and struggling, past curious onlookers and into an empty alleyway.

"What has gotten into you?" she chided.

Child, you have no inkling of the irony that statement holds.

Zara went cold. *Whose voice is that? Where did it come from? Why in the flying fuck is it in my head?!*

Bones stilled suddenly in her arms. *You can hear me?*

She stared at him, wide-eyed and pale.

"Bones?" Zara whispered. "Is that you?"

If the dog could have rolled his eyes—or, more accurately, if the disembodied soul inhabiting the hound could have rolled his eyes—he would have.

Yes, you silly girl, your brainless mutt has miraculously developed the ability to project his thoughts into your mind. Definitely sounds plausible to me.

Zara let go of Bones and slowly backed away from him. She sat very still for several breaths, then glanced up and down the alley before speaking again.

"If you aren't Bones, then who the hell are you?" she asked in a shaky whisper. Before Barros could respond, she added nervously, "And by the way, why would it be any more likely that someone or something has possessed my dog than it would be that he'd found a way to communicate with me? Both seem pretty unlikely in my opinion."

Maybe you're smarter than I imagined, Barros projected. *Probably not though. Who I am is of little concern to you —*

Zara raised a hand to cut him off. "Excuse me, I think it's of great concern to me to know who or what has taken control of my hound."

With that, she pulled a coil of rope from deep within the folds of her cloak and sprang forward to loop it around Bones' neck before he could react.

Impertinent little shit, Barros grumbled.

"I can still hear you!"

Right. Well, no sense in wasting time arguing. If telling you who I am is what it's going to take to get you to let me loose, we might as well get to it.

"Listen, I'll be thrilled to free my dog of you, if that's at all possible. But you will not be going anywhere with Bones." Zara gave the rope a quick yank to underscore her point.

Very well, then. But it may be best we take this discussion elsewhere. I fear our little tableau may be drawing unwanted attention.

Bones' snout pointed down the alleyway to where a cluster of servants who had been taking out the trash or having a smoke now stood watching Zara intently.

Zara's face grew hot as she realised how she must look, huddled in the alleyway talking to her dog. She stood and tugged on the rope securing Bones…and whatever had taken up residence in his body.

"Come on then."

Zara spent the afternoon listening to Barros' tale. She'd led poor Bones to a secluded building, long-abandoned, that served as an occasional hideout. She was still stunned by the sheer absurdity of the situation she and Bones had stumbled into.

But the ancient alchemist's story was fascinating. Like her, he'd been betrayed by someone he should have known better than to trust, though his choice had far worse consequences than Zara's. She shuddered at the thought of being trapped inside a pocket watch for centuries.

How had he not gone mad?

Or maybe he had, she considered. Maybe everything he was telling her was a lie; maybe the spirit possessing Bones wasn't who he said he was at all. But that didn't really matter, did it? She and her hound were in a bind, regardless. And the timing made sense given what Yuri had told her just the day before about the Queen selling Lestrange's belongings. Zara refocused as the alchemist's lament was drawing to a close.

And I thought I finally had a shot at vengeance. Yet, here I sit, resisting this mongrel's urge to lick its nether regions.

"That's the one part I don't quite get," Zara mused. "Lestrange was killed centuries ago. They hung the monster then burned him to ashes. I know that may have happened after you were, well… But you *had* to know he couldn't be alive after all this time. How could you possibly hope to get revenge on a dead man?"

Lestrange has done many things. Dying is not one of them. Not truly, at least. His body may be dust, but I knew that man better than most. I know what he was planning. And I planned ahead.

Zara frowned at him. "Translation please? I don't speak cryptic twisted soul."

The phylacteries weren't meant only for his victims. I suspected Lestrange meant to transfer his soul into one as well, as a kind of sanctuary where he could remain hidden until the time was right for a resurgence.

"Why would he have been so sure he could free himself at will?"

And I was beginning to think you really were smarter than I'd imagined. Grand Mage, remember? Strongest necromancer ever to live?

"Point taken," Zara relented.

Anyway, I believe he was successful. This wasn't quite the order of operations I'd hoped for, but when I realized what he was likely planning, I created a phylactery of my own. One imbued with power only alchemy could provide. I have no doubt it would hold his soul, keep it there for eternity. I just need to get back into the Palace to get it, and then track the bastard down.

"That sounds pretty complicated, especially since you seem to be stuck inside my dog."

Yes, well. That is a problem. It's also a problem that this mutt is flea-ridden. The itching is nearly unbearable.

Zara ignored the alchemist's complaint. She was lost in thought again, sifting through the many pieces of Barros' tale. Something had been nagging her since he'd told her he was an alchemist. It took quite a bit of pondering until it came to her.

"What kind of object was the phylactery you made for Lestrange?" she asked.

It was quite ingenious, actually. I used my key to our laboratory. It was always in my possession, so I had no concern he would stumble onto my plans. Why do you ask?

"Because I think I know where it is."

Zara told Barros about her recent job for Del—about the key with the ouroboros and Del's double-cross. It made sense he'd have such a hard-on for the key, even though he couldn't know its real value.

Getting a hold of the key to Lestrange's laboratory would be a twofold win. With a little inside help, Del could gain access to whatever was left of the necromancer's things. He could make a pretty penny off just about anything that came out of that room, even an old scrap of paper or rusty lab equipment. And when he was done, he could sell the key itself as a novelty to some vapid noble. It was ornate enough.

Barros was silent for some time. Eventually, he stood in front of Zara and held her gaze.

Perhaps we could strike up an arrangement of our own?

Zara raised an eyebrow. "Go on."

Take me to this Del. Help me get the key back and I'll help you rob him blind. Then go with me to find Lestrange. I can work as your accomplice along the way. In this body, I can gain access to places you can't—to information and objects, valuable objects, you couldn't hope to collect on your own. You'd never need to worry about money again, and I'd have the assistance I needed to capture and end Lestrange.

"Why should I trust you?"

You probably shouldn't, as I probably shouldn't trust you. But I'm not sure either of us have much choice if we want to achieve our desired ends.

"I don't much like you being in my head," Zara said.

I don't much like being stuck in the body of a beast that eats its own feces and has an unmitigated desire to hump everything it passes, but here we are.

Zara laughed in spite of herself. "Well, when you put it that way…"

She reached down and took Bones' paw in her hand, giving it a little shake for good measure.

The girl and the alchemist waited outside Del's hideaway until long past nightfall. They watched as his men took up their posts outside the front gate.

When one stepped away to take a piss, Zara was there to jab her dagger into his jugular while Barros used Bones' sharp teeth to rip out the throat of the other. They wasted no time entering the building and locating Del where he slept. Zara was glad to see his eyes open just as she drew her blade across his neck.

Then she rifled through his drawers, breaking open a lock box that held Barros' key and enough sheets to pay her squatter's fee for a year or more.

Zara dropped her bounty into her leather pouch and smiled at Bones, mischief in her eyes.

"One treacherous bastard down, one more to go."

The alchemist looked up at his unlikely partner, Del's blood splattered across her cheeks like gruesome freckles.

The hound's tail wagged happily as the pair headed into the night to begin their search for their final target.

Next stop, the royal palace.

THE DRAGON MEDALLION

NERISHA KEMRAJ

"*Come to me...* " a croaky whisper threaded through the town square.

Marilio heard it even over the bustle of the market and the cries of the vendors. He craned his neck to listen for where the voice had originated from. No one else seemed to have heard it.

"Hey, give us our money back!" one of his spectators yelled. "You aren't even doing anything, you silly boy!"

He glanced down at the small crowd gathered around his makeshift stage and the hand-painted sign read: 'Marilio the Magnificent'. They were still waiting for his grand finale, oblivious to the voice that had distracted him.

"Sorry, guys. Show's over today. I gotta go."

He grabbed the hat full of silversheets and scurried away from the folk he'd just swindled.

"You're no mage!" the outraged man shouted after him. "You little thief!"

Marilio couldn't hear him. He heard the voice once more.

"Come to me, dear boy! I have what you need…"

He followed the hoarse and urgent whisper towards one of the shops that lined the town square. He peeped in at the window to find that he had stopped in front of the local pawn shop.

"Come inside." The whisper sounded more urgent now. *"Find me."*

Marilio hesitated. The shop owner knew him to be troublesome. This was probably just another stupid elf prank. Some of them were nasty, little buggers, and he couldn't afford to get into another meddlesome battle with any one of them. He turned away, whispering voice be damned.

"I am not a silly elf, boy!"

Marilio stopped in his tracks. They could read his mind? What sort of magic was this?

"Who are you?" he asked aloud, returning to the window.

As if in reply to his question, a box at the corner, inside the shop, began to emit a green, glowing mist of light and shook open to reveal some sort of silver-black chain. A chunky pendant was attached to it. Marilio's eyes darted to the shop owner and the customers within. Was he the only one seeing this?

He exhaled slowly, realising he had been holding his breath, as the piece of jewellery floated towards him in plain view of both the magic, and non-magic folk.

He saw that it was some sort of medallion now, as it approached. It stopped just above his closed bag, waiting as the small duffel untied itself. Marilio's eyes widened as he realised what it was about to do, just as the shop owner caught sight of it falling into his bag.

"Stop! Thief!" he shouted, as the bag flew into Marilio's hands.

"*Run!*"

The voice erupted from his bag as Marilio broke into a sprint, away from the shop.

"What in the Void is going on?" he rambled, as they hid behind some walls a short distance from the pawn shop. "Who are you? *What* are you?"

"*Calm down, dear boy.*"

"Calm down? You just turned me into a thief?"

"*You were already a thief. And what were you stealing? Trinkets? Coins? I can give you what you truly desire. Magic.*"

"And how are you going to do that?

"*I am Dolfus, Grand Mage of Guardiana, appointed by King Vertice himself. You have already seen a taste of my powers. But I am trapped inside this Faith-forsaken medallion and I need to be set free. Only a young wizard, such as yourself, can help me. You see, I have been watching you, and I have sensed your magical abilities for a while now. I see the potential you have, and I have chosen you, out of all the rest. You are…special, you see.*"

318

Marilio *was* special. He'd always known that about himself. Grand Mage Dolfus. seemed to think he was also gullible and easily flattered. Maybe people would have fallen for that back in his day—whenever that was—but times had changed. You didn't survive on Kingsgate streets without some smarts.

"A Grand Mage, you say? So, why can't you get your sorry self out of that object, if you're so grand?"

The hoarse whisper grew louder with anger. *"How dare you question my abilities? Me, the most powerful mage of all time?"*

Marilio laughed at that. "If you were as powerful as you say you are, you wouldn't have gotten yourself stuck in a piece of jewellery, isn't that so?"

The medallion remained silent, giving Marilio enough time to examine the ancient jewel with fascination. It glinted with magnificence under the moonlight. He ran his fingers over the embossed front. The face of a dragon rose from the centre of the ancient medallion, its body filling out the rest of the circular object. It was so finely detailed that Marilio could see each scale that covered the body of the enchanting beast. But his fingers stopped at the side of the medallion, where a clasp held it together. It did not open.

"Does this open?" he asked aloud, not expecting an answer.

"It obviously does," Dolfus said, returning mockery in kind. *"Can you not see the clasp?"*

"Of course, I know that," Marilio retorted, embarrassed. "I mean, it clearly doesn't open now, does it? Someone even scratched the finish trying to pry it apart.

How *does* it open?"

Dolfus didn't answer. Marilio wondered if even he knew.

"For someone who needs my help, you're very rude to me, you know. And besides, how do I know you are who you say you are? I heard the Grand Mage to King Vertice, Darrian Dolfus, was a perfectly acceptable magician, until he got himself killed by the infamous Lestrange! Now *that* was truly a great mage. The power he had over the realm. Wow! He even had King Vertice in his back pocket!"

"Don't you dare speak about that traitor in awe!" the voice roared, as the medallion grew hot in Marilio's hand.

The dragon glowed a fiery orange, and Marilio dropped it to stop it searing the skin on his palms, but that wasn't enough. The dust around the medallion began to rise, lifting up in a tornado-like swirl. The hot sand lashed angrily around Marilio and he began to choke.

"A perfectly acceptable magician, am I? Should I give you a taste of my power?"

"Alright, alright, old man. That's enough!" He coughed, choking on mouthfuls of dust. Taking his flask, he rinsed out his mouth. Then, suddenly, something clicked in his mind. He knew he had seen that medallion before. "Wait! This is the medallion that was around the neck of Artemis the day he died!"

Marilio's eyes widened as memories of the previous week cluttered his mind. Artemis had been one of the richest, most egomaniacal men in the neighbourhood. He'd once hired Marilio to perform at a birthday party—

far beneath his skills, frankly—but the whole thing had been a prank. He'd wanted Marilio there to make fun of him, to taunt him for his stunted magical abilities. Really, he'd been an ass.

Artemis had made his fortune from dragon scales, a powerful and rare alchemical ingredient. He'd hired dozens of mercenaries to scour the Violet Range to retrieve scales, the fresher the better. His hirelings had died constantly, but the money kept rolling in. Just the week before, he'd gone to the auction at the palace with a fat sack of gold.

He'd died the very next day.

Marilio flashed back to when Artemis had rushed into the square, screaming indecipherable words as if he'd been possessed. The very same medallion had been clutched in his hand before a mass of flames had engulfed him.

Only they hadn't found the medallion on his body. Had the pawn broker pried it from his blackened fist before the guards had arrived?

"It was you who killed him, wasn't it? This is the cursed object of Alvard Lestrange, himself! That's why nobody wanted it! That's what Artemis was screaming about! He wasn't saying 'this is strange', he meant 'it's Lestrange!' I can't believe I didn't see it earlier!"

Slowly, the medallion levitated from the ground up to his face, silent.

"Are you Lestrange? Is that why you killed him? Because he figured you out. I saw him! I saw that poor man combust into flames!" Marilio saw now that it was true, it was indeed, the very same medallion. Artemis had been the one to try to pry it open and the charred marks at its edges were from the fire that had consumed him.

"It was you!" Marilio shouted, horrified, just as the medallion flew to his head and knocked him out cold.

When the young wizard awoke a while later, he found himself covered in blood in the middle of the forest. It was dark and the air was fierce with the buzz of insects. Light of a full moon shone down through the canopy. At least he wasn't blind. The sound of rushing water, the humidity, told him they'd come west, beyond the city gates. The medallion weighed heavy around his neck.

"Wh-what happened?"

"Ah, my young friend, I see you are awake."

"What did you do to me?" Marilio surveyed his blood-soaked shirt and hands, searching for a tell-tale wound. He tasted iron in his mouth.

"I'm sorry, dear boy. I thought that would work. It did not, sadly. You see, I have an insatiable hunger, it seems. I have tried to rid myself of it. Sadly, it is not to be."

Marilio picked up the remains of what used to be a wild rabbit. "Disgusting! You could have at least cooked it first!" he said, silently thanking the Circle that he was unharmed.

"My apologies. My abilities are rather limited from within this object. I will need your help to try and break free from it, even if it is just temporary. You see,

I am permanently attached to this medallion, and only Lestrange's chamber holds the secret to my ultimate freedom. We need to get to the palace."

Marilio let out a moan of disgust as he saw the bones of an old crow lying nearby. Only a few feathers were evident, and he gagged at the thought of what lay inside him now.

"Well, if you need to get into the palace, what are we doing here in Blue Haven?"

"Ah, yes, that is where we are. I should have guessed."

"Wait, are you able to see from in there?"

"Of course, dear lad. Whether a gift, or punishment, I do not know, but that evil traitor has allowed for me to keep all my senses from within here. I am, however, unable to...move on, as one would say. I am doomed to this unrest for eternity, or at least until all his plans are put into place."

"Plans? What plans?"

"His plans. Lestrange. Things did not end with his death, as everyone had hoped. He has waited for these moments from the beginning. The soulstorms are only the beginning. We *must* warn the others."

Marilio staggered backwards against a tree as he tried to stand. The medallion had done more damage to his head than he realised. "You sure are one powerful wizard, even in death!" he snickered.

"Actually, I prefer the term Grand Mage, if you please."

Marilio rolled his eyes. The old soul was kind of pompous, even trapped in a piece of jewellery. But a sudden thirst caught in his throat, and Marilio slowly made his way towards the sound of a nearby stream.

"Don't bother, boy!" the medallion boomed against his chest. *"That doesn't do me any good."*

"Yeah, it doesn't do you any good, but it does for me. I'm quite thirsty after all that raw, bloody meat you forced down my throat! How did you do that anyway?"

"It's quite easy, you see. You possess a magical strain that I am able to tap into. As long as I am placed around your neck, I am able to…take over your vessel, so to speak."

"WHAT?" Marilio turned away from the stream, aghast. "You mean, you *possessed* me?"

"Well, I must admit it was rather presumptuous of me, seeing as you did not give me permission. But you were 'out of it', as they say, and I had nothing else to do, you see?"

"That doesn't give you permission to wear me like a coat! By the Void! Do not, under any circumstances, do that again. Do you hear me?"

Marilio removed the medallion from around his neck and stuffed it in his pocket, then drank mouthfuls of water before stomping off in the direction of Kingsgate and home.

"Where are we going?"

Silence.

"I do apologise, young lad. I am only trying to save the realm."

"Save the realm by feeding me crow?! And taking over my body? It seems like you have an agenda of your own. A Grand Mage would not act in such a manner."

"Oh, are you so sure about that? This coming from someone in the same line of work as myself, who chooses to make a mockery out of the non-magic folk by swindling them of their money with those silly... 'magic tricks'!"

"That's not the same thing!"

"Sure, it isn't."

"What's that supposed to mean? Huh?"

"Nothing. Nothing. I was simply agreeing with you, my dear boy."

Marilio clicked his tongue in irritation. "Stop calling me that, will you? I am Marilio. Marilio the Magnificent."

The voice grunted in response. *"Where are we going?"*

"To my lodge. I need to catch a few winks, seeing as it's still the middle of the night. Anyway, can't you get us back to town faster? How did we get here anyway?"

"Why, we flew, of course."

"Flew?" Marilio hesitated. He'd never flown before. "Can you fly us back?"

"You know what you have to do."

Marilio sighed and looped the medallion around his neck again. Once again, he was no longer in control of his body.

"What's happening, Dolfus?"

"I'm getting us there faster, of course," the imprisoned Grand Mage said, in the voice of Marilio, having taken full control of the young fellow's body. "As you requested,"

With a single leap, they burst through the canopy of the Blue Haven and soared through the night sky. Marilio saw the walls of Kingsgate passing below. They landed with a loud thud in front of Marilio's tiny dwelling a short while later. Short of breath and exhausted from the takeover, Marilio staggered inside and collapsed onto his bed.

"Grand Mage Dolfus, a question for you."

A young boy approached, a curtain of black hair shrouding his ghost-white face. As usual, he put forth his question ever-so politely.

"An odd thought has struck me. The soul inhabits the body like a parasite, controlling it entirely, and both body and soul become useless without each other. Has anyone ever discovered where the soul goes once the body is dead?"

Dolfus shook his head. "Alas, dear Alvard, all of our natural sciences have failed to provide the answer. To hear the Faith tell it, all souls are part of the Circle, in a never-ending cycle of reincarnation, hoping to reach the Centre."

"But never learning from our mistakes. It's a pity the soul can't be captured and preserved before it is able to leave the body? Then, maybe, a new vessel could be found for it."

"That's bordering on necromancy, my boy," said a very young Grand Mage Dolfus. "Best be careful. What have they been teaching you at the Academy anyway?"

"I was just curious. The people want us mages to be able to answer anything and everything, no matter the situation. I know there are merchants and courtiers who'd love to avoid the Circle's judgement and they'll ask. It's alright, if you don't know anything about it. I guess the grand, old library will have to do…"

"No, no. Wait."

Dolfus took a breath. Alvard Lestrange stared at him with silent intensity, waiting for an answer. He was going to walk this path regardless, that much was clear.

"It is not that I do not know the subject. I am quite informed about it. It is my duty to research all threats to the realm, necromancy among them. It is possible to capture a soul, but not without immense pain, even in the vessel's last stage of life. It is even more excruciating when it is forcefully done. But I am not in a position to discuss such things with a young student. It is a very fine line to be crossed, if mistaught."

Marilio woke with sweat dripping down his face. His heart pounded into overdrive as he gulped in the entirety of his flask.

"What was that, Dolfus? I saw you. It felt so real. As if I was there."

"Yes, my dear boy. That was just a memory. A memory of how it all began. You see, young Alvard Lestrange was a student of mine. He was destined for great things, from the moment he arrived at the Academy, and I took him under my wing. Little did I know that, in all those years of training, he was actually readying himself to take my post. He learned from the very best and perverted my teachings so that he could take power and use the Crown's wealth to pursue his diabolical research."

An overwhelming weight of sadness blanketed Marilio, and he could not stop himself from trembling. He hastily removed the medallion and the sensation lifted just as quickly. Maybe it was Dolfus who was depressed.

The previous day and night proved to be a blurry memory as Marilio dressed, ready to face a new day of magic tricks to earn his crust. He might have believed he'd just dreamt the whole thing, if it wasn't for the medallion, now glowing as it made its way towards him.

"Just stop, Dolfus. You're staying here today. I can't take you with me. Everyone would know that you're the cursed trinket that killed Artemis."

"We need to go to the palace, boy. The realm is at stake."

"The realm hasn't given me anything but a shack to live in and a charlatan's routine. Why should I care?"

"You should care because you can't be Marilio the Magnificent if the whole city's been blighted by Lestrange. Besides, I'm going to make you rich and famous. You flew just last night. Imagine the magic we can do together today."

Whether it was because old Dolfus had used his name for the first time, or whether it was the pleading tone in the former Grand Mage's voice, Marilio didn't know, but he found himself agreeing, much to his dismay.

"Fine. We'll work some magic. Then we'll go and stop Lestrange."

Over the next few days, with Dolfus helping him, Marilio's magic increased tenfold. He found himself doing things he would never have succeeded at before. He managed to secure himself a nicer cottage in the village, and even became one of the most eligible young bachelors in town. The girls would flock to see his shows, which grew larger as the days drove on, and the crowds were astounded with his success. His swindling days were behind him. Finally, honest money.

At that rate, he'd become a great truly magician in no time. He might even have a shot at becoming Grand Mage himself.

However, even with all his newfound success, the cool steel touching his chest always brought him back to reality. He was only as great as the Grand Mage allowed him to be. It wasn't his magic.

"It's alright, dear Marilio," Dolfus said one day, sensing the boy's defeat, *"you will be just as great, even without me."*

"Just stay out of my mind, Dolfus. You know nothing!"

Marilio removed the medallion before sitting down at his new dining table to eat in peace. Dolfus watched the boy, but said nothing, giving him space until night fell.

"We need to get to the palace," he said, breaking the hours of silence. *"The soulstorms are worsening. He will only grow stronger, and then the realm will be his."*

"Just leave me alone. I don't need to do anything."

Wallowing in self-pity, Marilio turned away, unable to fall asleep. The newly acquired, soft and comfortable queen-size bed made him feel smaller as he sank inside his own mind.

"Let me go! I can't help you! This is wrong, boy! This is not the way. Please!"

An older Dolfus sat, restrained to a chair, brown ropes tightly bound to his neck, hands and feet.

"I'm sorry, old man. I did not wish for it to come to this, but it has to be done. It is the only way."

"No, it's not. I promise, Alvard. There are other ways. Please, listen to me. I can't take this anymore. I'll die."

"Die if you must, just not before I am able to extract the final bit of information from you. I'm so close. So close. I can feel it! There isn't enough time. This vessel is only temporary. I must learn how to safely preserve my soul. Sadly, it does take the sacrifice of others. And today, it is not your turn."

Dolfus watched as Lestrange dragged in a person with a brown sack covering their face. He lay them down onto the wooden table. Judging by his dress, Dolfus guessed him to be one of the stable boys.

"What are you doing, Alvard. Please stop. You can't do this! Help! Help us!"

"You know better than that, Grand Mage. I've already taken care of sound-proofing this room. You do know I'm quite capable. The star pupil of my time. Besides, the royals know that you have left us, gone onto the Violet Range, in search of more challenging endeavours, having grown bored of mundane duties at the palace."

A maniacal smile spread across his face as restraints magically tied themselves around the young boy. The latest sacrifice moaned, trying to speak, but the words remained inaudible, unable to scream thanks to the curse Lestrange had placed on him.

He forced a concoction into the boy's mouth, pressing one hand over his lips so that he could not spit it out, and muttered the incantation he had forcefully extracted from the Dolfus's mind.

"Alvard, stop…"

Tears rolled down Dolfus's face. He knew there was nothing he could do to prevent the poor boy's death. Before he could say anything further, with a swift movement of his free hand, Lestrange silenced Dolfus, as his lips melded into each other, sealing his mouth.

Lestrange stepped back from the table, a tiny vial in his hand. The boy's body began to shake. Foam ejected from his mouth.

Even without the use of his mouth, Dolfus projected words into Lestrange's mind. "Save him!"

"Silence, old man, or it will be your turn! Why is it not working? Tell me!"

He raised his hands and the ropes around Dolfus grew tighter, digging deeper into his flesh. He was interrupted by beams of light that shot out of the boy's body, as he began to scream wordlessly.

"Is that his soul? Is that light his soul? How do I capture it?"

Lestrange grabbed the vial, trying to trap the bright light within the glass. It passed through, continuing to seep out into the ether.

"How do I concentrate it into the vial. Tell me!"

Lestrange dug into his mind, raking for the answer buried in Dolfus's decades of experience. He writhed in pain.

The light tore through the boy's skin, pouring out from holes in his flesh, as he continued to convulse. Then he levitated, pulling tight against the magical shackles, and as the final bursts of life emitted from inside him, the boy exploded, leaving splotches of flesh all over the room and the two mages.

Marilio ripped the medallion from his neck, slamming it against the wall of his room as he choked himself awake. His eyes wide, his heart racing, he checked his wrists and his neck for the damage he had felt inflicted on them. There were no ropes. He was not bleeding.

"What was that? What happened to me? What are you doing to me?"

"I apologise, Marilio. You needed to see for yourself."

"I didn't just *see*! I felt everything! I was dying!"

"Oh, relax, boy! It was my pain that you were feeling! And that wasn't even the worst of it. Would you like me to take you further? Like say, the night my soul was stripped from me? I can tell you, what happened to that boy wasn't half of what he did to me in the end, once he'd perfected the process."

A cloud of rage swirled around Marilio, burning his insides, filling him with some of the anger contained within the Grand Mage.

"That was only the beginning, Marilio. There were many other victims before he became successful in actually concentrating the soul into a new vessel. After that, he became obsessed with trapping the souls in objects, marking them with his blood so that he controlled them. I was there to witness a few of the objects, but not all. I succumbed to death from his sadistic torture before he could perfect the soul preservation ritual, and so he was left to experiment further, on his own. I did not willingly give him what he required, as you may have seen. That man was no mage. He was pure evil. And that is why we have to stop his return."

"Do you think he actually succeeded? That he found a way to survive hanging?"

"I don't think, *dear boy, I know. I was there in the chambers, with the rest of them, trapped within mere objects, after my death."*

"So, what do you plan to do?"

"We need to get to the palace, to inform the royals that the time has come. Now that the trinkets have been removed from the palace, he will be free soon enough. We need to destroy him before he attains the unimaginable power he seeks."

The trek to the palace hadn't been as hard as Marilio had expected, and they encountered no hassle for much of the way, until Marilio stopped for lunch in a tavern named, ironically, the King's Head.

"Say, boy, where did you get that medallion?"

A royal guard of huge stature, accompanied by an almost carbon copy, cast their shadows over him. Marilio pushed his tanker away and tried to act casually.

"What, this? It was a gift from my mother."

Damn it! They'd forgotten to disguise the medallion. It looked like it belonged in the palace, not around the neck of a boy from the slums, no matter how prosperous a street magician he was.

"Yeah right." They exchanged glances. "Wasn't this the description of one of the objects Captain Merrick was muttering about?"

"Yeah, I say it was. You need to come with us, boy."

They grabbed him by a hand each and carried him out of the pub, around to where their cart awaited. Marilio noticed the alleyway was secluded and the medallion began to glow the ethereal green he had seen before, moments before he passed out.

When he came to again, it wasn't in the same place he'd been moments before.

"Where are we?" He noticed the blood on his hands and blanched. "What happened? Where are the guards?"

He grabbed hold of the medallion and flashed back to his encounter with the guards. This time, he was able to claw back some of the memories Dolfus had suppressed. He saw himself pulling one of the swords from a guard's belt with a hand gesture, before slicing each of them clean across the throat without even touching the blade. They had no chance.

"What did you do? Murderer! You're just like him! You killed those innocent men! I won't help you! I want no part I this!"

334

"You've already taken my help! All the riches you have acquired, that is because of me! You would be nothing but a low-life on the street if it weren't for me. You owe me."

"I owe you nothing. Take it all back."

He tried to remove the medallion from his neck, but it would not budge. Instead, the dragon burned a fiery red, and sank a fraction into his chest.

He screamed in agony. "Stop! What are you doing?"

"Will you help me? Yes or no? Or do you wish to end up the way Artemis did?"

The dragon medallion sank a little deeper. Marilio remembered the way Artemis had exploded into flames. So, this was what had happened.

"Wait! I'll sneak you into the palace, as promised. But that's it. Then we're done."

Before Dolfus could respond, thunder boomed overhead, and the sky turned dark. The air filled with a thousand screams.

A soulstorm.

"We have to get out of here, under shelter. Now."

Dolfus compelled Marilio's body, urging them to safety. Marilio stumbled like a marionette, trying to move with the pull of invisible strings. He glimpsed the storm's wrath upon some of the unsheltered residents, as they waited for the horror to dissipate.

"Can't we help them?"

The medallion's strong hold of him kept him where he was.

"We are helping them. We're going to stop Lestrange."

Dolfus's memories of the palace didn't match the reality. Three hundred years had added new corridors, new rooms, new walls. In the end, Marilio was running blind in a maze of opulence and splendour. Getting in had been hard enough—he hadn't wanted to give the old Grand Mage any reason to kill anymore guards—but finding their way to the Queen's chambers was proving impossible.

"Stop right there!" someone barked, when Marilio found himself at a new dead end.

He froze in his tracks and lifted his hands for good measure. It was a woman's voice, but the royal guard had just as many women as men. This probably wasn't a chambermaid.

"Who are you? How in the Void did you get inside the palace?"

"I-I work here."

"Bullshit! I'm pretty sure I'd remember if the queen had hired a jester. Turn around."

Marilio did as he was ordered and saw a woman marching towards him in full magister's robes. The same kind of robes Dolfus had worn when he'd still been alive.

Which probably made her the current Grand Mage.

An older man strode at her side, wearing the insignia of the Guard Captain. Marilio realised he was in real trouble.

"Who are you?" Marilio asked, the medallion etching him with courage.

"Who am I? Wow, you break into a place and you

don't even bother to do your homework? What kind of thief are you anyway?"

She was quite assertive for her stout build, but he needed her to shut up so he could tell her what was going on.

"I'm not a thief. I'm…"

She pointed at the scar on his chest, in the shape of a roaring dragon. "What in the name of all that's good and circular is that?"

"Oh, that? It's a…birth mark type of thing."

"Right. Because I was born yesterday. Merrick get behind me."

The man, Merrick, who'd had his hand ready at his sword the whole time, unsheathed it and stood his ground.

"Would you stop being macho and learn to follow orders? Get behind me *now!* That medallion's on the list. This is more of Lestrange's junk we're dealing with."

She lifted her hands. Flames ignited in her palms. Marilio remembered what had happened to Artemis.

"Wait!" he yelped, his own hands in front of him in surrender. The medallion revealed itself as it floated to take its place around his neck.

"Where did you get that thing from, kid?"

"It came to me."

"What do you mean 'it came to you'? Did you buy it? Steal it?"

She assessed his dress robes. Even now, after all his success, he probably didn't look like someone who could afford it. Only the wealthiest aristocrats had been able to attend the auction.

"It called to me and I picked it up. That's all."

"We are here to warn you, young lady."

"Who said that?" The flames in the Grand Mage's palms bloomed brighter, a warning. "Is someone else here with you? Tell them to come out slowly."

"Wait! It's the medallion. There's a soul trapped within, but it's not Lestrange! He comes with a message for the royals."

"A message for the royals? So, why are you heading in the direction of Lestrange's chambers?"

Marilio sighed. He knew they'd been going the wrong way.

"Do you want me to grab them, Magisty?" Merrick asked, flinty eyes glaring right at Marilio.

"Are you crazy? God knows what that medallion might do. We need to contain it. Now."

Marilio winced. There was no way Dolfus would let himself be 'contained'. Not again. With a rush of numbness, he took over Marilio's body and projected ice from his hands at the pair who'd accosted them. The Grand Mage threw out an arm and the wave of magic stopped short of her, shattering to pieces against a shimmering, rainbow-hued shield. The ice slammed into Merrick and threw him backwards down the corridor.

Dolfus had already taken off running before they could stop him.

They rounded the corner and slammed into the iron-braced door at the end of the corridor. Dolfus used Marilio's body to wrestle with the handle.

"Is this really Lestrange's study?"

"I have to get in. I have to make sure it hasn't…"

"Going back to the scene of the crime, huh?"

The woman slunk around the corner, palms still flaming. She didn't look pleased.

"Well, I learned my mistake last time and I sealed the fucking door. Nothing else belonging to Alvard Bastard Lestrange is getting free on my watch."

"We need to see if it's still in there. Please. We must stop his return."

The Grand Mage hesitated, like she'd realised she wasn't speaking to Marilio anymore. "Let me guess. Our friend from the medallion?"

"Listen, young lady, there is no time to explain. The soulstorms are getting closer, stronger, and more frequent. He grows stronger with them."

"What do you know about the soulstorms? Who the fuck *are* you?"

"If it will let us proceed faster, alright. I am Darrian Dolfus, most powerful mage of all time. Grand Mage to King Vertice. Tortured and killed by Alvard Lestrange and cursed to be trapped in this medallion for eternity, or until such time when he returns."

"So that's it then? You want to free him so that you can be free yourself?"

"No, dear lady! Listen! His soul! His soul is somewhere close. You must stop them from releasing him. He grows stronger with the coming of the soulstorms, and I fear it is only the beginning. He is gathering all that he needs for his final act."

"Y'know, that's exactly the kind of line Lestrange would feed someone if he wanted them to undo a magical barrier around his chambers. Just saying."

"I am not him!"

"Okay, fine. I believe you. Then which item is his? If you tell me, I can stop him myself."

"I don't know. I heard their voices, echoing in the study, but none of them belonged to him. And I witnessed the imprisonment of a couple of them. Not the chalk, or the game board. No, he would not be something menial, without meaning to him. But I do know that he is an object himself! That was why the others were sacrificed! They were simply a means to an end. He had planned the perfect soul preservation ritual, to preserve himself for eternity, so that he can return at will!"

"But why now? Why after all this time?"

"Why not? No one remembers his tyranny anymore. The time is ripe to try again. Perhaps he has been influencing matters from behind the scenes. Even a powerful mage such as he has limited abilities from within an object, but now the way is clear for his ascent. I cannot say for sure what his plans are, as I could not hold on for that long. But I do know that we need to stop it getting that far."

"And how can we do that?"

"You are a strong Grand Mage, yourself, I can sense it. I have faith in you. But first we have to—"

Dolfus, still acting through Marilio, flinched as an arrow thunked into the doorframe. Guards surged down the corridor to the sound of clamouring alarm bells. The new Grand Mage turned, throwing up a wall of force to shield Marilio's body from the attack.

"Hold your fire, damn it! This isn't—!"

Dolfus was already moving, leaping from the window, defying gravity with an effort of magical will. More arrows rained from the walls. Then there was a crack, like thunder, and something struck him in the flank.

"They didn't have devices like that in my day," he gasped.

His magic faltered, and he plunged into the rushing river below.

Marilio crawled onto the bank of the river, now aware of the water rushing against his feet. He could barely make out the palace lights in the distance. The river had dragged him a long way off. His head spun as he remembered how Dolfus had made him jump through the palace window.

Dolfus! The dragon medallion! It was no longer around his neck!

Trying to stand, a sharp pain shot through his side, dropping him to his face again. The hole in his torso pumped blood into the murky waters. He searched around, groping mud and leaves in the darkness, hoping to find the medallion. If he could find it, Dolfus could heal him.

His search was cut short as the thunder, and the screams of a thousand tortured souls rumbled over him. Covering his ears, he dragged himself into the shelter of a drain emerging from the filth-strewn bank.

Out in the open, he saw the soultstorm descending like a grasping hand, reaching out for something lying in the reeds.

A dragon medallion.

Marilio watched with watery eyes as a wisp of green light lashed out at the twisted maelstrom above, trying desperately to fend it off. But, like Dolfus had said, even a powerful mage had limited abilities from within an object. He needed a host, and if Marilio stepped out, he'd be devoured in an instant.

"I'm sorry, old man," he whispered, as the storm engulfed the medallion and ripped the imprisoned soul from within. "I'm sorry…"

Interlude Five
Shot Down in Flames
S.O. Green

"Hey, can I see that for a moment?"

The rifleman stared at Lyssa, bewildered. He and the other defenders had taken shelter from the sudden soulstorm in the tower and probably hadn't expected to be accosted by the Grand Mage.

Her smile lulled him into a false sense of security—and besides, she outranked him anyway—so he handed his weapon over without question. Merrick hadn't been quick enough to catch her racing up the stairs to the wall, which might have been because she was young and fit, despite being a mage, and also because she'd used elemental wind to cheat. That was why he wasn't there to stop her channelling the power of the earth into her arms to snap the fucking gun in half.

It had the desired effect. Every guard up there backed off a few extra steps.

"Are you out of your fucking minds? You just shot the best lead I had to find Lestrange before he kills us all! If anything happens to Camelia, I swear by the Circle, I'll—"

Merrick clapped a hand on her shoulder. She stopped, took a breath, realised she was making an ass of herself. Everyone on those stairs was questioning her suitability to be Grand Mage, either because she was ranting about a man who'd been dead for three hundred years, or because she'd just called the queen by her first name.

Besides, it wasn't their fault. They'd been charged with defending the wall. It wasn't on them that the best chance she had of defeating an evil that had been malignant in Guardiana for three centuries had decided to fly past them, within firing range, while the alarm bells had been ringing. Or that he was now somewhere in the river with a hole through him.

"Put a team together," Merrick ordered. "As soon as the storm's abated, I want you to search the river for any sign of the intruder or his medallion. Grand Mage Lyssa seems to think they can stop the insanity in our realm, so that means we follow her lead. Do you all understand?"

There was a hesitant round of nodding, and then some more affirmative shouts of "yes, Captain", before they all moved out to follow his orders. Lyssa looked at the shattered rifle in her hands and cringed. Where was her self-control?

Mages without self-control ended up like Lestrange.

"Are you alright, Your Magisty?"

"Fine, I just… I want this to end. All these little fires burning in our home, all these people getting hurt, and I can never help them. I thought maybe if I could find Lestrange and destroy him before anything else happened, there wouldn't be anymore deaths. Am I fooling myself? Am I not the mage everyone told me I was?"

"With respect, you are dealing with a power that has evaded capture longer than any of us has been alive. The more I learn about Lestrange, the more I'm convinced that he was a monster from the Void, not a man at all."

"No, he was human," Lyssa insisted. "Only a human could be this cruel."

She sighed and raked her fingers through her hair. It was getting dirty, tangled. She tried to remember the last time she'd taken a bath or slept the whole night. Dreams of being trapped in a worthless trinket, unable to stop the horrors being visited on her realm, tormented her in the black of night. She heard Camelia screaming every time she closed her eyes.

She could feel herself losing the plot. First, it was yelling at the guards and breaking their rare and expensive weaponry; next, she'd be putting the palace on lockdown and clearing out every room with fireballs.

Actually, that wasn't a bad idea.

"We have another complication," Merrick said.

"Do I look like I'm in the mood for complications?"

"You'll want to hear this. During the disturbance, someone else got into the palace."

"Do we even have locks on the doors?"

"They were found in the dungeons; in a crypt we believe was once used by Lestrange. We've been investigating anywhere he might have stashed more objects, as per your instructions. A young girl and a dog were loitering down there. They asked to speak to you."

"Me?"

"The Grand Mage. They said they had information about Lestrange, and you were the only one they'd speak to. No one else."

"Shit…"

Lyssa smoothed her hands over her face. Right now, all she wanted was to see Camelia smile, take a dunk in a washtub and roll into bed. Instead, she was going to the dungeons to talk to yet another intruder about her fucking necromancer problem.

"Okay, I'll talk to them. But they'd better have something interesting to say, or…"

She trailed off, too tired to even make a decent threat. She forced her head up, her back straight, and took off marching.

Alright, girl. Let's see what you've got to say to me.

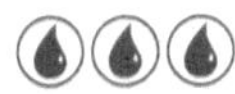

Down, down, down into the dungeon, where apparently Lestrange had performed some of his sickest experiments and the walls were still black from where they'd burned that shit out with good, old-fashioned, non-magical fire.

They didn't keep people in the dungeons anymore. They'd been used to house the crown's political enemies once—courtiers fallen out of favour, would-be revolutionaries, outspoken detractors—but Camelia's daddy had weakened the crown to the point that no one had a bad word to say about them anymore. Hard to generate controversy when you were basically toothless.

Most of Lestrange's victims had been taken from those barred cells. Kind of ironic that the person with information about him would have ended up there really.

She found the girl under light guard, which was fine because there was no way she was getting out of that cage. She looked about twelve, but Lyssa tried to keep in mind that malnutrition had a nasty way of making people underweight. She was sitting cross-legged, digging between the stones on the floor with a stick she must have found in the cell, which the guards had left her with because of its complete lack of offensive suitability. Sitting next to her was the mangiest mongrel she thought she'd ever seen. But she'd never met a bad dog before. Plenty of shitty owners, but never a bad dog.

"You had something to tell me," Lyssa said, folding her arms and taking what she hoped was an authoritative stance. "About Lestrange."

"Are you the Grand Mage?"

"No, I'm wearing these robes because I'm into kinky outfit stuff. Seriously, my patience has worn about as thin as you, girl. Don't keep me waiting."

"My dog wants to talk to you."

Lyssa's eyes flicked to the mutt sitting on the stone beside her. Its posture looked awkward, like it didn't quite understand how to articulate itself, and there was something about the gravity of its stare. It wasn't panting or scratching or doing any other doggy things. It was just…looking at her.

"Tell him to speak up. I must be going deaf."

The girl sighed. "Right… He says you haven't found Lestrange's phylactery yet, else you wouldn't be running yourself ragged. And he says—just a second, I'm telling her—that even when you do find the object with his soul inside it, you won't know what to do with it, because you're not a necromancer like he was."

Lyssa cycled through a number of emotions, through surprise, then concern, then creeping horror, and finally annoyance, where she'd started. She scowled at the girl and the dog she was apparently translating for.

"All of which is true but could also just be good guesswork. You need to give me something more than that."

Silence. The girl turned to look at her dog. She assumed they were having a conversation. Nothing she could do but wait.

Eventually, the girl said, "Lestrange didn't just use magic to imprison people in objects. He used an alchemical process too. In the same way you can transmute lead into gold, you can turn the soul into wood, or glass, or silver. The problem is, Lestrange wasn't an alchemist. He needed help to perfect the process."

The girl's tone of voice had changed, like she was reciting someone else's words as they were spoken. Lyssa was beginning to believe that there was more to this simple picture than met the eye. And she caught the implication in the girl's—the dog's?—words.

"Someone else knew how to do it."

The girl nodded. She reached into her cloak and

withdrew a plain, brass key. It looked like the kind they used in some of the doors in the palace. Gold and silver, though pretty, were too soft and had a nasty habit of warping in the locks.

"Where did you get that?"

"Someone paid me to steal it, but…my dog told me how important it was, and that I needed to bring it here, to you."

"Why?"

"Because this isn't a phylactery. It's a prison. It was built for Lestrange. If you can channel his soul into this, he'll be trapped, powerless, just like all the others he's imprisoned."

"So all I need to do is find his phylactery and… what, just tap them together?"

The girl nodded. "It should be just that simple. It was supposed to be revenge. Barros' last laugh."

She lapsed into silence. Lyssa eyed her through the bars for a moment.

"Who was the dog? Before?"

"Does it matter? He's my dog now."

Lyssa scoffed. Of course it mattered, but… Didn't she have other things on her mind right now? Bigger problems?

She took the key out of the girl's unresisting hand and tucked it into her robes.

"Any idea where Lestrange is hiding?"

"Somewhere in plain sight, he says. Somewhere he could watch everyone scurrying around, trying to figure things out, and laugh at them when they failed. Somewhere no one would think to look."

Lyssa thought she knew where Lestrange was. His gauntlet was still sitting on his desk in the study. No one had taken it for the auction. It had gone completely overlooked. Even she had glimpsed it the last time she'd entered, then gone straight to her list of missing items. She'd barely spared it a second thought. What was that? Some kind of spell? A glamour? Or were their minds just cringing from the wretchedness of the soul lying within?

"I think I know where he is," she said, and turned to leave. But she hesitated at the dungeon door and turned back. "I'll send word to have you released, once I know your story checks out."

"Don't worry about me," the girl said, curling her arms around herself. "I can take care of myself."

"Sit tight," Lyssa ordered, and she might have been talking to her, the dog or the guards.

She had a necromancer to imprison.

In Plain Sight

S.O. Green

Lyssa rolled up her sleeves and started to undo the warding around the study door. The brass key burned in the folds of her robes, and she wished she hadn't been quite so thorough with the enchantment.

In fairness, I didn't think I'd ever want to go back into this godforsaken dump.

"Are you sure he's in the gauntlet?" Merrick asked.

He already had his sword drawn, like he could hack Lestrange's soul into oblivion. His reliance on the physical would have been funny if it hadn't been so dangerous, but he'd had her back throughout all this and she'd developed newfound appreciation for the old grump.

That was why, as the magical barrier dimmed and faded, she said, "Whatever happens, stay the fuck behind me."

Rather than argue with her, he gave a tight smile and said, "Yes, Your Magisty."

She shouldered the door open and swept inside. In one hand, she held the staff of power she'd bought in the Adventurers' Quarter. In the other, she clutched the key.

The gauntlet was right where she'd left it, and where countless other Grand Mages and servants had left it for the last three hundred years, ever since they'd pried it off Lestrange's arm so they could clap him in irons. She imagined he'd cut quite an intimidating figure, prowling the royal court with those black steel claws. Maybe folks would have listened to her more if she'd had a similar accessory. Maybe a threatening codpiece or something.

She waved a hand over the gauntlet, searching for a trace of Lestrange. A smell of sulphur, a taste of ash, some remnant of the black void that was his soul. She couldn't sense anything, so did that mean he wasn't here? Or did it mean he was hiding, and she wasn't strong enough to root him out?

"Your Magisty?" Merrick asked, agitation clear in his voice.

"I'm looking, alright? Give me a minute."

"No, Your Magisty, it's…"

The way he trailed off made her flick a glance back, and she saw Camelia standing in the doorway to the study, a bemused look on her face. Lyssa growled. She didn't need more distractions right now.

"Camelia, please, I'm—"

"Lyssa, I summoned you. Where have you been?"

"I've been trying to save your bloody country! This

could be it. What I've been looking for the whole time. I might be *this* close to fixing all this and then no one else has to die, so please, just go back to your throne room and I'll—"

"Are you dismissing me?"

"Yes," Lyssa snapped, "for your own good."

Camelia sighed. She looked at Merrick. She lay a hand gently on his arm, and Lyssa wondered if she was going to enlist the captain's help in dissuading her from her appointed task.

Instead, Merrick dissolved.

The whole thing took a single, horrifying second. The Captain of the Guard was there one moment, gone the next, turned to a pile of ash and flakes of rust at Camelia's slippered feet. Skin, bone, armour, clothing, all gone. He didn't even have time to scream. The next time a breeze blew through that room, there'd be no sign he'd even existed.

"What the holy *fuck*?!"

"He was older than I expected," Camelia muttered, inspecting the dust on her fingers. "I wonder how long he had until retirement. Oh well. I suppose it doesn't matter now."

Lyssa had loved Camelia from close to the first moment she'd laid eyes on her, and there'd been times when she'd have been happy to spend the rest of eternity in the palace with her queen and blow up the outside world. But, right then, she aimed the staff of power at her pretty, little head and snarled, "What the fuck is going on, Camelia?"

"The queen can't hear you right now, Lyssa. May I

take a message?"

Lyssa's pupils dilated. The world, previously unfocused and confusing, clicked into sudden, terrible clarity. Things made more sense than they'd made in quite a long time.

"It's you, isn't it?"

"Yes, it seems as though the game is over. You've found me."

"Has it *always* been you? I mean, is she…?"

"You want to know if your beloved queen actually exists, or if I've been playing you for a fool all this time using the voice and the body you yearn for? Don't fret, Lyssa. Camelia has been the one blundering her way through ruling this country, half-blind to your romantic overtures, the whole time. I might have helped her, here and there. Planted an idea in her head to take root whenever I needed it to. The infirmary she built? Actually, that was my idea. I even suggested a way she could fund it. A little charity auction. Well, I needed to make some space, didn't I? This place was cluttered with so much garbage. Failed experiments and the like. It was time to get my personal effects in order."

The staff of power hadn't felt that heavy, but keeping it levelled at the face of the person she loved made her arm waver. She should have known. Someone like Lestrange could never be as kind or as loyal as Camelia. He couldn't even fake it. But he'd taken advantage of her—just another old dickhead trying to exploit the queen's generosity and the fact that she gave a shit— and if Lyssa could have ripped him out of her body and hurled him into oblivion, she would have. She wouldn't even have thought twice.

"Why?" she growled. "Why now?"

"Because I was ready. I've been watching over Guardiana for three hundred years, waiting for the time when a Grand Mage might actually surpass me. I've had to watch the title pass down from one decrepit, senile idiot to another over and over again, and then *you* came along. Quite a breath of fresh air, actually, and with an abundance of magical power that you haven't even *begun* to tap into."

So that was it. It was all about her. She'd become Grand Mage, with power enough to rival even him, and he'd plunged her realm into anarchy. He'd *killed* people. Maybe everyone would have been better off if she'd never been born, never been carried off that ship all those years ago.

Ma'am should have just hurled her into the ocean.

Scratch that. I'm fine. Lestrange is the one who should never have been born.

Her eyes flicked to the coronet perched among Camelia's brilliant, golden curls. What was it the girl had said? Somewhere in plain sight? Somewhere he could watch and laugh?

The prophecy in the Tenes board. *Crown. Death.*

"So that's it, is it? You've literally been controlling the Crown of Guardiana from beyond the grave."

"You have to admit, you didn't see that coming, did you? But it wasn't about vanity. I needed something consistent. Something with staying power. One king dies, a queen rises, both wear the crown. Even if there'd been an uprising, a coup, they'd have kept the crown jewels.

Heritage pieces. Maybe I would have had to prod them in the right direction, but I doubt it would have been a hard sell."

"You're a real piece of shit," Lyssa grunted.

Camelia—no, Lestrange in Camelia's body—took a step towards her. Lyssa thrust the staff at him with more conviction than she felt.

Maybe if she could get the crown away from him…

"What are you going to do, Lyssa? Kill your queen? Could you live with yourself? Well, no, actually, you'd be executed for treason, but even if you escaped, you'd be haunted by it, wouldn't you? Your heart would be broken until the end of your days."

"You're right," Lyssa said, and she tossed the staff aside with a scowl. "No matter what, I could never hurt her."

But maybe I don't need to.

"You've made the right choice," Lestrange insisted, stepping closer still. "The world will be better off this way. The soulstorms will stop. I think it's probably time to reap the harvest I sowed all those years ago. There must be thousands of them up there now, waiting for me to just reach out and take them, and I've missed that hungry, little sliver of myself so much. Once I take control, everything will seem like a strange dream, just like it does for Camelia right now. Who knows? Perhaps you'll even wake up now and again in the queen's bed. Think of it as a reward for your obedience. There's no reason why we can't both get what we want out of this."

"You have no fucking idea what I want."

He ignored that comment, because he thought he'd

won. But he hadn't seen the key, so all Lyssa needed was for him to bring the crown close enough for her to use it. The moment he was in reach, before he could grab her, she grabbed first. She seized Camelia by a fistful of blonde hair and jammed the key against the crown.

It would work. It *had* to work.

It didn't work. Lestrange blew her off her feet with a gust of wind so strong it slammed her into the wall and sent the furniture scattering all around them. She heard the clamour of voices, and suddenly she realised exactly how many of Lestrange's possessions contained other people's souls.

Lestrange flexed Camelia's hand, looking at the way the skin had purpled and split. Magic from a non-magical body. If he kept using it, he'd tear Camelia apart like wet paper.

"Oh, is that Barros' key? Yes, that was an interesting plan he hatched. Of course, he taught me a lot tricks during our time together, and the simple ones are the best. I had someone find the key for me and soak it in sage water, just in case it found its way here. It turns out I was right to be cautious."

Lyssa pushed herself up, tried to summon the air into her palms, tried to turn her rage into a flame she could wield, or tilt the stones under Lestrange's feet and take his balance. She couldn't focus, couldn't concentrate, with Camelia's face her only target.

All the pain, all the suffering that he caused was going to be on her, because she wasn't strong enough to stop him.

He flicked his hand—Camelia's hand—and flipped

her off her feet. She landed hard on her side with a groan. Before she could get back up, he was on her, pulling the coronet loose from the queen's magnificent hair and driving it, upside down, onto Lyssa's head. The jagged ornamentation pierced her skin, the gems and jewels scraping down to bone. Blood trickled between her eyes and over the bridge of her nose.

"This is what it feels like," she heard him whisper, in his true voice, "to be a soul trapped in an object."

She tried to fight back, but her body wouldn't obey her anymore. She could feel herself shrinking, slipping out of her fingers and toes, her arms and legs, like a costume that suddenly didn't fit anymore. She went blind, lost the musty smell of Lestrange's study. Pretty soon, it didn't even hurt anymore.

Camelia, she gasped, but the words didn't make it to her mouth. *I'm sorry.*

EPILOGUE

Who lingers in undeath, sees all and can do nothing?

The Circle is real. It is unbroken. We have all come before and we will all come again. Those are the teachings of the Faith. All things are cycles, repeating. Lives, conflicts, peace, love and beauty. Nightmares. The nightmare is beginning again. He shudders from that knowledge, within his prison, but he will learn eventually, when his own circle repeats.

Who sees what happens? Who knows its meaning?

It's him. She knows it's him, because who else could it be? In a world of mad and unreal things, she is certain this one, terrible thing is real, this insane torrent of souls pouring forth from the anguished sky, screaming and crying and lavishing itself upon the highest room of the tallest tower of the palace of thieves and monsters. Yes, he is back, and she dances with joy and wails with misery upon the Kingsgate rooftops. Perhaps she'll get to kill him this time.

Who will do what must be done?

The others stand and stare. The sight of the storm has struck them dumb. So close to the palace? To the centre of power? Is nowhere safe? Is nothing sacred? She already knows the answer. Her grip tightens on the new blade. Silently, she turns away. It is a long walk back to the cave, and a difficult bargain she will have to make.

Who has seen this? Foretold it?

Always the same final tile. It never changes, repeating into infinity. Is this what they meant when they talked of a Circle? He thought it was supposed to be a happy thing. Another chance at life, at paradise. He swipes the game board from the table, scattering her dainty finger bones. The game is over. They have all already lost.

Who does not see and does not care?

She plays the most beautiful swan song for the soul she replaced. Her new fingers are nimble, her new ears keen. What happened to the girl? No matter. This second chance would be worth any sacrifice. She is free to make beautiful music again. The nobles and merchant kings adore her and soon she will forget the sad, old man in his tumble-down cottage. She dwells in manors and palaces that never see the sky.

Who entertains in a different way?

The woman wears a hangman's noose upon her shoulders and the crowd watches her with rapt attention, until the storm gathers, and the clouds putrefy. With their eyes turned away, she recalls the blade in her sleeve, and sees the executioner's back. She smiles.

Who doesn't care for the city and its problems? Who has secrets of their own to keep?

The eerie light can be seen as far off as the small shack beside the ruined field, brighter than even the fire of the Red Land Wall. He watches, for a time, but he has more important things to do. The strange happenings in Kingsgate have agitated his boy, and he does the fatherly thing, tries to soothe him with kind words and a gentle embrace. None of this concerns them.

Who sees opportunity among the chaos?

To think that they had once looked down on elves. Jealousy, he assumes, for now he knows what it means to be one of the fairer folk. To be agile and swift and beautiful. Eternal, or close to it. No need for Lestrange's magic now. Except that storm, that maelstrom, above the palace. Could it be? Another chance to know what the necromancer knew? And from the source this time. A wellspring indeed. The time has finally come.

Who is blinded by their own vanity?

This face is better. This face will do. He left the others in ruins and perhaps it was all just a test. A trick by the mage who once scorned him at court. He can't even recall his name. There's chaos in the streets, but only the mirror matters. Only his beauty. Whatever happens, he will survive. Thrive. The lion, ever on the hunt.

Who knows well the darkness in their soul and in the souls of others?

The dungeon couldn't hold her. She's glad she isn't

in the palace anymore, that she can watch the storm rage from afar. She wants to clutch the dog tight, but it wouldn't feel right anymore. He doesn't offer comfort the way he once did, but he has knowledge and skills and advice. He'll see her right, he says, but the hard work she'll have to do on her own. She'll have to get her hands dirty. She looks at the blood under her fingernails and in the lines of her palms, just dark smears in the pervading emerald light. Can they get any dirtier?

Who has lost everything?

He convalesces in the home of an admirer—heavily intoxicated, wound inexpertly bandaged—but for how long? When will they realise that the powers that made him beloved have deserted him? He pulls the dragon medallion from under his shirt, heavy on its chain. No words come. No magic at his fingertips. It is just jewellery now. How much will it fetch? How much ale will it buy? He thinks of the scream he heard, as the storm wrenched his mentor away, and drains another bottle.

Who stands to lose so much more?

Camelia had never slept on the floor in her entire life. She'd fallen asleep in the throne a couple of times, waiting for Lyssa to come home, but this was new. Unprecedented.

But then, they were living in unprecedented times.

She was cold and the window was open. She tried to adjust her gown around her to keep warm, but the fading screams of a passing soulstorm prickled her skin and put terror in her heart. How many of her subjects had perished this time? It ached to wonder.

Her hair was loose and tangled. She reached out,

searching for her coronet, wondering how she'd dropped it, and…

And why there as blood on it.

"Lyssa?"

The other woman—her Grand Mage, her best friend, her most trusted advisor, really there was no word to describe her—stood at the window. Dangerous, if there had really been a soulstorm, but then, she'd always been fearless. Confident. Maybe it was why it was so easy to trust her.

Lyssa turned from the window and the confidence was there, as well as something else. Her eyes shimmered with vitality, her skin practically glowed. Her smile was small but potent, and Camelia didn't think she'd seen her so pleased in some time.

The dried blood on her face was shocking, but she didn't seem to care.

"What happened?"

"It's over, Camelia. Lestrange is gone. It looks like we won. We don't have to worry about him or the soulstorms ever again."

Camelia managed a smile. "I knew you could do it."

She tried to stand, but her hands ached, bruised and painful. Had she fallen?

Lyssa caught her, helped her to her feet. She fell against her chest and, for a moment, her Grand Mage cradled her there until she felt able to rise. Lyssa took her hands gently and, slowly, the pain ebbed away, soothed by magic.

That was when she realised that Lyssa was wearing the clawed gauntlet from the desk. It encased her left arm from shoulder to fingertips. Camelia felt like she should have been intimidated by it, but… Actually, she found its touch comforting in a way she couldn't explain. Like there was something familiar about it.

"No sense in letting something like this go to waste," Lyssa said, by way of explanation. "We should respect the items in this room. After all, some objects have souls all of their own, don't they?"

ABOUT THE AUTHORS

Marcus Bines is a family man and teacher of religion, ethics and philosophy. His parents encouraged the reading of Tintin but covered his eyes over the gross bits in Indiana Jones. It's okay though, he's seen them now.

He writes fantasy and horror, with a penchant for strange creatures, unusual worlds and avoiding the Oxford comma. He has a few short stories published in anthologies and is working on his debut novel.

Many things take his fancy: movies, animals, the power of belief, unanswerable questions, languages, nature, ideas, veganism, sci-fi, indie rock, ancient tales, pyramids, myths, aliens, words... Oh, and human beings. They're pretty interesting.

Links:

https://twitter.com/marcus_bines
https://www.facebook.com/marcusbinesnovelist/
https://marcusbines.wordpress.com/

Jessica Chanese is a speculative fiction writer living in Queensbury, NY, USA, with her husband, two kids, one giant, cuddly pitbull, and one adorably demonic-looking puppy. Her short stories have appeared in Black Hare Press' Lust and Envy and Cloaked Press' Fall into Fantasy 2020, among others. Jessica's first novel, Minivan Warrior: The Odyssey Begins, available through Kindle Unlimited, is a quirky contemporary fantasy featuring a suburban mom, a minivan, and demons. She may one day get her act together enough to have her own website, but until then, you can find her on Facebook and Twitter.

Holley Cornetto was born and raised in Alabama, but now lives in New Jersey. To indulge her love of books and stories, she became a librarian and English professor. She is also a writer, because the only thing better than being surrounded by stories is to create them herself. Holley is a regular contributor at The Horror Tree. She can often be found lurking on Twitter @HLCornetto.

K.B. Elijah is a speculative fiction author whose work features in dozens of anthologies about the mysterious, the magical and the macabre. Her own short fantasy novellas with twists, The Empty Sky (collection), Out of the Nowhere (collection), Whispers in the Dark and Metaphoria, are available now.
Join her on Instagram @k.b.elijah for book reviews and upcoming stories.

Clint Foster lives in southern Iowa with his wonderful wife, Nik, and their herd of four cats and two dogs, along with a jungle's worth of houseplants. He has dozens of published stories in genres ranging from science fiction to horror, epic poetry to hundred word drabbles, and is always looking for another challenge. He has written for several different publishers before including Nordic Press, Dragon Soul Press, Black Hare Press, Electric Spec Magazine, Cloaked Press LLC, and more. He enjoys exploring new styles and genres as both a reader and writer and loves getting new recommendations.

Carrie Gessner received a BA in English from Carnegie Mellon University and an MFA in Writing Popular Fiction from Seton Hill University. She writes speculative fiction and is the co-host of the Positively Pop Culture podcast. When she's not writing or reading, she likes to go for walks in the park with her greyhound.

Simone Oldman Green (they/them) is a genre-fluid writer and editor living in the Kingdom of Fife with husband, John. Author of the post-apocalyptic novelette, Sin Chaser, published by Eerie River Publishing, as well as over 70 works with imprints including Dragon Soul Press, Black Ink Fiction and Nordic Press. They won 3rd Place in the British Fantasy Society's Short Story Contest 2018. Writer, vegan, martial artist, gamer, occasionally a terrible person (but only to fictional people).

Website: https://thebasementoflove.blogspot.com/
Facebook: https://www.facebook.com/thebasementoflove
Twitter: https://twitter.com/SOGreenWriter

Aaron P. Hansen has been working as a web developer since 2015, writing code and frequently wondering how it works. He is a graduate of Algonquin and Mohawk College in computer-related things.
Between working, raising his daughter, and playing fetch with his dog, Aaron has written two published short stories and is currently working on a post-apocalyptic novella.

Aaron works and lives in Hamilton, Ontario.
Facebook: facebook.com/aaron.hansen.376695

Instagram: Aaron.P.Hansen
Website: www.aaronphansen.com

Joel R Hunt is a writer, librarian, ex-teacher and part-time human currently residing in the UK. He has a passion for horror, science fiction and all things bizarre. Joel's drabbles and other short stories can be found in a range of anthologies by Black Hare Press, Eerie River Publishing and World Weaver Press, among others, and he posts daily microstories on Twitter. Updates and examples of his work can be found at https://joelrhuntauthor.wordpress.com/

Nerisha Kemraj resides in Gauteng, South Africa with her husband and two daughters. She has over 200 short stories and poems published in various publications, both print and online. She has also received an Honourable Mention Award for her tanka in the Fujisan Taisho 2019 Tanka Contest.
Nerisha holds a Bachelor's degree in Communication Science, and a Post Graduate Certificate in Education from University of South Africa.
Find her here: https://linktr.ee/NerishaKemraj

Kimberly Rei does her best work in the places that can't exist... the in-between places where imagination defies reality. With a penchant for dark corners and hooks that leave readers looking over their shoulder, she is always on the lookout for new ideas, new projects, and new ways to make words dance

Her debut novelette, Chrysalis, is available now.

Kim is happiest behind a keyboard or doing anything at all with her beautiful wife.

studio-rei.mailchimpsites.com

Alanna Robertson-Webb is a writer and lover of dark fantasy, horror, and high fantasy. She has been featured in over eighty-eight different collections, and even co-wrote a sci-fi novella. As of the time of this publication Alanna has edited eleven different books, and she one day aspires to run both a LARP and a nerdy-themed restaurant. Her day job is a burial coordinator at a cemetery, which means she gets to spend her hours around two of her favorite things: books, and spooky places.

While not nearly a complete list, you can find her more recent writing and/or editing fingerprints on these publications:
- It Calls from the Forest (volumes 1 and 2), Eerie River Publishing, 2020
- Afromyth Volume 2, Afrocentric Books, 2020
- Forgotten Ones, Eerie River Publishing, 2020
- Blood Crown, The Great Void Books, 2021
- Castles and Kimonos, BWWP Publishing, 2020
- What Monsters Do for Love, Soteira Press, 2019
- 13 Guests, Black Ink Fiction, 2021
- Clockwork Dragons, Zombie Pirate Publishing, 2019
- Infected, Blair Daniels, 2018
- Daughters of Darkness, Black Widow Press, 2018

- Adventure Awaits Volume 1, Nordic Press, 2021

Websites:
https://arwauthor.wixsite.com/arwauthor
Twitter: @mythologyhorror
Facebook: Alanna Robertson-Webb, Author

MORE FROM NORDIC PRESS

Novels/Novellas

Face of Fear by C. Marry Hultman
9789198671001

Dawson Junior G3 by Brian Wagstaff
9789198671049

Boy in the Wardrobe by Esther Jacoby
9789198684018

New Life Cottage by Esther Jacoby
9789198671056

The Wait by Esther Jacoby
e-book:https://books2read.com/u/4Dgz8Q

Liebe ist Warten by Esther Jacoby
9789198671070

Das Cottage by Ester Jacoby
9789198684070

Musing on Death & Dying by Esther Jacoby
9789198671063

Earth Door by Cye Thomas
9789198671025

An Odd Collection of Tales By Cye Thomes
9789198684124

Graffiti Stories by Nick Gerrard
9789198671018

Punk Novelette by Nick Gerrard
9789198671087

Struggle and Strife by Nick Gerrard
9789198684049

Murder Planet by Adam Carpenter
9789198671032

Generation Ship by Adam Carpenter
9789198684063

Cold as Hell by Neen Cohen
9789198684094

Six Days to Hell by E.L. Giles
9789198684087

Hell Hath No Fury by Chisto Healy
9789198750706

True Mates by E.F. Vogel
9789198750713

Anthologies

Just 13
9789198684025

Lost Lore & Legends
9789198671094

Wicked West
9789198684193

Adventure Awaits

Volume 1
9789198684124

Volume 2
978-9198684155

Volume 3
9789198684179

Mortem Cycle

Death House
9789198684117

Death Ship
9789198684148

Death Beyond
9789198684162

Death Cuisine
9789198684186

Coming Soon

Soldier's Song by C. Marry Hultman

Murder, Mystery & Mayhem

Rise and Fall

Worlds Collide

Find us at:
https://www.nordicpresspublishing.com/